the
chief
of
rally
tree

a novel

jennifer
boyden

Skyhorse Publishing

For Ian and Gavia
and in memory of my father, Thomas Oakes—
planters of trees, all.

Skyhorse Publishing books may be purchased in bulk at special discounts for sales promotion, corporate gifts, fund-raising, or educational purposes. Special editions can also be created to specifications. For details, contact the Special Sales Department, Skyhorse Publishing, 307 West 36th Street, 11th Floor, New York, NY 10018 or info@skyhorsepublishing.com.

Skyhorse® and Skyhorse Publishing® are registered trademarks of Skyhorse Publishing, Inc.®, a Delaware corporation.

Visit our website at www.skyhorsepublishing.com.

10 9 8 7 6 5 4 3 2 1

Library of Congress Cataloging-in-Publication Data is available on file.

Cover design by Erin Seaward-Hiatt

Print ISBN: 978-1-5107-3269-8
Ebook ISBN: 978-1-5107-3270-4

Printed in the United States of America

outsourced memory. Adopted by corporations. He was asked for a sound bite, but produced a critique.

So what if people had "lost the fluency that had once positioned them as highly sensitive receptors of earth consciousness, capable of reading tiny vibrations, wind shifts, and bark flakes as a language which held deep personal significance?" Wind shifts? Bark flakes? Why was he talking about the feelings of trees? People turned their television channels back to the grizzlies. They were feeding on something large and steaming.

People no longer spoke bark flake. So they weren't good at living without a store nearby and should turn off their lights earlier, get some sleep, try dreaming in the languages of other species. When Winter said such things to the interviewers, they usually responded with blinking, a repurposing of attention as their eyes wandered off to consider his moss-toned shirt, what the fiber was, who made it, if there were more in stock.

But Winter said one thing that stuck, a name: Lin Strickland. She had written the book that called him away from his project; indeed, away from himself. He needed to talk to her: Lin Strickland.

The moment Winter said her name, Lin's books sold and sold, the presses of them suddenly churning out piles that dwindled and reappeared each day. Few people had heard of her before, but in Winter's wake, she was said to be a writers' writer, a readers' writer, a writer of the ages, a benchmark writer, a writer who carried a compass that pointed to truth's perfect north, a writer of internal calamity and certain recognition. A writer Winter had read, though it had nearly destroyed him to do so.

That, from a man who had endured years of winters naked, worked among his pack to take down grown elk and deliver the death press to the flexion of their necks, torn mouth-first and ravenously into the body, run miles of territory daily, and been swept down a mountain in a landslide. He woke up to darkness which gradually sifted into a slow tunnel of brighter and brighter white as his pack dug him out, curled around him and licked him until he understood that to stand on your own is to die. That the man who stands most firmly is the one who has died of darkness and been restored by belonging.

CHAPTER 1

Winter returned. The first time he'd appeared in national consciousness was eighteen years ago, after he spent the decade of his twenties living as a member of a wolf pack whose territory ran from British Columbia to the Yaak River Valley. When he entered the spotlight then, no one had yet heard of him or missed him while he ran the miles, pissed the boundaries, howled the moon, attacked the elk, slept the afternoons. Then he stepped out of the woods, muscled, wary, and sharp, and fame was an umbrella that opened over him. First, the book of his wolfdom caused a sensation. Then the movie, a foraging cookbook, and an endorsement of a low-impact footwear line whose launch he didn't care about enough to stick around for. By the time it was released, his farewell letter was in the hands of the press. They reported its contents: he had a date with isolation. He needed to save himself so he'd have something left to give his new secret project.

And he was gone.

The world moved quickly on. It met the grizzly bear man, the horse woman, a crocodile wrestler, the migration simulators, and the cat woman with whisker implants. It was crowded. The goat walker, the hyena trainer, the man who orchestrated braying.

They had to move over when Winter reemerged after spending ten years on his secret project. The shine-producing light of the studios made him glow. His hair scattered light like a new season. The world held its breath and adjusted the volume to hear him better.

But what he said made no sense. Syllables of mandates and urgings, coalescences of them until they became long strings of ideas that had nothing to do with wolves. There were no mammals anywhere in his new project. Now it was all about people being numbed by overdependence. Enfeebled by

"But Lin's book," he said, "it left me uncertain. My plan is to meet with her to see if I can regain my confidence and so become whole again. I need to assess whether I truly know myself or not."

He wouldn't say what his new project was, but it demanded such self-knowing. Whatever it was, he was willing to say that it involved entering realms of a once-foreign dimension, which one could only do if one were truly and only oneself. His agent revealed a bit more, if one understood what it meant to be "dedicated to accessing ancient consciousness." Winter believed most humans had a buried capacity to do what he was doing, but lacked the proper channels to access the ability. It was like a room with no doors, a sky in a box of sky.

Nevertheless, the project was going well. Or had been, he said. Until Lin Strickland's book.

And now Lin was invited to her students' parents' time-share islands, to deliver keynote speeches, and to spend weekends on sunny coastlines teaching workshops for the ecology and arts centers. Talk shows, guest appearances, cook-offs, ESP posters, international conferences dedicated to consciousness in the age of the corporation.

Lin was available, her schedule one of possibility, large and small. If someone crossed campus with a soccer ball, Lin had time to kick it, her inexperience made adorable by how just getting close to the ball increased her joy, her usually steady gait becoming a feisty pitch of elbows as she closed in on the ball. If a student brought a dog to campus, she'd teach it to stay. When students stopped by her office, they'd chat for hours about—what? Recipes for steamed pumpkin. The recurrence of teeth in a dream. The how-do-you-say *I feel awakened* in Urdu. Her door was always open, so from his office next door Roal Bowman heard it all.

She and her students talked as if the afternoon clock were a field of sky, nothing beyond those hands but the everness of atmosphere, an amnesia of numbers, no purpose in its pointing. Her office glinted with bright voices. When the reporters came everyone wondered how much longer Braddock

College could keep Lin, how much longer she would stay before moving toward greater prestige.

By then, the award stickers crowded the cover of her book and her interviewers asked where she'd go next. It could be anywhere. But instead of moving to watch the sunrise of her next ambition, she paid the rent on her house and helped the neighbor repair the fence between their yards. She returned from a reading tour, adopted a fish for her office, framed a tapestry, and stayed at Braddock.

She stayed through the winter and into spring as if she didn't know that Braddock was so remote, so immodest with overwatered green in contrast to the dusty wheat fields around the town best known for its onion festival.

Everyone waited for her announcement, waited until the last minute of the last week of classes when the students climbed the enormous limbs of the Rally Tree to call out for their causes, dropping down their last postcards of the year to urge summer action for their favorite causes. Meatless Weekdays. Ride a Bike. Lose the Lipstick. Recycle Your Life. Get Fertile with Farmers.

But here it was, the end of the year, the Rally Tree cards spent, and Lin with no indication of a plan to go. Instead she shared one of her favorite letters from a local reader:

Lin—

I am wondering if any of the other letters you've received have told you joy makes an actual sound? It sounds like cobwebs snapping. But perhaps it's not the cobweb, but the sound of light breaking, one end of it being separated from the other. I would make that sound if the experience of your book were removed from me. It is one light that connects to my own. People say your book redefines what a book is, but I think that misses the point. A book is only always a book. I hope it redefines focus into fractals, and fractals into tessellations, and tessellations into waves. Because we hear in waves but think we understand in focus. Anyway, congratulations. And thank you for the filaments of light.

Even after receiving letters like that, it was as though Lin didn't know that Braddock College was where people stayed only when their wilt of ambition revealed the flower of relief.

Margi Wright in sociology stayed, Margi with her mother who pretended to remember.

Or brilliant Dick Lockham in his elegant suits and arrogant beard who could be counted on to be sober during most of the weekday morning classes.

Or Jean Tellar whose decades-old analysis of stuffed animals as porn for children could not find the traction she knew it deserved.

And Roal. Of course Roal stayed too.

Though lately, there had been changes. A few others had begun to stay long enough to pass the stories from one year to those who arrived the next. Quentin Hoover improbably stayed after recalculating the distribution rate of dust-borne viruses. Gary Stone became Division Chair and stayed, and Tony Guzman looked comfortable too, unwinded by his relentless publication schedule and private early morning Pilates. In the past they'd have returned their job like a book they wouldn't remember reading. But now they said they loved the town, enjoyed the weather, could walk to work, raise a family. And they kept their ambitions: they published, outreached, served. They gathered and procreated, took flexible schedules, formed clubs, installed outdoor kitchens. And stayed.

CHAPTER 2

Time swung a lazier spiral over Roal Bowman. He stacked another pile of papers at the edge of his desk. They would be finished by the end of next week, when school ended and the students spilled from buildings, dropped their sweatshirts on the lawn, and revealed that all along they had been bodies and mouths and pourings of amber.

Roal made his comments in green: there was no other color that would work for these students. They would soon leave for a summer and come back with their insistent, terrifying smiles when they said the words *future* and *hope* and *want*. Roal had tried red pens. And pencils. But the students did not need a crisis of red or the erasability of graphite. There would be life enough for both.

His notes on their papers were crafted as tiny script in the margins of their work. Notes about tone, passages of pieces the work called to mind, semicolons, why etymological origins made certain words incompatible with others, explanations about why the characters ought to reconsider their motives. His notes were copious, labored, nearly affectionate due to the amount of time invested he spent with each word. The precision of his letters, sharp-cornered *E*s and *R*s that flourished where they trailed instead of drooping. His belief that they would understand his allusions and references. He bloomed on their pages and encouraged them to do the same, and so students found touching the rift between his distant in-person self and the intimate proximity of him of the page, touching in nearly the same strange way that the Heimlich maneuver can remind the arms of tenderness.

Roal shut his door gently to the students gathering in Lin's office, the festival of anticipation. Students used to stop by his office, too. A few of them, anyway, until his own little book went quietly out of print. The last few copies lay on his bookshelf: *Every Good Thing Must*. The covers were still crisp enough, but the pages' edges had yellowed like hospital tubing. When students asked him to sign a copy he felt how thin it was.

Twenty years at Braddock, tenured, and with a steadily delivered income, *Professor* had a certain ring to it. The Bell of Inertia. The Gong of This Is It. Though the college seemed to want a little more. Demanded it lately, in fact. Tagg Larson, the dean, said Roal would need to do something that could be put in Roal's next evaluation packet.

"Anything—" Tagg said, "a paragraph, a review, an article about writer's block. A—a satirical cartoon. Just publish *something*. It doesn't matter what. It could be a poem." Tagg rolled his hand in the air as if to usher in more ideas, more possibilities. Tagg was so small and delicately proportioned that he looked like a child playing the part of an ambitious accountant. But his little wrists were creased and hairy just like a grown-up's, and his suits were expertly fitted. This tiny precision lent Tagg's authority a chilling quality, like watching children organize a gun cabinet.

Not likely, Roal explained again. His first book had been a kind of mistake, a surprise orchestrated by his wife, Dina. It wasn't even what Roal had intended with all of its stories cut in half so only their beginnings were left, and then published as a book of lessons for beginning writers. They read the first half of the stories and then wrote the second themselves. Sixteen years later, Roal had recovered from the surprise of the book, but not the sting of it. There would not be another.

Tagg threw up his tiny hands before leaving, "You don't get it, Roal, I'm not asking. I'm telling you how it is." Roal imagined tiny confetti coming down over them both.

But Roal knew how it was. He had tenure, one book, decent class sizes, and at a solid six-five stood too tall to take arguments from Tagg seriously.

Plus his students really did almost like him—they couldn't say why. Something about how he shook his shaggy black hair from his face when he had an idea, like a swimmer proudly rising, chin angling out as his mouth opened for air. When he spoke, his lids remained low and heavy, giving him a reputation for being droll and unflappable. He was rarely funny, but did not seem exactly serious. Solid. Patient as a whale heart. His height was an authority they trusted. And when they searched his dark eyes for a message beneath those lids, for a flicker of humor or a shuttering of displeasure—anything to read what he said—they were struck by the impassive gaze of them, how they accorded all things equally, all things worthy or unworthy of the same kind of consideration. It was the look in the eye of a fish pulled from the water and laid on the bank, the spectacular eye turned slightly to look at the world of air, taking in the overhead birds, the trees, the people, and the grass with the same unblinking calm. When the fish would be done trying, its eye would lose focus, its wilderness congealed.

As for most tall men, particularly those whose looks became more etched than softened over time, people stepped aside to make room for Roal, then looked up to see his appreciation for the favor they'd provided. But the look of gratitude they hoped for was rarely present. Because Roal had always been treated with special consideration, he assumed it must be so for everyone: the world a place where the gifts always exceeded the earnings, where the corrective measure was to guard against the mindless excesses of generosity. A world of the tipped-up, waiting face where people thanked him for the favors they provided.

In this grateful air, Roal loved to sit with the students who brought him their work, silence crepitating importantly between them. In his office, the air felt substantial, and the ticking of the second hand profound. His lamp's green seep of light siphoned time, and the desktop sand garden with its miniature rake made them giants of possibility.

After students left, Roal's office stayed with them like a portable sanctuary. They entered it throughout their days of sun and traffic, of tabloid covers, of news from home of dead pets, of the microwave's timer announcing the readiness of their next meal. It was the important silence of a large and solid man who sat still as he held their work in his own steady hands.

But now it was Lin's students whose voices Roal heard, beak-sharp on the drywall between their offices. Roal sank onto his cushion in the corner. Another burst of laughter. He closed his eyes and prepared to meditate. His first *ohm*-hum was weak, a wire-thin sound that was separate from him, that originated somewhere removed from his solar plexus. He started over, locating the center of the next humming *ohm* inside his head. He pushed it deeper, down into his chest where he wanted to feel the vowel gather his body around it. He intoned again, this *ohm* extending past the sound of Lin laughing as she told a student how to catch a taxi in Prague. It filled his office, inhabiting one second's clock tick and then spreading into the next and so on until each *ohm* was an elastic length of hum.

Roal loved these moments—the imagined nowhere and nothing on either side of him. Not his growing unease about how his father would sometimes call too early just to talk about how beautiful eggs were, not Tagg's overeager interest in his upcoming evaluation, not the way Dina seemed to go still and lost when he reached to smooth her hair. *Ohmmm*—the sound was tantalizing: enduring, stable in a world that kept rearranging the furniture in the room of his comfort. The distance between one *ohm* and the next got farther and farther away, eventually stretching impossibly. Into sleep. He slept.

The knock on his door woke him, his office still dream-crowded and warm. The delivery woman peeked in, bashful to find him sleeping on his cushion. She had deliveries for Lin, but Lin had gone to class. She asked Roal to give them to Lin when she returned.

"Flowers," he called, when he heard Lin's key in the lock. He took them to her: "For you."

Lin beamed, "Dahlias! Thank you, Roal—oh, they remind me of a little place I used to go that had nothing but dahlias and bagels. How lovely." She cleared a tangle of twine and set the flowers on her desk, then read the card as Roal waited to hand her the package. Lin laughed, "Ah, I see. Ha—I thought these were from you! No wonder. But thanks for delivering them." She tucked the card back into the flowers and reached for the package.

"No wonder?" asked Roal. "Why's that?" Lin turned her face toward him. It was clear and ovoid, pulled slightly sharp at her chin. She reminded Roal of a boat, of something headed for a vastness of blue. Her faded green eyes, the sturdy prow of her upturned nose, even some silver in the spray of the springing curls of her hair. She had water in her past.

She looked at him quizzically.

"You said 'no wonder.' No wonder what?" Roal looked down at her.

"Oh." Lin gazed at the flowers, thinking. "I guess I meant it literally—as in, if the flowers were from you, it would make me wonder. But they're not, so there is no wonder. No. Wonder."

When Roal handed her the package he saw his own return address in the corner of it and made a move to try to grab it back. His elbow caught the edge of the mask next to Lin's door, and that in turn hit the rain stick above it. It clattered onto Roal and then to the floor, the sound of its rain sullen. The return address was clearly Roal's, written in Dina's firm-pressed writing.

Lin watched him with an openness so frank it engaged her whole body. She set one hand squarely on top of the package and the other under her chin. She did not lean over to pick up the rain stick or offer to show Roal the package. Roal hesitated, then picked up the stick himself and hung it on the ledge where it rained for a few seconds. Lin's crowded office was exactly the kind of room he tried to never enter. Things balanced atop other things, the cascading potential for shift and slide enormous. Entering further would make things wobble, and trying to steady them would set off an avalanche of falling. He would have to back up to get out.

"Anything else?" Lin asked.

"No. Maybe. I wonder—" he paused. He and Lin rarely spoke. Time, schedules, closed doors, then his long habit of nodding at her in the hallway which had at first been intended as polite recognition but had come to stand for entire conversations. The nods were almost the only words they shared. He glanced at the package again.

"Just, congratulations. On your book," he said. "I mean, you've been so busy I haven't had time to congratulate you. I'm sure once I read it it'll be worth flowers. Then you may have to wonder after all." He smiled down at her uneasily, ready to back away. He needed to call Dina. Except Lin was looking at him with something like amusement. The intention of being amused.

"Oh," said Lin. "That was awkward."

"Awkward?" said Roal. "What?"

Without a trace of the awkwardness she suggested might be present, Lin said, "I think what you said was awkward because now I know you haven't read the book—I'd assumed you had. I wonder if you will. I've read yours. And everyone's who's here. But," she continued, warming up, "what I think is really awkwardly interesting is why your reading the book would in any way determine whether or not it's worth flowers—for me, that's actually the most fascinating part." And she went on, testing awkwardness as a doctor might test a muscle to determine its precise source of pain. "Also, maybe this conversation feels awkward because it's rare. You know, we haven't had a personal conversation yet, and I've been here for three years. And all because of dahlias."

Roal's laugh was brief, embarrassed: "Fine, I won't get you flowers."

"No?" Lin mock-fluttered her eyelashes and pressed her hand to her chest.

"No." Roal said irritably, "Or if I do, it will just be to deliver them to the name on the card." He returned to his office, firmly closing his door with a satisfying click. It reminded him of his mother's cigarette case, how he used to feed her cigarettes so he could feel the click of the case: open, shut, open, shut. When it snapped shut, it always felt so final, the last answer the silver box might ever get to give. He didn't want to send Lin flowers. He would not send Lin flowers. He reached for the phone as Lin opened his door and poked her head in.

"No harm, I hope?"

"None," Roal said. " Everything is fine."

"Anyway," Lin continued, "Tell Dina thanks for the package, and what I can bring tomorrow."

"Tomorrow?" Roal turned to Lin. "What about Dina?"

"We're having dinner at your house. At six. But I can't stay long because the next day I go to meet Winter Patent at his yet-to-be disclosed wherever." With that, Lin waved and disappeared. Roal stared after her. Dinner? He called Dina.

"Lin says she's coming to dinner. What does she mean?" He heard water running. A metal spoon in a metal bowl.

"We invited Lin to dinner tomorrow. Wait. Just a minute." The water turned off. "Okay. I need to go. I'm feeling a pull toward the not-phone world."

"I mean," Roal explained, "how do you know Lin?"

"Really?" Dina's voice caved a little. "Lin's my walking partner? Around the reservoir?" The reservoir sounded familiar. So did Lin's name as soon as Dina said it. Lin. Lynn. It clicked. He had heard it, but as Lynn, a random neighborhood anybody. To hear the name fixed to Lin, his colleague, it was startling. How long?

"Plus," Dina said, "we should celebrate her book. I mean, it's a little late but still."

"Have you read it? Do we even have a copy?"

He doubted Dina had mentioned that she and Lin *Strickland* were friends. He'd have remembered that. It seemed, anyway, like the type of thing he thought he would remember. If he had heard it.

Dina was saying. "It's sort of absorbable, really, more than readable. It makes you feel permeable."

"Also Lin had a package. From you." Roal said. He was not yet sure what he was asking.

"That was fast. I'm glad it got there." Dina said.

"What's in it?"

"Just some things for a book she's working on. A photo I found at the thrift store, a pamphlet from the chiropractor that seemed to relate. Oh, and a funny cheese stick wrapper. Just random things that will be useful." Sound of a cutting board being set on the counter.

Roal was horrified. "A pamphlet that 'seemed to relate'? You sent Lin Strickland *a funny cheese stick wrapper*?"

"I know. Strange, right?" She paused to consider, "But who knows how these things work? I need to get dinner in the oven and get back to the yard. Something is going on out there. Everyone is quiet. I'll see you soon."

When Roal walked through the front door later, Dina stepped into the kitchen doorway, giving a quick wave, her hands wet and flecked with cilantro. Roal regarded her as if this were something new.

But then she speculated that someone in the neighborhood was spraying their lawn so the grass was withdrawn and she was herself again. Roal studied her with a question he felt he could answer purely by looking: but nothing had changed. Her plants, her cilantro hands, the way she spoke as if they'd been having a conversation all day long.

He was grateful later to have looked for so long at her, to have worked to see something he might have missed before. It was this vision of Dina that Roal would remember after she'd left.

There in the doorway of the kitchen, her two braids were wrapped neatly up over the top of her head and then around the back. She looked at him directly with her wide-set eyes, gathering great expanses of space with her gaze. The scar on the side of her face puckered the skin and pulled the left side of her face into a slight permanent smile. She wore an old button-down shirt of Roal's over a summer dress, with an apron over that, and she looked spare within the layers. The house smelled like dinner. Like lemon chicken and green beans and layer biscuits. It smelled like there should be a swing on the backyard tree and a dog running in with slippers.

Roal poked around in the living room brushing aside the trailing plants. Dina called that if he was looking for Lin's book, it was in her project room. He found it near her chair, nestled into the piles of notebooks and papers that lay in soft sloping mounds, animal and quiet.

Lin's book felt thick and substantial. No author picture. He wondered why. Lin was strong looking, with good, deep lines around her mouth that suggested a habit of humor.

Her bio stated she had grown up in Wisconsin. This was her first book. Double major in Psychology and Physics, then a degree in Creative Writing. One reviewer noted that the book's "narrative sequences allow readers to experience dimension and space as a set of lived properties." Her acknowledgments thanked a writing grant, a dog, the amygdala, her parents, and the university lab where she'd done research on sound and vibrational resonance. 582 pages, ending with the words "imprint of a double." The first word was "According" and there were 118 chapters, a few of which began on the same page. Roal sat down and leafed through: some single-sentence chapters, some equations, a picture of sheet music. The paragraph he started reading alternated between the phrases, "Night pitch dropping" and variations on the word "Resonance." It seemed to him like the kind of book where you had to keep going back to the beginning.

"Take it—I'm done," Dina said from behind the chair, startling Roal.

He accidentally upset a pile of papers that slid in layers sideways, like an archaeology experiment.

"Whoa, a landslide!" Dina's surprise sounded guarded, the way one might say give happy hello to a friend's ex-husband before remembering you'd already agreed to despise him. She kneeled down to gather the papers. But then she turned to Roal and said, "Well here you see it—my life's work I guess!" She indicated the scatter in her hands.

Roal nodded with a look of apology. Papers littered the floor. Scraps of paper, really, some with Dina's writing in the margins: annotated recipes; yellow-page service listings for heat installation; white pages with street names and last names circled; musical scores; an invitation to join the Episcopalian church; grocery store receipts. Lists. Roal had an aversion to the inanity of scrapbooking, artifacts useful to no one alive, mundane details of those whose archived pages increase in value the longer they remain forgotten.

Scrapbooks defeated the now of Roal's Zen by looking over the shoulder of *is* for another glimpse at *was*. He didn't want to sift through an evidence pile of their life. But he'd plundered the space and did not have the right to comment on the scrapbook as a pedestal for the moments he believed had earned the right to disappear so there was room for the present. He helped her shuffle the papers together, gave them a final pat, and stood up.

They looked at each other, Dina's lip raised in a permanent question of collaboration, and Roal smiling back, though as the moment stretched he became less certain of what he was smiling about. The moment grew rather than shrank, as if Roal were approaching the moment rather than leaving it. Something was required of him, a guessing game he hadn't read the rules for.

"So," Dina said, "that's my latest project. I can tell you where it's heading if you'd like." Roal turned to her with mock seriousness.

"We already *are* where it's heading—I was there the first time. I am sorry I messed it up though. I hope I didn't completely undo the timeline."

Dina looked puzzled, "What do you mean you were there the first time?"

"Just that I'm here now. You know what they say: 'The past steals from the present.' I'm not much for reminiscing with scrapbooks. But you can—it's just not for me. I'm sorry though, that I messed it up."

Dina gazed up at him. Roal later tried to recreate her expression, but it was a mix of two things he couldn't quite place together. Relief and pity? Distance and longing? It was the look given to those who can't possibly guess how their life will change. Her hair was a loose frizz near her temples. When she spoke again, the expression had faded.

"Oh no," she said, sounding certain, perhaps thankful. "No, don't worry about that. You didn't mess it up. No," she said, still thinking, "your answer is . . . useful. I think it is good now, so thank you."

The way her eyes took him in was tender, but they also looked far past him, as was her way. Perhaps she saw a faraway Roal on a horizon. Perhaps it was just that she always seemed to enjoy the solitude of distance. He remembered later how lightly she'd taken his elbow to lead him from the room, how she squeezed his arm once and tenderly, then closed the door behind them.

CHAPTER 3

On Thursday, Lin complained that the reporters were getting in the way of her "exploration halls," a term Roal objected to because it disregarded the beauty of "lecture"—a beautiful word rooted in *legend*, a word which tied Roal to an ancient practice.

The reporters wanted to scoop the Winter Wolf Reintroduction, though Lin knew no more than they did. She'd been told only that she would get in a car, be taken to a location, meet Winter, and later be driven home. The end.

But the reporters came anyway: the stakes were high. They pretended to lounge on campus, disguising themselves as students and springing into aggressive chumminess upon a sighting of Lin. At the end of the day, she jumped into Roal's office and closed the door breathlessly behind her.

"Hey—saw a reporter closing in just as I tried to escape. Mind if I take a second here until he leaves?" Roal waved her in, *okay, okay*.

They heard the knock next door. "Professor Strickland?" he called, "I just saw your light a second ago. You in? Miss Strickland?" Then, more softly, "Professor?"

Lin exaggerated a grimace and mouthed *My light?* Roal shrugged in commiseration. They waited, their eyes on the door. The reporter sighed and knocked again. Then they both jumped when they heard the knock on Roal's door. Lin pressed herself to the wall behind it. Roal leaned back and called, "Yes?" The door opened. The reporter looked in and rubbed his pale chin pointlessly, then looked again down the hallway toward Lin's office.

"Yes?" Roal repeated.

"Dr.—" The reporter looked at the nameplate on Roal's door. "Dr. Bowman?"

"Professor Bowman." Roal corrected.

"Really? I wouldn't have known." The reporter sounded surprised.

"Yes," said Roal, "just Professor."

"Okay—do you know where I might find Lin Strickland, the author of . . . ?"

Roal's interruption was swift: "Yes, I know. You just missed her."

The reporter groaned, then wrote down his contact information. When Roal reached for it, the reporter said, "You look different."

"From what?" Roal looked more closely at the reporter.

"A class about twenty years ago, I think? I almost didn't recognize you—you had long braids then and taught writing."

"Still do," Roal said. "Teach writing, that is."

"Yeah. And Indian too, of course," the reporter joked. Roal flinched, grateful the door was between him and Lin. The reporter clearly assumed that Roal was, in fact, still an Indian, and the joke would therefore be funny. But Roal had cut his braids, and hoped that his phase of allowing others to believe he was Native American had been severed as well, a forgetting that was possible given those early days of the faculty's rapid turnover. Aside from Dick Lockham, there was no one else around who could hold him to his old habit. And who knows what Dick remembered? Less and less each week. Roal had wrapped that chapter of his life, along with his braids, in tissue paper and laid it in his dresser drawer, perhaps a dare to his own future reckoning.

Roal pointed to the small sand garden on his desk and the low cushion in the corner, "Well, now I simply am what I practice. I'm just working on being where I am." He began to close the door.

Lin's choked snicker was likely mistaken by the reporter as Roal settling back into his chair. Without looking at Lin, Roal thrust the reporter's contact information toward her and wished her luck getting to their place for dinner. When she left, he breathed until the breathing did not scrape his stomach like a spoon accusing an empty bowl.

* * *

When Lin showed up, she held a giant bouquet of forsythia and two bottles of wine.

"I wasn't sure which to bring," she breezed, "good white or bad red. So I brought both." Dina ushered Lin into the kitchen, the forsythia bouquet an armful of light. Lin complimented Dina's apron, and then remarked how quickly Dina's little jade plant was putting on leaves. Roal froze. Lin had been to the house before. She knew Dina's plants—how else would she notice a change in the leaves? He paused inside his study so his surprise would not be on display.

From there, he could hear Lin talking about the car parked in front of her house, how it hadn't moved since Tuesday. Dina said she'd already walked by the car but couldn't see anyone through the tinted windows, and Roal listened, trying to absorb that Dina and Lin were friends. Really friends. Friends who noticed when each other's plants put out leaves. Friends who scoped out each other's stalkers and mused about mixed flatware and whom among the people they knew was most likely to live on a boat with a lover for one week of each year and tell no one. Friends.

"Wine!" Lin called out from the edge of the kitchen. And Roal went in.

All night Roal felt himself standing just outside the circle of light cast by the conversation. It was a conversation laced with familiarity and understandings of how things worked from the inside. He could not find a way to ease himself in, so sat like a newcomer at his own table. He reminded himself they should have company more often as he was out of practice. Or less often. He wasn't sure which.

When Dina served Lin ice cream with her pie, but gave Roal a piece of pie without it, Lin recalled that Roal was lactose intolerant. When Lin suggested that they all visit the lavender farm at the edge of town, she quickly apologized, saying she'd forgotten that Roal was allergic to bee stings, so the trip might not be a good idea. Dina took no special notice of Lin's little claims to knowledge, as if Roal's medical history were not an intimate history opened now by Lin. Lin's questions to Roal were conversational. Casual. Close. Have

Epi-Pen injectables gotten any easier to self-administer? It's been years now since your mom died, right?—do you think your father will date again?

After a while, Roal stopped cataloging the things Lin knew about him. The answer was evident: everything—his mother died from a cancer she didn't try to beat, his father was alone, his wedding gift to Dina was the reading chair still in her project room, his first bike still hung in their garage, their backyard tree had begun as a start that Dina took from the yard of Roal's childhood because, as Dina said, it already knew him, so would grow better than a stranger. Roal and Dina had no children, didn't travel, kept separate bedrooms because Roal needed to fall asleep to television and Dina needed to have her glaring full-spectrum light blast on at four a.m. so she could be properly awake by five, and together they needed new carpet in the living room. All of it. Lin was in on it all.

Lin wanted the story of how he and Dina met, and Dina nodded toward Roal so he could tell it. He began stiffly. He couldn't remember the last time they had told he story. He started with graduate school when he would finish classes and head to Kenner's Lounge. Dina had been part of Kenner's since, what? Twelve? Dina nodded. She was twelve and the school bus dropped her at the wrong place, which happened often with all of her address changes. She had no idea where she was, but Kenner's was open, so she went in, did her math, and fell asleep in a booth until Big Ken found her. She couldn't remember her new address or the names of her new foster parents, but she had the name of her case worker who came to pick her up. By then, she and Big Ken were friends, and he had a list of jobs he needed help with. She became his unofficial assistant and, later, when she was released from the foster system, Big Ken gave her a job and the room above the bar.

"She hadn't thought what to do next," Roal said, "She'd been there forever." Dina nodded. As her addresses and the people she lived with changed, her family was Big Ken and the dim gloss of the bar. The thin cushions. Chessboards in the corner, Ribbit the dog chasing birds in his sleep by the jukebox. Roal was often there after class, in part because he knew Dina would be—something about her, he said. One day he handed her a story and told her that since she had inspired it, it really belonged to her.

"I don't think I'd inspired anyone before—it felt daunting," Dina confessed.

Roal smiled, then explained to Lin, "It's not one of the stories in my book."

"Was it her hair that inspired the story?" Lin asked Roal, though she was looking at Dina. Roal nodded, surprised. Lin was right. Those impossibly coiled braids.

"I can see it," Lin said. "Those are some impressive braids."

"Heavy anyway." Dina looked like a woodcut from an old-world story-book. Twenty years ago, her braids had glowed nearly gold. Now, silver streaks cast a halo of white. Roal was grateful the topic of his own braids had not come up. He finished the story of how they met. When Dina continued it, he was surprised there was more. He hadn't heard her version before.

Dina said, "Anyway, when I gave his story back to him with some comments I couldn't tell if he was compelled or offended. We started dating."

"Oh, so that's where you got your start," Lin said, looking at Dina.

"Yes. Roal's story. It was the first time anyone gave work to me—just specifically to me. It made me *feel* specific. It felt, I don't know, grand. I was indebted for being seen that way. I really owed him for that."

When Roal replayed that sentence later, he heard Dina's use of the past tense, the soft thud at the end of "owed" like a bird hitting the window from a room away. But he could not have known just yet to select that one sentence from among the many. That is the regret of regret.

Roal smiled, casting back into the memory of Dina's studio apartment where she began to read more, then wrote letters to writers about their work, beginning with those long dead. At night she read aloud her letters to Proust and Dickens about where their lines were over-stuffed or where they had made an obvious statement when the more subtle one had already done the job. Roal listened to her read—the outrage and subversive hilarity of her attempts. He fell asleep as she read, his own hair unbraided and mingled with hers, a dark shadow in light water.

The night Dina met Roal's parents, he lay down exhausted as Dina unwound her braids from their coils. They hung past her waist, the ends of them twitching as she unraveled the braids while staring at the wall. This ritual meant nothing to her, simply one of the thousands of times her hands had traveled the path. When she came to bed, Roal draped her hair over him. It'd been a long night, he said weakly, drained and drifting off. He later woke to Dina pushing him off her hair, which he had pinned beneath him when he rolled over. After that, she kept her hair braided and piled above her pillow as she slept, which prompted Roal to ask her to marry him. It was the logically irrational move of a man who did not want to lose her and so thought he should marry her before she declared other parts of her life out of bounds.

His professors had already assigned him a new depth because of his relationship with her. His classmates analyzed it with the open wonder of foreigners who witness the tossing of bones. His father welcomed it as a sign of maturity, and Helen, his mother, was relieved Roal would not be alone when she died.

Helen shared her relief a few evenings later. She liked to speculate that somewhere in her ancestry there might be a Native American who was buried, she thought, in Vermont. Roal wanted it to be true so he could stop pretending it was. But Roal's father, Chet, cringed.

"Helen," he interjected, "all of my relatives are from Michigan, and Latvia before that. We have dark hair. All of us. That's where Roal gets it."

"Yes, but they weren't much for running, now were they?"

"Neither is Roal." Chet insisted.

"But he didn't stick with it!" Helen protested, her chin drawn toward her chest. "He could have been really good if he had stuck with it." Chet didn't argue. Not over something that brightened Helen as she spoke about it. Helen was a few years from fifty, which was a few years past the time the doctors had given her, so it seemed uncharitable to correct her.

But Helen's sister Nettie, the dark one, swore they were not Indians (Native Americans, Helen corrected) and didn't care that Helen remembered something about Vermont and a treaty—which one? Helen wasn't sure. When Nettie heard Helen going on about high cheekbones, she'd mutter, "Jesus, Helen! Come *on*."

The night Dina met Helen, Helen nodded tepidly, and then looked at the glass of water just out of reach. She cleared her throat to make an announcement, her eyes on the glass of water as she spoke.

"It's nice to meet you," she began. "You should know that if Roal is part Native American, there isn't any paperwork. So if you have children they probably won't get a break on college."

"Mom!" Roal spluttered.

"That's alright, Mrs. Bowman, it's nice to meet you, too," said Dina.

"I'm not an Indian," Roal protested.

"I don't know where I'm from, either," said Dina.

"Native American," said Helen.

"Fine, whatever," Roal said to Helen. "But I'm not," he said to Dina. Helen's face sank at Roal's betrayal, and Chet stepped in to show Dina the back yard, leaving Helen and Roal alone.

"Mom?" Roal asked, his shoulders suspended in a shrug of disbelief.

"Sorry, honey." Helen's chin trembled. "I just got so wound up trying to think of how to explain."

"Explain what? I never told her I'm an Indian."

"I didn't want her to think you were lying. That can put a lot of strain on a marriage."

"Marriage? Our kids getting college scholarships?"

"It's coming. I can tell." Helen frowned, annoyed, "Oh, why is it that the people who are going to get married are the last ones to know it? It doesn't make sense."

"Mom, when Dina comes back in, let it go. Please. We're here for dinner. Let's have dinner with regular conversation. Please?"

"She's young. Who did you say her people are?"

Then Chet and Dina stepped back in, and Helen was ready to talk.

When Helen asked Dina what she did, Dina told her: she took care of her plants, twenty-seven of them now, most of them from starts she got from people who had been kind to her when she was in foster care. She had rigged up a little irrigation system that ran from her kitchen and bathroom sinks throughout the studio, along the shelves and ladders and tables.

When Helen asked again what Dina did, Dina told her: she listened to music a few hours each day before work. She thought the music might help to build an internal structure like a Jesuit memory palace. She thought it could help for when her work seemed mundane. Helen looked at Roal.

When Helen asked if Dina did anything else, Dina told her: she liked to walk in the evenings when the air temperatures shifted and changed places. She liked the currents of that hour. She knew every block of the town, every alley, every dumpster. She knew when the food for the restaurants was brought to the back doors, and who would sell their house next based on what types of repairs were under way. Roal smiled encouragingly as if he didn't notice Helen's gaze stuck to him.

Though Roal cringed when Helen pushed, "Anything *else*, dear?" Dina was calm, and told her: She wrote letters to writers, and credited Roal for the inspiration.

And finally, desperately, Helen exclaimed: "But what do you *do*, dear? What do you *do*?"

And Dina understood: "Oh. I work at Kenner's. Kenner's Lounge where I met Roal. I've been there forever." Helen, who at last received the answer she already knew, sat back.

"I see," said Helen. Dinner was served.

As Roal now listened to Dina and Lin talk he knew with certainty—had known for years, if he had to admit it to himself, which he knew he should—that he didn't know Dina well. The small pieces of conversation Lin and Dina traded seemed so small, such intricate ornaments of knowledge. He couldn't find a way to enter, though Lin asked him questions and Dina's talking included him. He waited for them in the living room feeling like an overlarge cellular presence as Dina and Lin tidied the kitchen.

Roal had assumed that to live with a person was the same thing as to know a person. He knew the taste of Dina's cooking and the sounds of her mornings. But he had not known she would walk by a stranger's car to get a glimpse of who sat inside or that she tested melons by closing her eyes and feeling the water-dense heaviness travel from her hands to her shoulder. That was another Dina. What did one say to a Dina like that?

If Lin and Dina were a story he and his class were studying, the class would describe their conversation as the essential work of building interstices, the supports to hold them together across the spaces between themselves. If they built enough such spaces, they would, eventually, have a structure that could support them.

Roal felt something swing into a new position inside himself. The essential work.

He heard Dina exclaim in the kitchen, "Really? Yes. Yes. This might be the answer to asking what might happen next. This is perfect!"

And Lin answering, "Oh, thank God. But tell no one." And Dina said of course, the timing was incredible, she had no plans.

When they came out of the kitchen they were glowing, certain of something. Roal would ask Dina about it after Lin left, a small question toward building the interstitial on a night that was clear from his house to the stars.

When they were alone Roal turned to thank Dina for the evening. They rarely entertained, and he hadn't known what to expect from Lin, but was happy the dinner had happened and that Dina was friends with someone he knew.

"Quite a surprise, though," he said. "To find out so all of a sudden."

Dina looked at him swiftly. It was late, and her eyes seemed to have faded from a snappish, inspired blue to one paler within just a few seconds. He wondered if that happened each night, to everyone, or if it had happened years ago and he was just now catching up on her face. Dina searched Roal's eyes, and he understood she was trying to see if he had been joking. He was not. When he broke her gaze, Dina turned to head other room and said it hadn't really been very sudden.

"I mean," said Roal, "I just didn't connect it before—I didn't know you meant the same Lin. I thought you meant a *Lynn*—like a general Lynn with a *y*. A different Lin."

"It's strange," she yawned, "why you thought that. Oh well, I better get going. Lots to do and I'm already tired! Good night."

He tried to explain further, "I think I hadn't connected that your Lin and my Lin were the same person because I didn't know you knew her—like really knew her. I don't really know her."

Dina stopped. "Does it make you curious," she said, not sure how to ask it, "I mean, about all the rest of it? All of the hours in the days? Do you want to know?"

He was grateful the weekend was so close and there would be time to get into it. He could do that: step into the details of another life. But at that moment, halfway to hungover, and early asleep, the thought of answering yes right then would mean more than he had time for. It would mean the floodgates. The hours.

Do you want to know?

"Dina," he said. "Right now I'm beat. Let's go there later. When I can really pay attention."

Dina smiled and gave a single, slow, generous nod of understanding, "I loved it too, Roal. You are dear to me. Good night."

He was warmed by the tenderness. Tomorrow, he would tell her he understood finally that knowing is demonstrated by awareness of what is small and intimate, and he would like to get better at it. He could say that. He believed he could.

He could also admit that it is embarrassing to come by these moments of enlightenment so late, and to see that everyone else already knew what he only just discovered. If he were feeling particularly fearless, he might reveal his main insecurity, which is that there are so few people in the world who allow us to get to know them deeply, and he might not have what it takes to survive the depth.

He would develop these thoughts. At the edge of sleep, when the world is both possible and far away.

When Dina later came to say goodnight, her braids were down, and he saw by the light of the television that they were thin but lovely. He told her he had much to tell her. She leaned down to kiss his cheek. He reached up to touch her shoulder. One of his eyelids drooped more than the other with wine, and the news was terrible behind her.

CHAPTER 4

Dina's note was next to the coffee pot.

> R:
>
> Lin didn't want to go alone to meet Winter, so invited me (!) to go with her. An adventure! Their meeting might go until Sunday (!!), but she could be ready to come back as early as tonight, or tomorrow. She'll have to see how it goes. I sense a whole new beginning awaits! Wish me luck!
>
> I do love you ever Dina
> PS: Whatever you'll need is in the freezer.

Roal read, reread, the note. Even as he poured the coffee and pulled the chair from the table, Dina was now riding shotgun to Lin Strickland, world-famous writer on her way to meet, and perhaps to heal, the famed Winter Patent. The other Dina. The one he didn't know quite yet. Roal counted Dina's exclamation points: six (!) and for a moment was embarrassed by their overuse, though under the circumstance, Roal supposed she could have gotten away with more.

Roal drank his coffee. Dina would meet Winter Patent. The house settled around him, the shift in the wind noted.

Roal touched the phone. He listened to the dial tone, its tonal hum announcing that the world was ready to receive, the lines were open.

He could call his father, but Chet would need to know more than Roal knew and would also need to know why Roal knew so little. He set the phone down.

A luxurious privacy opened inside him.

More than wanting to tell anyone that Dina was about to meet Winter, Roal wanted to savor that he alone knew what was happening. He now knew something about the Winter Patent story that had not been anticipated and could hardly be guessed. His wife would meet the legend. And after she met him, there would be interviews. There would be phone calls and knocks at the door.

He too was now included in the story that, when it broke, would spill onto him and include him. A burst of cameras. Questions called out from a crush of reporters.

As he dressed for work, he paid new attention to the crisp but worn collar, his jacket's baggy pockets. The details would be important. When Roal passed others on his walk to campus, he noticed how their faces did not yet hold the story. He alone knew and so he was not among them.

On campus, Roal felt unknown and surprising. He flexed with a purpose that waited to be required.

When Felicia asked him how he was doing, he replied "Fantastically!" so vigorously the word expanded to include his walk to campus, the car Dina rode in as the distance stretched between them, the moon still in the just-blue sky. There was not yet anything more to say. But there would be. Roal breathed in, and his lungs felt like giant fur-lined rooms where he could bask in interior luxury.

Angela stopped by. She was also separate, had something others did not: she was a returning student, older than the rest at twenty-eight, an ex-stepmother of one. As she spoke to Roal about her final draft of a vignette series, her statements turned into upturned questions.

"I'm worried the leaps between sections are too . . . personally intuitive? I don't want to turn it in if you won't like it. I can meet this afternoon? Here?" The pages smelled like detergent.

"Angela," he said. Her eyebrows tweezed themselves into a question. She'd had enough lousy luck to see a no coming. Roal assured her that her vignettes were fine. Excellent, actually. Secrets she shared past her ability to outrun them. It was her strength. But he couldn't meet her later. He tasted the information about Dina under his tongue. It was like a key.

Metallic bite delicious as a storm. Explosive once exposed to air.

"I can't make it. Not today," he said. "Sorry. Something has come up. And don't worry—you know this work is good." He handed her back the pages and she took them, flushing at either the rejection or the compliment. She mumbled a return of high hope for his own weekend and fled.

Roal wondered if the power of *no* was greater than Zen's power of *now*, as *now* had never made him feel so rushed through with authority. No had just cleared his afternoon. He surged into it, gave it his full height as he walked to class. And then it held him aloft all the way to the faculty lounge.

There, Tony signaled to be quiet and closed the door. Roal recognized the look Tony was giving him: Tony was about to make a confession.

"Hey, Roal, so, have you seen what's going on with Gary?" Tony rubbed his close cropped goatee to appear casual, but it only made him look greedy.

"Something's going on with Gary?"

"Yes. And Jill. Something is going on—I saw them talking in a way that definitely made me wonder about the bigger story."

Roal's curiosity shrank. Gary, Division Chair, father of two, prone to wild gesticulations and wearing shorts well into winter. Gary didn't usually elicit gossip because he couldn't keep secrets, blurting out exactly what was going on as soon as he learned it himself.

"Easier that way," Gary always said. "Who can remember what you're supposed to know or not know? Just out with it."

Roal doubted Gary's secret would last long if there was one. And doubted, too, it would come to much when it spilled.

"It's probably just whatever people talk about. They're married, so having a conversation doesn't seem suspicious. Just talking." Roal said.

But Tony reported the facts: Jill stopped by Gary's office, which she almost never did. Then the two of them walked out to her car, together, talking too low for Tony to overhear. They exchanged papers. Or not exactly exchanged, Tony explained, but examined. Jill gave some papers to Gary. Gary pointed to something. Jill made a note. They squinted at it. They were definitely tense. Tony knew that.

"Tense how?" Roal asked.

"Like an in-the-shoulders, in-the-mouth kind of tense. Furtive."

"Maybe they're buying a house."

"No, I asked. I sort of asked. I hinted at it, but Gary didn't bite. It's not a house." Tony leaned in to tell Roal what else he had found out, each fact marked by a finger he held in the air: "And it's not a car. Jill just got the new minivan, and Gary is never giving up the Scout. And it's not a baby either—Gary's been fixed and Jill is afraid of having twins again. Plus it's not a new school for the boys—I hinted about that too but got nothing. That leaves divorce, which doesn't seem logical. Or health. But they looked fine. Maybe it's a will?"

"Maybe. It's not the kind of thing I would know." Roal was careful. He wondered what Tony really wanted. Tony who rolled his eyes when Roal spoke in the meetings, and Tony who wanted to measure whether Roal's creative writing students actually emerged from the class as better writers than when they went in. Tony volunteered to devise the metrics, as well as to sit on the committee needed to approve the whole process. He was in his twenties and said he'd helped streamline departments before, but no one had asked him before what. Tony was the one who, just three weeks after arriving, asked Roal when he would retire so he could let his friends know about the position. He was shocked to learn Roal was only forty-six. Roal would not be leaving.

Roal suspected it was also Tony who had urged Tagg Larson to get to the bottom of how Roal had been hired in the first place, much less tenured so quickly. No one from Roal's original committee was still around to ask, so Tagg had had to ask Roal directly. It was true the process had been unusual, but it had also been legitimate. Expedited, yes, Roal admitted, because the college was trying to stabilize in the face of mass departures. While others jumped ship and headed back to Connecticut, Seattle, San Francisco, Madison, the college stepped up its incentives, reached out, tried to save what remained. They needed Roal to stay.

Tagg said it must have been quite a different time back then. Roal didn't admit it to Tagg, but it had been a different time. Most definitely.

Today's incoming faculty ran circles around Roal, but Roal had remained, and that was worth something too. He had arrived before it was popular to live among wheat fields and teach classes wearing muck boots and dinner-plate belt buckles as a statement of ironic authenticity.

The other thing Roal didn't admit, and didn't really know himself whether or not it was true, was that he may have been a minority hire. No one had asked him if he was Native American outright. He remembered, though, telling a colleague he hated having to declare his race on job applications, but in the end had checked the "Caucasian" box anyway. He didn't say he should have checked something else, but the way he had said he'd checked the Caucasian box made it sound as though he had done it to be subversive. To assimilate. He couldn't really remember. He was in his braided twenties then. He hadn't yet worked out that life would continue as a series of events, utterances, actions, and gestures that would eventually reveal a pattern. Each moment then had still seemed like the only one, discrete and modular for when life needed to start over again.

"It's possible though." Tony pushed Roal to entertain the idea of Gary and Jill's impending divorce.

"Anything is possible, I suppose." And then Roal brushed past Tony, opened the door, and left. How simple to just end the conversation. How clearly necessary. It was like an invention Roal was surprised he'd been living without. Fantastic. Tony poked his head in, right behind Roal.

"So, if you hear anything, let me know, huh Chief?" Roal allowed the use of "Chief" from the Dean, who called everyone either Chief or Big Guy, but he wouldn't accept it from Tony. Roal suspected Tony knew that Roal used to allow others to assume he was Indian. It was the kind of information Tony would find valuable.

"Right? You'll keep an eye on it?" Roal felt the earlier glow of his secret spread its wings and fan him. He knew something that Tony did not, and the fact of that connected Roal to Gary, who also knew something Tony did not. Roal was connected now to the world of all people whose business is private and guarded because it is their own. Roal looked at Tony thoughtfully, expansively. He felt close to Tony, too, who knew things, who gathered and made a currency of secrets. He spoke for this secret part of Tony and of everyone when he answered.

"No. I won't keep an eye on it. Absolutely not."

Tony's eyes widened, impressed. In the after-utterance, Roal sat down alone, a taker of stances, a definer of space and time. After no, the cliff-drop into whatever might happen next seemed charged and noble, a hang glider over the landscape of his life. Remarkable, really, the view.

CHAPTER 5

Roal eyed his house as he walked toward it that afternoon, wondering if he should try to spruce it up for the TV crews, pull the clover from the lawn, clean the siding to brighten up the once-blue now bleached to a cadaverous gray. At least the yellow shutters were bright. The thought of taking on the house scared him. He still couldn't believe he owned something so large, with that much surface area. Small cracks from settling had appeared in the walls, and sometimes at night the whole thing creaked and popped. It lived its own life right over his head.

"Modest" was a word reporters might use to describe the house. It was a modestly sized rancher whose internal layout was apparent from the outside where it sat on a modest lot that featured a few clusters of modest trees and one incredible backyard willow. Whatever word they chose to describe the house would depend on how the story with Winter went and whether they ended up liking Dina. The picture windows were too ambitious for the house's proportions. But Dina liked them. She clustered plants in the windows, and they took over, fighting for light and making the living room a dim and private jungle.

Inside, Roal leafed through a book without seeing it. It felt good to have something solid in his hands. Mostly, it was important just to stay in the front room in case it all happened at any moment: Dina and Lin bursting through the door, and then lights on the lawn and interviews, perhaps a feature story about their life on Bridge Street which would reveal—which would surely reveal—Roal faltered.

There was no angle he could think of for a reporter to take. Perhaps just the ordinariness that made Dina and Roal such unlikely candidates for meeting Winter Patent. Dina, anyway. Roal was a story accessory, not the catalyst.

More shoelace than shoe, more clasp than jewel. He might answer the phone, but they would be calling for Dina.

The street returned its cars from the day, neighbors pulling in and disappearing into their homes. An occasional child on a bike, mothers pushing strollers in an efficient hurry.

The longer Real waited in the living room, the less he felt he belonged in it. Its little makeshift tables next to the chair that rocked once you pressed a lever. The couch with its back to that wall so it had a view of the plant-filled shelves and ceiling hooks that surrounded the window. Overhead lights spaced too far apart pressed the ceiling down where it went dark between the reach of the bulbs. It was a room to be walked across to get to the other rooms. His living room was a hallway, and he felt that its refusal to accept him there was the price for not having taken it seriously. He wrapped a vine around his finger, studying how its leaves darkened at the center. A small note was tucked underneath its pot. Real unfolded it: *Dancing.*

A single word. Then he saw that each plant had a note attached to it. Sometimes one word, sometimes more:

How bold to build your dreams among fast-moving stones.
Webs are spun from the point of pivoting. Stillness can weave them into
    a rope. Then climb.
Avalanche of space.
Space.
Always you. Always hearing.
Push me toward the next gathering.
If you're ever lonely, expand the sky.
Lift.
I hear you.
Mother. Asking.
Drenched in the spill of overpoured succumbing.

Dozens of notes on scraps of paper no larger than the promise of a fortune cookie. He quickly returned the notes to their plants, unsure of what he had just read. A boundless loneliness bloomed in his chest and he stood looking around the room until night lost its shapes.

Hunger. In the kitchen, he read again the note Dina had left for him. Not tonight (!), he thought, and headed to the freezer for a meal, chewed it down like it was the last.

Roal wore himself out with waiting again on Saturday, worried, never far from the window or the phone. He occasionally read and gently returned the little notes, no idea how long they'd been there or what they meant.

> *Star glittered rimrock of your original self.*
> *Yearning.*
> *Broken from removal. Staying.*

He sat up late, watching, prepared, distracted. He spent hours wishing he and Dina had gotten cell phones, wishing Dina had told him ahead of time of her plan so he could have told her not to go, wishing Winter Patent would call to apologize for keeping Dina so long and then talking with Roal about his life in the secret location, wishing Lin's tires would go flat at the meeting with Winter so Roal would have to drive out and rescue them, wishing Dina safe, wishing Dina home, wishing his waiting didn't feel so deliciously selfish and wounded—the entire day and night so diligently nursed and attended to, each minute hovered over and then regretted for the waste of it. He sat until the waiting legitimized a growing annoyance over being tethered to a window through which he had to take whatever light the plants didn't want. He breathed out. They breathed back. It went on.

Dina didn't return that night either, and despite watching the news past exhaustion Roal couldn't fall asleep. Fitful half-nods into sleep were interspersed with the sudden and excited local coverage of a cougar attack on a dog just inside the city limits. The owner fought it off with a can of cooking spray and her gardening shoe: "I just grabbed the first things I could get my hands on! I mean, it was a big cat, for sure, but it had our daughter's dog, so I didn't have a choice. I threw the shoe and started spraying and screaming for it to get. I don't know what scared it the most. Probably the combination."

The dog slept with his sedated head in the daughter's lap as she stroked his speckled face. Her face was pale except for the blotches under her eyes. When they asked her what she thought of her brave mother, she asked, "Do you think he'll be okay? He hurts all the way into here." She touched her stomach. No one answered.

The mother said she was going to stock up on pepper spray and teach her daughter to use it. The girl didn't appear to hear.

The experts doubted that would help. Most cougars just drop down from above, they said. You never see them coming.

The news cycled all night: protests over free trade, ice cap melt, bombs that colonized death in the Middle East. Winter Patent and Lin Strickland were meeting, though no one had heard from them yet. Helmets were recommended for children on tricycles. Stocks down, foreclosures up, cancer holding steady. Roal dreamed he needed to purchase a share of Winter's royalties before an office closed. He couldn't find it but kept looking in narrow buildings until the doorbell rang and woke him from a jaw-clenched sleep.

It was too early to focus. The air felt soft, his shoulders heavy. Again, the doorbell. Roal remembered the agitated waste of Saturday and sat up, a sore and sudden anger blooming in his heart and clearing his disorientation. Dina should have called. Dina should not have left him alone to worry, distracted and foolish, all weekend left out of the loop. The doorbell rang again, again, twice fast, and once more just as he set his hand on the doorknob. Yesterday's tenderness had burned itself out, leaving just a husk of a pride: "Hell yes," he planned to say: "I damn well *do* want to know."

Roal swept the door open, ready, his mouth ready to spring, to be sprung by Dina's half-smile question. He leaned through the door.

And he knew.

It wasn't Dina. It was Lin. Of course. Why would Dina ring the bell to her own house? Lin shielded her eyes from Roal as the morning air passed between breezed past his legs and into his boxers. He was not wearing enough to be as substantial as Lin's expression told him he would need to be. She turned away, and Roal fled back down the hall for clothing. When he came back, Lin still stood just inside the door. They greeted each other formally.

"Good morning, Lin."

"Good morning, Roal." She was looking at the gutter over his head. If she had more to say, she wasn't ready yet. Neither was Roal.

"How are you?"

"Okay, and you?"

"Well."

"Good, good."

"Great," Roal croaked. They stood there, each with something to say or ask. But terrified.

"Coffee?" asked Roal.

"Please." Lin's relief broke their frozen postures, and they headed to the kitchen.

There, Roal made the coffee as if rehearsing a play: *Now I fill the carafe. Now I add coffee grounds. Now I turn the switch to On. Now I wait in a bruised silence. Now my hands tremble but I feel it in my stomach.*

Each stage of the production delayed the coming moment, the moment of the play when one of the characters does or says something unaccountable, and one of the other characters gets handed a new set of lines without a chance for rehearsal. *Now I watch the coffee drip. Now I get two cups.*

Then Lin said it: "She stayed, Roal. She's not coming back."

Once she said it, it seemed so simple. That was all. Roal's hands relaxed. He could talk about the word stayed. It was a shape he knew.

"Stayed?"

"With Winter. On his project. She said to tell you, I mean, she asked me to let you know she won't be back. She thought she would be when we left, but then we got there."

"Where is she?"

"I'm not supposed to say. I can't say. Won't." Lin rubbed her eyes, blocking out Roal. He felt like two selves were listening as Lin's news reached him. One self floated over the other and maintained its usual form, conveyed a detached intrigue, a gentle inquiry into Lin's awkwardness. Roal noticed bark on her clothes and reached to brush a fir needle from her shoulder. The other self felt deflated. Losing air. Was he about to have a conversation with a colleague about his wife leaving him? He should have remained in the entryway, exposed in his boxers and midlife starter breasts. His two selves uncomfortably greeted each other, disoriented in the meeting.

"Stayed?" When he said it this time, he no longer understood the word. It could have been a specialized surgical instrument or a stabilizer for foam insulation. "She lives here. All her things are here."

"I know. But she did stay. I'll tell you what I know. Dina said you'd probably take it well." Lin said that hopefully, holding her coffee just under her chin, shivering, her hands wrapped around it for warmth.

"No. No, I don't think I will," said Roal.

But he did. They drank coffee, and Roal's hair was combed, and he wore a single-pocket pale green button-down shirt, a braided belt holding up his olive weekend pants, and double-knotted shoes. He sat up straight, did not interrupt, and nodded at intervals; he offered sugar and cream and, eventually, toast.

Lin's directness was without pity, hope, or judgment. Roal appreciated how this allowed the news of Dina's decision to be presented like a traveling exhibit they could point at and discuss. Objectively. From many angles. From far away.

Roal recognized the life they examined, but the pieces were out of order now so felt like they belonged to someone else's life. As if the air they were breathing hadn't been provided by Dina's plants, and the food they ate hadn't been selected at the store by Dina, and the table they had their arms on hadn't been stripped and finished by her.

Exhibit A: Winter Patent. Exhibit B: Dina Bowman (née Stokes). Exhibit C: the connection, the instantaneous and irrefutable and undeniable charge of the connection.

The air they breathed: Dina. The plates on the counter: Dina. The note bearing her handwriting: Dina. The hanging onions, the gleaming floor, the sugar in the bowl: Dina, Dina, Dina.

* * *

Roal showed Lin Dina's note.

"Look," Roal pointed. "She wrote 'I do love you ever Dina'? How should we read that? There isn't any punctuation. The emphasis could be on any of those words *love* or *do*. Or *you*. It doesn't seem like the kind of thing she'd write when she's planning to go off with Winter. And she says right here that she'll be back—maybe by tonight."

Lin interrupted, waving away the analysis.

"No," said Lin, "This has nothing to do with Winter. She didn't even know Winter when she wrote the note. Forget the note. It's just about Dina. What she wants to do."

Roal's high school girlfriend had broken up with him through a friend as well. Roal didn't even think his girlfriend had written the breakup note herself. But her best friend delivered it just like Lin was doing, using the perfect logic of the person once-removed. It all made so much sense to the friend. He protested now, as he wished he had then.

"But Dina," he explained to himself and Lin, "is with Winter. So it seems like it has something to do with Winter."

"Actually it's irrelevant. Sort of. She's there for the project. You're not following." Lin was getting flustered. Lin, who had driven Dina into an undeclarable woods and left her with a man who had lived for a decade as a wolf, attacking elk and howling invitations to the pack to join him over the body of a fawn and shitting scent trails from Canada to Utah.

"Then what," Roal asked, feeling exposed and mean, "then what is the point? Since when does someone's wife leave him for Winter-fucking-Patent, and the husband misses the point?"

Lin shook her head tightly: "That's what I'm telling you. She didn't leave you for Winter. What she left you for—oh, it's strange, I know—she left you for the trees."

CHAPTER 6

The sheer absurdity of Lin's announcement burst the tension between them, sending them into laughter uncontrolled and desperate. They laughed themselves weak and wrung. Laughed to prolong whatever would happen next. Laughed to forget the thing which had already happened, whatever that was. *Dina*, Lin gasped, and they'd start again. *Trees!* Roal snickered, and hilarity gathered them in its fist, squeezing hard for keeps.

Their laughter whimpered to a stop and then gave up altogether. Something was coming. Lin tried to get out of its way by standing up and brushing debris off her sweater, an attempt at a look of *Not me!* innocence. It nearly made Roal start again. He didn't even bother to sit up. He just lay on the floor in the path of the reckoning thing, crushable and reckless.

"The trees! Oh. Oh my God. A tree . . ." Roal chuckled, waiting for Lin to tell him the truth.

But she had, and it wasn't changing. In fact, it got a little worse: Dina was convinced she could inhabit trees and heal them. She discovered this was all she had ever wanted to do, but she just hadn't known it was possible. The project was incredibly powerful with implications so fantastic it was clear why Dina—or anyone who could do what she thought she was doing— would stay.

"When you say 'inhabit a tree' what do you mean?" Roal's tongue was wooly. His head needed water. The floor trembled under his pummeling heart. He covered his eyes.

"It's hard to explain. I think I understand it, but it's still hard. Basically, Winter has been acquiring forests that have died. Forest dead zones. He works to help them recover. But it's tricky."

Roal snorted, "Come on, Lin. Why does everyone think that whatever Winter says or does is a breakthrough moment? Restoration isn't tricky—the park service does it every summer. With high school students!"

"True, people do forest restoration. But Winter's up to something different. And, for the record, dead zones *are* tricky. No one knows exactly why technically healthy forests just die and don't regenerate. But Winter has had some luck bringing them back. He's been helping forests that have been dead and incapable of production for at least ten years. That's where he was all that time. It takes a long time to do this kind of work." Lin said this like it was the end of the explanation. Roal uncovered his eyes. He wondered how much of what she told him had been rehearsed.

Lin went on, "Winter seeks out forests that he believes have lost the will to grow—the will to invest more energy in what our dimension understands as growth."

"Right. Our dimension." It was more a dismissal than a request for clarification.

"Winter says people tend to think that growth is defined by mass. You know—measurable growth. When we think of nonhuman life, like trees, we tend to equate their growth with profit potential." A look at Roal's rigid face made Lin trail off. "Actually, I don't think this explanation is helping. For now it might just be easiest to think about the project as forest rehabilitation, except Winter uses consciousness instead of traditional planting methods to restore the forest's will to live." Here, admiration lit her eyes, sparking Roal's anger.

"I don't understand. I don't get any of this," Roal charged. "Why are we even talking about Winter? Who cares? Where is Dina? How long until she's coming back? I don't care about Winter's project. Where is *Dina*?"

"I can't say where. It's a secret. But she's fine. You don't have to worry. Not about her safety anyway, anyway. I mean. . . ." Lin trailed off, embarrassed. Roal understood: Dina was not in physical danger, so he didn't need to worry about her safety. His worry would need to be more personal.

"Oh, what? You can't tell me? She's my wife. Everything's great for twenty-whatever years, and then she just goes off and I shouldn't worry? Why?

Because Winter Patent 'has a project'? He's a goddamn wolf! I'm choosing to worry about Dina. Where is she?"

Roal couldn't recall his last real anger. He swallowed and was surprised at the smooth machinery of his throat, how good it felt.

Lin seemed torn and took her time deciding what to say next. "Look, I know it's shock. But it's not my fault. And I don't have to be here. I mean I didn't have to come. I did it as a favor to Dina. She asked me."

And then she added, "And everything has not been great for twenty-some years."

"No. Things have been good. You and Dina have been friends for, what?— less than a year. Big deal. We've been fine. And I do need to worry about her. She's with a stranger. She can't just go."

Lin pushed aside a plant to read the clock behind it. When she faced Roal again, she looked cheerlessly committed to finishing her work. She searched at his face. The pouches under his eyes, his chapped lips, the unknowing. Roal felt his cheek twitch. He looked away.

Finally Lin sighed kindly. "Roal, you're right. I'm sorry. I only know what she told me, or maybe what I thought she was telling me. When we met she needed a friend. She said she hadn't had one for years. I'm just here to tell you what she asked me to say. Let me finish and I'll be out of your space." When Roal said nothing, she went on.

"Dina wants to stay because the project is a great fit for her. She's truly enthralled by it, and excited that Winter recognized she has a natural gift for it. He's been looking for someone like her." Roal looked at her sharply, and Lin rushed to correct herself.

"Not like that—Winter's interests are more . . . I don't know. He still has a magnetism, but it's not personal. Dina stayed because she thinks the trees need her. He project is interesting. She says this is her next phase, the natural next step. She didn't know until we got there that that's what it would be."

"I don't even know what you're talking about." What had been Dina's first phase? He was tapping his fingers against each other because they were cold and shriveled and felt strange. Lin was explaining the project again. It sounded bigger than Roal could bear.

"It's huge. Really huge. And, if you can get past the shock of Dina leaving, it's really interesting. Somehow he's getting trees to transfer their consciousness to him. Dina can do it too." Lin eyed Roal. He stared at her blankly, his mouth sulky.

"He says he can access their blocked emotions and heal them. The way he describes it is pretty squishy from a scientific point of view. But I think he's probably figured out how to have a different kind of dimensional access and is healing them in their own reality. Actually, it could be both. I wonder if it is both. Hmm. Emotion *as* dimension—now that's interesting." Lin took a notebook from her pocket and made a note.

Roal cleared his throat, but Lin kept writing without looking up. When she finished, she closed the notebook and looked back at Roal as if it were difficult to place what they'd been talking about.

"Sorry. Back to Dina. So Winter says he can feel the forest's suppressed will to grow, then he clears the blockage, and this allows them to accept that growth is generative and productive rather than a threat to their survival. And then they can heal by allowing new growth to happen for the next generation. Which is interesting, because if you think about it, it's the tree's own success with growth that gets them killed. For the wood."

Lin admitted she didn't understand it intuitively more than logistically. "And what I do know is that it seems to be working. Winter's documentation is impressive. The places where he has worked show significant greening inside of otherwise dead forest areas."

"I still don't see what Dina has to do with it. What's her talent? What does Winter want from her?"

"Well, he wants a partner—someone like Dina who can tune in differently. And who doesn't have an ego. Someone who can work for the good of the project and not her own ego. She's a rare person. Winter needs help so he can work faster and get the forests going before it's too late. He is, after all, just one man. Even he needs help."

"No," Roal finally said softly. "Dina needs help. It sounds crazy."

"Well, yes," Lin said affectionately, "which is perfect for her. She's a little nuts, but in a completely wonderful way. All her crazy, perfect care packages for my characters. And the notes she writes to her plants just to cheer them on, or to give them something she's worried they need to keep them strong? Yes, a little crazy. I mean, look around." Lin gestured. As she did so, she gently rubbed the fuzzy leaf of the primrose next to her. "Yes. Winter's project is exactly her cup of tea. And she wants it. Roal, it just really speaks to her—to who she is at her core. She has a purpose again."

"A purpose?" Roal scoffed. "To listen to a tree. If she needs a purpose, why not bike across the state for MS? Other people bike across the state. Gary and his wife did. Or French. She could learn French. Or—what's the name of that girl who plays the violin downtown to raise money for flood victims? We could get Dina hooked in with her. If she needs a purpose, I mean. If that's what she needs. We can find her a goddamn purpose."

Roal was suddenly flooded by an awareness of purposes: whales, polar bears—anything going extinct, really. The world was waiting to be served. It was a giant held breath of purpose. Roal sat, nearly crushed by his sense of the world's enormous need.

"If Dina needs a purpose, I just think we could find her something where she doesn't have to live in a dead zone and, and, for God's sake, photosynthesize with a wolf. I mean, really," Roal protested, "we're just setting her up for failure. Bring her back, and we'll find her a purpose."

Lin stared with a kind of fascination that made Roal feel fully visible, though he wasn't sure of what was being revealed. The laughter that couldn't be turned away earlier was now beyond summoning. Roal stood up and angrily straightened his shirt. But the world pressed its thumb upon him and he slumped over the counter. It would be a heavy, heavy day.

"Roal, I hate to say it, but I don't think you have any idea. Let me back up."

Lin started at the beginning. With when Lin met Dina. With their friendship. With Winter Patent, and with whatever else was missing.

Lin met Dina at the reservoir. She recognized her from some college faculty party and felt obligated to walk with her since they were heading the same direction. She was relieved that Dina walked in such easy silence. Lin surprised herself by talking into it. The less Dina said, the more she talked. Boyfriends, walking shoes, color of the sky, trail dust, farmer's market. Talking and talking, more than she knew she had to say. Dina didn't have much to say back until Lin revealed she hoped the walk would shake loose an idea for a chapter she was working on. Then Dina started asking questions. Really listening. Lin perfectly imitated Dina's habit of listening with a quiet, reflective lean. Roal nodded in a pang of recognition.

"Then I felt guilty," Lin admitted. "I'd hogged the entire conversation but when I finally asked Dina a question she said she was having such a nice time she'd rather just have me keep going. She's funny. She said it would help avoid the awkwardness of my having to try to appear interested in whatever she might say. She's so direct and vulnerable. It was unexpected."

Roal nodded, recognizing Dina in this too.

Lin remembered one of Dina's comments in particular: "Most of what I love to do is of absolutely no interest to anyone but me!"

Lin thought she meant it in a self-deprecating way but Dina hastened to correct the impression: "Oh, no—not like that. Not at all. I can talk about what I like to do, but it's a conversation killer. It happens all the time. Then other person looks all frantic for a way to leave the conversation. It's awful. And I'd like this conversation to go on."

"I think she meant it," Lin said. "She takes a lot of pleasure in the luxury of a deeply private life that an appearance of boringness made possible."

"She never complained about things being boring."

"She meant it more like just doing things that she finds exciting but that are usual and mundane: reading, walks, letters, houseplants. Things so regular that anyone who sees them looks right through, like a window. But Dina said that for her, that window was a mirror. She could see each thing clearly and it felt deliberate. Everything was a choice she got to make. She wanted to live deliberately, but not visibly. What an amazing description. And that was all in our first conversation." And so they were friends.

Lin paused uncertainly and then, as though she and Roal were friends enough for her confession, said, "And I have to admit—and I'm sorry—but

I thought at first that her focus on the deliberate-life thing was more of that Zen bullshit you're always after, and that you were both drinking the same Kool-Aid. It's so insufferable how you always use your Zen shtick to get out of responsibility." Lin laughed, remembering, "Before I knew her, I was worried I'd have to listen to more of that 'in-the-moment, transparent-being' crap, but with her, it's real. And it's pretty amazing."

Roal stared at her, scandalized. That Zen bullshit he was always after? Transparent-being crap? Roal wondered if profound embarrassment could produce a state of shock.

Lin raised her eyebrows in suspicious disbelief at Roal's surprise. "Oh, come on, Roal, I can't be the first one to mention this to you. Anyway, Dina isn't like that." Lin trailed off, having forgotten where she was going. Then she remembered: "You know, I don't think she ever talked explicitly about Zen, but I think she lived it."

Say goodbye to *namaste*. The prayer flags of his practice were in tatters, and *ohm* was just a way for those with low pain threshold to moan in public. What about how he had discovered that naming activities gave them meaning: Peeling the Orange, Adding Paper to Printer, Inhabiting Chair at Meeting. Or the soothing desktop sand garden with its little rake and small stones which always appeared to be sleeping? Zen impressed him. At its merest mention, arguments would simply recede, a black eel in a pool of dark leaves. In this, Zen was stronger than any other form of rhetoric—standing above Aristotle's well-mapped realm.

"Interesting," he would say at meetings. "We had this same conversation years ago. Different details, but the same disagreements. We should change this pattern by giving up what we think the outcome should be and try to figure out what's at the core. The building topples when the foundation shifts." As he cast a look of wise appeal around the table, the sharpenings of argument dulled and his colleagues looked away. Then Tony would roll his eyes and the meeting would end in silence. Roal now understood the silence. Just as he now understood why, following such meetings, Tony's door was closed and the voices within his office sounded like they belonged to most of the same people who had only just left the meeting.

Roal looked around the room at the plants. He disliked them suddenly for how he hadn't thought before what it meant that Dina liked to speak to them. She gave them names and said they had preferences about what they were next to. Before she chopped vegetables, she would hold them until they stopped resonating with fear and accepted her thanks. Roal had assumed that this was just a quirk and everyone was entitled to a few of them. Now he feared he should have questioned it more, perhaps should have had it assessed.

Had others already known? He had often seen her at faculty events standing alone after just a few minutes of conversation. She joined the other spouses who sat together discussing children or the cities they had in common as a result of being dragged from one place to the next by a faculty spouse swinging from job to job. Dina, without children to speak of, or other cities she had lived in, had little to add for comparison.

Lin was still talking, now spelling out one of Dina's theories about how famous people actually had less interesting lives than invisible people. "Famous people constantly have to interrupt their present lives to promote their work, which is all in the past. But she thought that because their fame is usually the result of a single action or talent, famous people get framed one-dimensionally. Then all the conversations are supposed to revolve around that one thing. So she thinks it's likely that famous people have fewer conversations of actual interest than non-famous people do.

"I mean," Lin admitted, "it is true. How often do we have to answer the usual list of questions about our work: Who are your influences? From what do you draw inspiration? How did you begin? Which of your characters do you think is most like yourself? Blah, blah, blah. We never get asked about anything the interviewer doesn't already know. Like what song from our youth influenced a rebellious decision. Or what factors influence what we buy at a grocery store. Or whether we really want to know what all those medications are for in our parents' medicine cabinet. Life-stuff. Stuff normal people get to talk about. It's interesting." Roal drifted in and out of listening.

He was still piecing together flashes to see if he could find one where another person looked fascinated by Dina.

Here Lin sighed. "And you know, Dina was right. I'd kill to be interviewed by someone who didn't care about my book. Next week will be the six-year anniversary of my divorce from a one-year marriage. Last week I lost a toenail. It hurt like shit—the divorce and the toenail. Well, and the marriage, too," Lin admitted. "Anyway, no one ever talks about that stuff with me except Dina. It's like my life is an irrelevant footnote to the paper it produces. I hadn't realized how much I missed real life stuff until we were friends."

Roal wondered if it were shabby of Lin to complain about the burden of her fortune. Though the way she said it seemed to suggest that she saw him as an equal in the great arena of singular genius, and he was flattered to be included.

He also wondered if Lin's reference to the pills in the medicine chest were a specific reference to the time Dina asked Roal why Chet had so many pills in his nightstand. Roal said if Chet hadn't mentioned it he probably didn't want to be asked. But Dina did ask and said Chet was glad to tell her—he thought if was good for someone else should know in case he forgot. Chet had so many pills that they came with their own calendars and charts. Like a preschool program for pills, with times and amounts and conferences scheduled to check on progress. Roal wondered now if he should have asked what they were for.

Roal said, "All of this—your friendship and the things she enjoyed—all of that sounds really good. It sounds like a purpose."

He insisted, "I mean it sounds like she was enjoying herself. Not bored. I don't get it. When do you think she'll be back?"

Lin seemed startled, as though she had forgotten why she was there. When she answered, her tone was soft.

"I don't know that she'll be back, Roal. She seemed hooked. I got to watch as she and Winter practiced together, and I tried it, but I just didn't get it. Besides, Winter had already changed his mind about me. He didn't want to talk to me after all. Just Dina." Lin sounded disappointed. "Dina said the experience of the work was deeply gratifying—like some kind of reciprocal feedback loop, and Winter said the feeling would only intensify and deepen as her work progressed. Winter thanked me for bringing her and told me to go, and I left."

"That's it?" Roal was sure he'd missed something. A few weeks of something. He summed it up to be sure he had the basics covered: "So Dina practiced becoming a tree for a few hours, Winter said thanks, and you left Dina standing in an amazing feedback loop in a dead zone. Does she need help?"

"No. I mean, I don't think so. Plus, I didn't leave her standing. They lie down. But anyway."

Roal turned away from her, huffing.

Lin snapped at him, "Roal, she's an adult and can leave home, you know. She is allowed. People do it all the time. Like a lot, actually, if you look at statistics." Then she took a deep breath.

Roal knew what such breaths meant, deep calming breaths before you say the hard thing you haven't said yet. He tried to brace himself: *ohm*, he intoned to himself. Though now it sounded hollow and only confirmed that his tolerance for pain was low, and it scared him.

He turned his face away from Lin. He did not want to be seen. But then he turned back to Lin and narrowed his eyes, "You probably really think you're being a friend to her. What a joke." He laughed a brief, bitter breath.

Lin unraveled. "It wasn't as if—"

She started again: "It's not like . . . Okay, forget it. Roal, this isn't about you. And you're not the only one this affects. I brought Dina because I thought it would be fun. That she'd be good to have along. She was supposed to come back. With me, after I had talked to Winter because he asked me to come. It wasn't supposed to be the kind of weekend where I returned home alone, and humiliated. That's right—the reporters will want to know why Winter sent me back without so much as asking me anything. I have nothing to report. That will be fun to tell the reporters. Do you think this is all about you? Do you think I won't be embarrassed? It doesn't matter. I have nothing to give the reporters. And now, here I am, trying to explain to you what happened, and every time I try to explain, you either deny or purposely trivialize what I say. As if people didn't get left by their partners unaccountably all the time. As if you've never noticed that you're constantly given more than you've earned. Big man. Big man at the head of the line. Oh for God's sake! Forget it!"

Lin sounded feverish, her voice dry-reedy, teetering between giddy and delirious. Her skin was patchy across her cheeks, and red dots of bites or heat rash prickled her neck. She apologized and insisted. She hadn't slept all night. She cried. She waved a finger at Roal and accused him of having left Dina alone for twenty years and then getting angry when Dina finally got the message and left.

Anyway, the Winter Patent story was over for her. It ended when Winter had asked her to leave, and the driver materialized and took her back. She was supposed to drive directly to her own house. But instead she headed back to Winter and Dina. She parked, then crept back to the forest site, watching from a few hundred yards away. She had to see more. Winter and Dina lay on the ground, arms outstretched, silent, taking in the news about the old root system from the mycelia beneath them.

After a few hours of Lin's watching from under an itchy bush, Dina turned her head in Lin's direction and called, "You are still here. It's okay. I understand. But the oncoming growth has revealed you, and your need is blocking them. It's time for you to go. They want you to go." Her eyes were closed the whole time. Then a branch fell a few feet from Lin, and she fled, terrified, back through the forest, half lost until she hit the road and found the car. She drove straight to Roal's house. Here to tell Roal everything, everything. Because Dina had asked her to. Only Dina hadn't warned her that Roal wouldn't be able to hear. She said he would take it well.

Lin raved on, speaking about Roal as if he were out of her muttering's range, and Roal was frightened. Lin looked pinched and dangerous in her flecked clothes and wild sproinging hair. He saw a gray hair on her chin. He noted a twitch in her eyelid. Her hand shook as she reached for a glass and filled it with water. She sighed. It passed.

"And there's more, Roal, but it's awkward. Awkward because we work together."

"More awkward than it's already going to be?" Roal imagined the news anchor asking him how he felt now that he lived alone. He'd be a sleazy side story feature about being less compelling than a stand of dead trees, and the four-foot stack of his writing in his office would document the fact that he had been living alone for years and hadn't known it.

"Good point. Plus, work is already awkward. All that weird Indian-slash-Zen-slash-writer-who-doesn't-publish shit! Why? I mean, why? Oh, anyway."

Low pain-threshold sound in Roal's head. Animal soundwave of prey to predator: *I am wounded*. Roal would have done anything to be not-here, now.

Lin apologized, embarrassed to be so snappish. She was overwrought and snappish. She had been unkind. She was sorry, really sorry, but still.

"Still what?" Roal asked.

"Still, it's awkward. I'm annoyed that Dina even asked me to do this."

Roal bit his tongue.

Finally, Lin asked, "So I guess what I need to know is this: Do you want to know what Dina told me?" He did want to know, but felt it was unfair to have to ask for something that would hurt.

"Yes?" Roal said, his voice reluctant. "I need . . . to know." If Lin could tell him, and he could listen and really hear her, then they could go to Dina and bring her home, maybe get some help. He could rise to knowing, and their life could make room to hold them both.

"Okay. First I'll just get the big thing out of the way. Dina knows you hated your book. She feels bad about that. She thinks you're stuck on it. When she reframed it as a book of starts, which was a great idea, she thought she was doing you a favor. But then you took it as an insult because it was published as a teaching tool, not literature. But it's good for what it does. She feels bad about that.

"The second thing is that she said she couldn't live with self-erasure any-more." Roal flinched, deeply scandalized.

"Self-erasure? I don't self-erase. Lin, I do not self-erase." His voice was pleading.

"I think Dina meant her own self-erasure," Lin said. "She said she needed to start giving her attention to something that would respond. When she worked with the trees, she said she felt like a partner in something bigger."

Roal couldn't plan what to do with his face. Shame? Rigid inscrutability? His entire posture waited to hear how to behave and he was immobile while he tried to think. He felt like a game show contestant who finds out too late that none of the other contestants are competing naked as planned. Lin, mistaking his paralysis for permission, went on.

"What I mean is, you don't show curiosity or doubt. You never want to know more. And you back out of any kind of difficult conversation by misusing Zen. You know," Lin said offhandedly, "Zen isn't supposed to grant you immunity from substance."

Roal wondered if Lin knew she was speaking in present tense. For Dina? For herself? For the college? Or perhaps for the whole town, which apparently had grown so tired of Roal that two years ago the phone book had misprinted his number and when Roal complained, he got left out of last year's book altogether. "A technical glitch," they said. "We thought you meant that printing your number was a misprint. Sorry." And so just like that, he no longer lived in his own town.

Dina was engaging in self-erasure—she was his wife. Wasn't she erasing that? It was true that Roal hadn't wanted to know more. He knew that. The plants and the reading and the walking around and around a reservoir. *Do you want to know?* He had to admit—not really. He struggled with how much energy it took to generate interest. So exhausting.

"It just seems shabby," he said tiredly. "She should be telling me this herself. I don't honestly know if I can disagree with what you're saying, but I wish you weren't the one saying it. But maybe that's the point. Maybe that's how far gone it is."

Lin softened. Nodded. "I know. I really do."

Lin said it might not make things feel better, but Dina's epiphany was probably as close as Dina would ever get to what new parents experience: they love something else impossibly, suddenly, in a way that physically changes their brain chemistry. Dina couldn't leave it. Not even to come home. She was afraid to leave the forest alone. Even though Lin could grasp the technical details of Winter's project, she didn't understand it from a resonant, gut-yes flashpoint. Though Dina did.

And, Lin said, "It turned out that's what Winter had been looking for after all. A partner, someone who could understand, because he said there isn't much time left and he needs help. So Dina stayed. She wants to be there."

Roal took it as a bad sign that he was relieved to be talking again about Dina and Winter and not about himself. Still, his face presented a problem. He wasn't sure of how to arrange it, of where his eyes should be going and whether his mouth should be held like that—drawn like a string on a sack full of ransom money: careful, decided, though already aware that delivering the money was a bad idea, half of it counterfeit anyway.

CHAPTER 7

Lin desperately needed sleep. She was tired past coherence, and her words tangled and slurred. She didn't want to go home where the press awaited her return. They needed the Winter Wolf Reintroduction scoop.

After a nap, she could answer Roal's questions and finish what she needed to say. But for now, a nap, she yawned, a nap.

She wandered off to Dina's room, leaving Roal alone in the kitchen where he wondered what to do next. He went through the details of Lin's story. It was quite a fiction. And it could be wrong. Or Dina could be wrong—mistaken in her belief that she wanted to stay in a forest. A few nights there might change her mind. She could be back before evening tonight. Or tomorrow. Next week, at the latest, if she were going to change her mind.

Roal looked into the backyard. The willow tree was the hopeful green of all trees after they've had a few months of spring. The hostas looked meager, but they would recover from winter and their leaves would thicken. Roal was surprised to know so many of the plants by name as he surveyed the yard: Cliff, Mrs. Johannson, Terri, Piper, Sister Catherine. Each plant a named for a person whose kindness Dina remembered. The years of hearing the names had made them so familiar that Roal could have joined in the conversation at any time.

He wondered what would have happened if Dina had chosen to learn Russian, if at their meals she had practiced her first words in a new language instead of delivering an update on the plants. Would she be fluent by now? Would he? Over seven thousand dinners together, a new word at each one. Think of it. They might have traveled to practice their new language, wandering around villages, tasting borscht and varenyky dumplings, slipping on frost-lined cobblestones and wearing rabbit-fur hats on their pink-cheeked heads.

Would they have had more to say to each other if the language they shared was one that did not come easily to either of them? Then, even the simplest things they might have said to each other would have seemed tender and difficult, interesting and endearing. They might have tried anything out in their new language, pointing to water or light, declaring dog and shoe and desire, insisting heart or feel. All of it becoming more and more clear over the years instead of getting further and further away as he knew they had been, but he didn't know how to anchor.

He used to think about the anchoring, but then the drift became the journey. So they drifted. In new languages, all the beginning words are so basic to survival they shape the speakers as an extension of the necessary: *Bread, want, water, please. I you go us here.* Roal had meant to be necessary. He guessed most people hoped for at least that. He looked again at the plants. Jemmie in a lavender bed next to Ms. Ida and Teacher Sarah. The Crandall Family just coming up in the feathery new shoots of their spring.

Roal winced to think of all the things that Dina told him, things for which he could not imagine a response: Chet had an expression he wore only when he tried to mask his excitement about an upcoming chess move; she had sent letters to Charlie and Pilar and other people whose names by now seemed so familiar they might as well be famous.

Lin was right. Roal had not shown the least curiosity. He had thought of Dina's evening reportage just a kind of dropping the loose ends of the day into a bucket. Roal was the bucket. Being Present. After what Lin said, though, it was clear that Being Present was very transparently not the same as Being Available. Available was harder.

Questions. They weren't difficult to ask. In fact, once they got going, they bloomed like a field of jellyfish rising. They take less time, and require no knowledge. Just listening. Interminable, make-way-for-others listening. What is the expression my father reserves for the anticipation of a clever chess move? When you see the expression does it change your strategy? What did your letters say?

* * *

"No," Lin was awake, and crisp to the edges where sleep had filled her in.

Roal revealed his epiphany: he had not asked Dina enough questions. It was no wonder she felt uninteresting and burned out on the night after night effort to raise a question with bait well displayed.

"Dina didn't feel uninteresting." Lin's laugh of dismissal reinforced her sharpness. "Jesus. I think, and this is my interpretation, but I think in the end her talent was being wasted."

Roal snickered, and Lin straightened up like she'd been slapped.

"You're an asshole, Roal Bowman. You really have no idea who Dina is. What she does. She's a muse. Or a savant. She's—oh, fuck off. How's that for your Zen moment? Be *there*." Lin turned unexpectedly and started scanning the room for her bag. She found it slumped by the door.

Lin dug through her purse for her keys, and said she'd rather go home and face the reporters about her failed meeting with Winter than sit around all day with Roal. "Twenty years!" Lin cried. "I can't even last a day!" She headed to the door.

"Wait." Roal was alarmed at her sudden change.

Lin paused with her back to him.

"Dina can't not be back. I mean, she can't just leave. She is coming back."

Lin turned to size up Roal and let out a breath of disgust. Roal could feel how much she was choosing not to say, "Who knows, Roal? Dina's a big girl excited about a big-girl project. She's ready to devote herself. Completely. It's a big deal. She's working with Winter. He's incredible. She wants to be there. And she didn't say she was sorry." She shook her head sadly. "But I am. I am sorry to lose my walking partner."

Roal knew she had nothing left to say. He tried one last time, using the kind of good-cop voice he thought would work for a hostage taker, careful and specific: "I want to know where she is—I want to talk to her. Before you say anything to the press. I don't want the press making anything definite."

Lin's eyebrows twitched at the mention of the press.

Roal reassessed, dropped his voice to a quiver: "Please. She's an orphan. She's my wife." Then he insisted, "She's my *wife*."

Lin looked at Roal flatly, then with a sympathy so open Roal believed he had a chance. But a calculation passed behind Lin's eyes, and her mouth angled into a dangerous, competitive smile: "Yes, and who knows better than she does what that means? She is your wife. And more, Roal. And more. You really have no idea. But you'll see."

She trailed some final advice behind her, "Watch the mail, Roal. It won't be what you expect, but keep an eye out for it! And thanks for the coffee!" The door banged shut.

Roal still didn't know where Dina was. Or, now, who.

Roal recalled a statistic he'd read about couples who stayed together. Couples who stayed together shared in common that they typically conversed a minimum of five and a half hours per week.

Three hundred and thirty minutes. Less than that, and the chances of making it were slim. That was an average of fifty-five minutes per evening, six nights a week. That left one night off for a late meeting, a headache, or a movie. Fifty-five minutes of talking on a daily installment plan. Not silent sitting, not "Good morning" in the early brush-past of one body against the other in the hallway between kitchen and bathroom, not nodding while the other person filled you in on the details of a plotless day. But back and forth talking.

When Roal had come across the statistic, it hadn't applied to him. It applied, he thought, to couples who were looking for a way to make it. Couples carrying their time like oil in a spoon as they tried to cross the room of their marriage with it.

It seemed to make talking an ulterior motive, which struck Roal as suspicious. Imagine, Roal pointed out to his fiction class, how much hangs in the balance of each word, the pressure on the conversation that couples are hoping will get them to the next respite of their lives together.

But the students disagreed. Didn't he think the statistic might not be about couples trying to *save* a marriage, and instead be about couples who already had a successful one—before the saving was necessary? And didn't

Professor Bowman think the *reason* might be irrelevant? Because wasn't it the *practice* itself that counted? After all, such nightly practice of conversation would then make real conversation a natural extension of the marital unit. Like meditation, one student insisted from the back, as if to remind Roal that he should at least agree with an argument when presented in his own lexicon.

Roal was about to respond when another student's outburst stopped him. Alyssa didn't get it—fifty-five minutes a night? That's *it*? She was outraged. Her parents were getting a divorce because they couldn't find fifty-five fucking minutes six fucking times a *week*? Her mother took salt baths that long every night! Her father played golf! Alyssa and her boyfriend couldn't *stop* talking when they were together and texted when they weren't.

"What happens?" she asked. "What happens when you get old? Do you just run out of past to talk about or something? Do you just stop caring?"

Roal changed the subject to divert the accusation the entire class now leveled at him based on the evidence of midlife wrinkles and the streaks of gray at his temples. He had meant to use the statistics as a tool to teach character development, but the conversation had flooded past that point. Now students were breaking into the safes of their personal stories to illustrate the failures of the previous generation—Roal's generation—with its misplaced priorities and stupid, undisciplined approaches to everything from marriage to salt baths.

Roal took little pleasure in his certainty that one day they would understand. That when they arrived home every evening after working with people they would not otherwise choose to know, and entered the calm of their own homes already exhausted and talked out, that what they would hope for was a cushion of silence, a look of understanding, a couple of questions whose answers were and would be forever the same, a meal, and a remote control that could command the angle on the news.

In the meantime, Roal thought, let the students dream, let them exhaust their vocal chords and debate breakfast cereals and the framings of political advisors. Impressed by their earnestness, he applauded their questions, reinforced that such challenges were the stuff of strong writing, and sent them off to explode against the pages in their dorm rooms where, no doubt, they'd demand silence or earbud music delivered precisely on their own terms.

Fifty-five minutes a night. It did seem small, though Roal couldn't remember the last time he and Dina had dragged so many words into the space between them. Their silence felt natural to Roal, not strained or tense. It was conversation that strained. Even when his mother died, there wasn't much to say, so they hadn't said it. Dina had checked in with Roal, but he was fine, really.

Helen had been ill for years, and she'd said it was her time. Roal tried to accept that. She always said she wouldn't feel right getting all greedy for more than what she'd been given. But his father suggested she might try to fight a little bit—maybe just to look for a new specialist or to look at the research. There were new medications that looked promising.

But Helen disagreed, "It's death, honey. No big deal. I mean, life is fine, but I've sort of done most of the good parts already. Plus, I don't feel good, and that's not going to change. Who wants that?"

Chet took a chance and called to ask Roal if he would grow his hair out. He knew it sounded silly, but could Roal even just tell Helen he was planning to grow his hair out again? Give her something to look forward to? Roal was grateful Chet couldn't see him wince on the other end of the line. Plus, Chet reminded him, the braiding would help strengthen her hands, and she loved telling stories as she braided.

Before Roal could answer, Chet rushed to assure Roal that Helen's stories about the Indians were just stories—that for God's sake, there was no more Indian in Roal than in a root beer float—but the stories made Helen happy. "Please," Chet asked, "I know it's a stretch, but she's not even trying anymore."

Roal said he'd try. "But remember," he said, "it will take years to grow it long enough."

But that too was part of the plan: Chet wanted Helen to wait for years. To want to wait. In the meantime Dina dropped by so Helen could braid her hair.

Dina shook her hair loose from the braids, but Helen complained that there was too much of it and it was impossible because it was so long. She said it hurt her hands and sat back. Dina rebraided her own hair and told Helen of the dim memory she had of someone braiding her hair when she was young. She thought it might have been her mother before she disappeared. Dina recalled a hand and the bright pull of her hair as the braids tightened against her scalp. A wooden chair and an enamel-top table with chrome legs. It was one of her only memories of a person who might have been her mother, and she kept the braids for that reason. That hand on her head, attached to the person who stood behind her and braided, that was her ancestry. No face, but soft hands, and a table clean and well-lit.

Helen died before Roal's next haircut. His relief about that was enormous, which added to his shame.

In the days after the funeral, Chet couldn't speak to Roal. He couldn't bear to find out if Roal was going to turn out to be a quitter like Helen. Helen was the kind of person, Chet sobbed, who would rather eat poisoned food than offend the cook.

Chet apologized. For everything: for doubting Roal, for the silence, for not working harder to get Helen to try another course of treatment. For being so easy on Roal his whole life. Too eager to give Roal whatever he wanted. Toys, a playhouse, ice cream, a car.

"I wanted you to be happy," Chet admitted with regret.

"I was happy, Dad," Roal said.

"I know. You weren't unhappy anyway. Maybe that's good. Just remember, though, that when things are hard, it's fight or flight. Not sleep. And not death. That's it. Got it?"

Roal nodded. But Chet worried elaborately, figuring that since giving up on life could hardly be a dominant characteristic, Helen must have been a double-recessive for passivity, so Roal surely had at least one of those genes.

"The question," he said, pointing a knuckle at Roal, "did I pass on a recessive gene too? We don't really know. We just don't know."

Roal said Chet could rest easy.

"Just think about it, Roal," said Chet. "Just keep it in mind."

After carrying Chet's challenge around for years, Roal wondered if it was wrong to now feel relief and excitement mixed in to what he felt about Dina leaving. Dread, shame, an ingrown throb of anger. But relief too. He would lay his father's question to rest by going after her.

Lin had said to check the mail: one postcard reminder for Roal Bowman or Resident to remember that Lawn Care is Good Neighbor Care!; one thick manila envelope and one small, thin letter, both for Dina. Nothing that looked like the answer Lin said was coming his way. He looked more closely at the letters for Dina, curious. They were real letters, with real ink and script from the hand of one person who shook, and another who asserted. Roal read the return addresses and paused, frowning. He found it strange that the names should match so closely—so exactly—names he knew so well. Names everyone knew so well.

Roal read the names again, sure they were only very close, only approximately related to others so famously similar.

Roal dropped the mailbox lid then stepped back in and locked the door. He wanted the mail out of his hands. He set it down quickly. He needed to think. He would figure out what to do with the letters in a moment. A moment long enough for a shower and a drink, a moment to tighten the squish of his knees and belly. A moment, he thought, to prepare for the moment of answering the real question of whether he wanted to know. And then, and then.

CHAPTER 8

Roal opened cupboards and drawers, pulling cans and bags of food onto the open counter. Foraging. Roaming. Procrastinating. He eyed the letters on the kitchen table, then inventoried the food on display in front of him, his belly a census taker with a memory for the details.

It seemed foolish to open the letters right away. Invasive, if not premature. Hadn't Dina's note said she'd be back tonight at the latest? She might have meant it. It was Dina's word against Lin's at this point, and Lin was an unknown.

Roal swiped another chip, de-lidded the pickled asparagus, delivered dry cereal to his wet mouth. It would be embarrassing if Dina came home and Roal was reading her mail. And it really was Lin's word against Dina's, Roal reasoned, and Dina was his wife—it was Lin's job to spin fiction as a daily practice out of dark matter, and dark matter was, after all, theoretical. He steadied himself.

Roal straightened the letters. He touched the small envelope. Smooth, thin, invitation-sized, with spidery script addressed to Dina. He allowed himself to glance again at its return address, then at the other envelope. Allowed his stolen glimpse to linger. He prickled with a nervous, wet chill: Pilar Engoscue. Matthew Ulysses Chafee. Names so famous they couldn't help but be familiar.

Lin had said the answers in the mail might not be what Roal expected. If they held an answer, Roal wondered what the question might be. Roal thought he should start with the small envelope, reasoning that difficult news would employ concision, not abundance. Plus the elderly rarely wasted time getting to the point. He began with that one, suddenly proud to say he could face it, though shaking as he opened it.

The envelope tore unevenly along the edge. Frail, thick, old paper. Smelled like cedar. No way to hide that he had opened it if Dina did come home at just that moment. He, Roal Bowman, was opening a letter from Pilar Engoscue. Trying to do it slowly, as if he were accustomed to such a name passing through the front door of 528 W. Bridge Street, kicking its shoes onto the beige living room carpet, taking in at a glance the plants and the long blue couch—Pilar, a name already familiar with the breakfast counter where Roal now sat, a counter where writers might gather as casually as mail was received, as if, as if.

But the letter told Roal nothing. Pilar Engoscue, the great poet of wreckage and loss, now in her mid-eighties, had written just a few lines in her insectile scrawl, in a voice casual as sisters:

> Dina—I got back from the coast to find your letter—my reward for doing these dreadful workshops! How do they always seem like a good idea when I agree to them? I am an old dog who does not learn. Anyway, I loved what you said about the tone of that last piece, and stayed up all night listening to *Flamma y Flamma*. You're right. It's perfect. Perfect! But you can't fix my new flock of chickens. They're so nearly bald with some kind of mite infection that the dog is ashamed to be seen chasing them any more. I'm working on a collaboration now with Clarisse. Sort of. She's doing the heavy lifting really. I'll tell you more later, but for now just thanks and thanks. P—

No last name. Just P—. Familiar, friendly, old Pilar with a loathing of workshops, and a stereo that played late into the night of her return because of something Dina had recommended. Roal cataloged familiarities. A mention of new chickens assumed knowledge of old chickens. The Clarisse (Clarisse Abertine, the sculptor? Lombardi, the journalist?) reference implied a shared friend. The tone of what last piece? It seemed Dina had written to Pilar about her work? What tone? What work? Dina, Roal nearly shuddered, what have you gotten us into?

More questions than answers. If the thin envelope contained mystery, Roal, surmised, perhaps the thick one would produce an inspector.

Roal seized the thick package, return address name and origin of Matthew Ulysses Chafee, Provincetown, MA, the new novelist whose first semi-autobiographical novel sizzled the ears, if not the long underpants, of the Christian missionaries introducing the people of foreign countries to the glory of their God and other, more fleshly encounters which felt unspeakably divine and lasted about as long as any other revelation. And became just as sought after.

Opening the package from the new up-and-coming didn't seem nearly as frightening as the letter sent by Pilar. Not that Matthew's presence in his home wasn't daunting: Roal was suddenly conscious of the worn path of carpet leading from front door to kitchen, how everything was clean enough, but dated. Aware too of the porcelain salt and pepper shakers whose flower pattern made them naively unaware of their overtly phallic shapes. Matthew Ulysses Chafee would likely know exactly what to make of them and, shaking them vigorously up and down, would probably not stop until the salt was empty.

But Roal could handle Matthew Ulysses Chafee. For now. As long as he was confined to the pages within the envelope. The tone of Matthew's letter was not as familiar as Pilar Engoscue's. More formal, which seemed foreign to the voice Roal connected to Matthew, whose fiction read like a jungle of language rain and lexical vines. Characters running through the pages with giant leaves, alligators on poles, skirts full of mangoes, and buckets of quicklime. The letter-writing Matthew greeted Dina from a distance, though closed the gap as it progressed.

Dear Ms. Bowman:

Thank you for the care of your last letter. I was pleased at the thoroughness and breadth of attention. You obviously have a clear sense of where my book might be headed and what it's mired in. I understand you cannot guarantee results, but can provide only recommendations and ideas about possible direction. All of this, I greatly appreciate.

I must admit that I found some of your requests odd and, frankly, invasive, which is why it has taken some time to respond. I apologize for the delay. I hope you might still have time to accommodate my work. I will also admit that I contacted Jonathan H. to learn more about how you work, and he was able to address my concerns in full, including the confidentiality, and said he remembered having exactly the same reaction I did, but was glad he overcame it. Please forgive me—I did not know what to expect. I am guessing you know how I feel and have likely received such letters before (Jonathan wonders if you remember his?). But . . . here we go! This is actually the first time in months I have allowed myself to look forward to diving back in. To be honest, my life is a wreck, and I have been afraid to make it worse by going ahead with this next book. But it's also my last hope, and I am grateful at least to have that.

Enclosed you will find the materials you requested. Please contact me if you need more or have questions. My difficulty right now is the same as before, and so the focus of what isn't working remains unchanged. If anything on your end has changed, like your availability or preferred method of contact, let me know.

I look forward to working with you, and am very hopeful. Somewhat fearful too. But that must mean the hope is real. In the meantime, thank you for all of your attention, thoughts—and even the very unusual if not (now anyway) completely endearing requests.

Sincerely,
Matthew Ulysses Chafee

Roal was stunned as he went through the enclosed papers, knowing he should put them back, should definitely stop looking, but unable to stop. He sifted through the entire content of the envelope, conscious of the oils on his skin, of how his fingers handled the pages. He got a soft feeling in his stomach, heard his heart near his ears but felt it in his hands. It reminded him of when he used to take money from the change jar on the neighbor's cookbook shelf, how doing that had similarly softened him even as it attuned him the settle and shift of the house beams, to the slow filter of dust as he kept track of where everyone was in the house, agonizing over the tiny disturbances to silence while he picked out the quarters and dimes, his ears attuned and his stomach weak and loose.

Roal sifted through Matthew's medical records, which bulked up over the months when the kidneys became worrisome and the medications had to be adjusted. Medications for the immune system, for anxiety, depression, and sinus infections. Copies of transcripts and report cards dating back to grade school. Photocopied recipes from the Saint Cecelia Unit of the Greater Lake cookbook, with several recipes including handwritten notes about who made them and what dates or celebrations Matthew attached to them, Minnesota hotdishes and things to do with mini hotdogs, canned soup, and chow mein noodles. Tax records. Photographs of open kitchen cupboards, clothing closets and drawers, and bookshelves. Matthew's? Was this Matthew's life? Was the photo of the slightly uneven café table in that studio kitchen window the place where Matthew Ulysses Chafee, the author of critics' accolades and missionaries' death threats, ate Kix cereal from a thin white bowl? Did Matthew Ulysses Chafee eat each morning looking at those humming electric wires just outside the kitchen window? Receipts for groceries and services. Names of bank tellers and childhood streets. The court ruling that declared his father incompetent.

Roal was concerned for Matthew. He considered how Dina might fit into this. Old friend? Lost family member? Therapist? Literary confidante? Roal's chest collapsed a little around his heart. Such fantasies! He eyed the pickled asparagus and took a shot of vinegar straight from it. The shock of it opened his chest again. Breathe, breath, breathing. Better. What was Dina up to? And for how long? Medical records? Insurance files? Annotated casserole recipes?

Roal thought he should have been more demandingly curious about Dina's time. What did she do the nine hours of each day he was away? Her end-of-day reports of walks and letters and reading, of music and plants, it all seemed like enough to fill a day. But then again, it all might only take an hour or two. He reviewed his days: to the office and classes each day, from eight until five. Then home to Dina (had she been there all day? what time did the waiting begin?). Unwinding with a drink. Dinner just past six. Writing until eight. Student papers or reading until nine. Checking the doors and turning off the day. Bed. News until sleep. On weekends, sleeping in and mowing or shoveling, first at home and then at Chet's. Reading papers. Reading a book. Writing. Dinner with Dina and, every other weekend, Chet. Chet and Dina at dinner talking about chess and gardening, the drives Chet wanted Dina to take him on and the ones Dina wanted Chet along for. Bed. News until sleep.

Roal tried to imagine Dina's days. He could see her in his mind only when he placed himself in the same room with her. Left by herself, she'd flick off like a light. Step in, and she reappeared exactly where he'd left her.

And each evening when he came home, she stepped from the kitchen like a clockwork miracle. The nightly coming into being, the reset button of the house pressed each time he rounded the last corner and approached it: the flowers along the sidewalk fresh. The refrigerator stocked. Blank paper restacking itself next his printer just as the supply ran low. Toner cartridges that never ran out. Somehow, for Roal, Dina had kept it all going without requiring an existence that extended beyond his presence. Who was she when he left and she disappeared?

I do love you ever Dina. What did it mean?

Do you want to know?

From the pictures he had just seen, Matthew's life looked poor and struggling. A crappy kitchen, a kidney that might not make it, a family he visited only in the form of the recipes he cooked to taste where he came from. But something about his letter vibrated and lived. He was looking to make something happen, and no one was lining up to guarantee that it would. He was grateful for hope, he said, and that would have to be enough.

Roal remembered what Lin said: he was given more than he earned. Had Dina been given less? Had she been happy? Unhappy? She had told him some years ago that her time was like a river: it kept rushing into whatever new spaces opened, and the ease of how it rushed to fill the void amazed her. Roal said his time was like a stone, and it hurt his back to push it uphill. Dina kept digging in the back yard and said to him, "In my river, water can always handle another stone."

So much of Dina's life with him had happened under the surface of the pond he skated on. Unimaginable fish, shadows thrown deep by surface leaves, sediment fine and claylike.

It had struck Roal as sweet when she quit her job waiting tables and thanked him for the time it would free up, "so I can really apply myself to my work." He assumed she meant the work of the house and her reading, and of the occasional faculty party where the spouses were expected to job-share the complaint load about the administration and student entitlement, while adoring the faculty for their academic service.

Those nights, when the party's kitchen emptied itself into the living room, and the snacks came out, the spouses mingled. Gary's wife, Jill, often waited out her time cheerily from the couch, but never weighed in on the inside conversations. And, likewise, no one had questions for her about her fund-raising campaigns. And Janet's husband, Rich, had stopped coming to the parties altogether because he said he could drink more at home and not be expected to answer clearly. Janet had laughed with everyone else, but stopped when Rich added that though the parties were presented as social occasions, everyone knew they were really an extension of territory into the homes of others.

And Dina went too, and said hello and helped prepare the food, then wandered on her own. The fact that Dina hadn't ever mentioned Pilar Engoscue or her contact with Matthew Ulysses Chafee at parties seemed shocking to Roal. And astonishingly disciplined. The discovery of it embarrassed him, not only because it made obvious how little attention he paid, but also how little of his attention she needed.

In the morning, Roal would have to go to work. And though nothing had to be said or not said immediately, eventually it would come out that Dina had left him, and there was more to her than Roal had known. An explanation would be required. Zen would not be enough.

If he were honest and said that he'd shown an appalling inability to share in her life, things also would not go well for him.

If he lied and said he was the one who left, he would look ridiculous especially because Winter Patent was part of the picture. He would not survive that lie at full height.

Somewhere in the suffering over how to tell the story, he remembered that in Zen the source of suffering is clinging to a story of the self that does not match the reality of the self. He was having a true Zen moment, a real one: the awareness of which came to him like enlightenment.

He said it out loud: "This, this is that moment."

To stop suffering, he would need to let the old story go by no longer clinging to the story of himself as a man whose life included a wife and the expectation of a wife. He would need to become a single man open to whatever public scrutiny revealed and the ability to go on without Dina. He would respect Dina's path and let her go.

But then Chet's challenge loomed. He would not—could never—tell Chet he had given up. To accept the reality of his own story might give him his own life, but it would ruin Chet's.

And then he understood what his story needed to be: he and Dina had been happy, over twenty years with hardly a fight, they were married young but had no regrets, and now she was gone and he couldn't imagine why. He hoped to find her soon.

Dad, Roal thought, *I will not let you down.*

And so as he stood in the darkened hallway, his back pressed against the wall, Roal told himself again the story he had been believing for years without even knowing it was a story: twenty years ago, he met and married a waitress, saved her from a life of hanging clothes on fraying clotheslines outside a college bar. Instead, they had been happy. Dina with her garden and her books, in the home they had selected together. That's how it had always been. Until it wasn't. He wondered if this story would be acceptable, if it would do as a little raft to cling to. He wondered if little rafts were allowed, or if the ocean's sheet of blue had to wash over everyone sometime.

Dina wouldn't be back. Not tonight, anyway, just as the new idea of her was forming in her absence. Tomorrow would come, and he would suffer at work. He knew. But at least the view of the world from his desk and the front of the classroom would not be as new as the view from his life tonight. He could arrive and wait out the day. And the next day too.

Roal put Matthew back in his envelope. He folded Pilar and put her away too. Then he turned off the lights with a heavy hand, and night filled the rooms, small dots of green surge protectors lighting Roal's way to bed. He dropped his clothes at the side of the bed and crawled in like a child, holding his knees a moment before reaching for the remote. He turned on the news.

Lin's voice pushed its way into his bedroom. The light from her face, enormous and looming on the screen, seared him as he sat up: Lin had something to say.

The makeup team had removed all evidence of the exhaustion left by the two sleepless nights in the forest, as well as any of the doubt she had shown earlier about what she would say. Roal watched the pre-interview clip, which tantalized viewers with the interview they'd been waiting for: Lin Strickland reveals the Winter Wolf Reintroduction (coming up in the second half of the news!). And then Lin disappeared, replaced by a local news image of a cougar leaping from a tree, its front paws spread wide, claws bared and ready to rip apart the unaware world below.

A family of cougars had been sighted, deep inside town borders. They were growing bolder, Del Brand of Fish and Wildlife reported. Their increasing numbers in the hills were pushing them into populated areas. He was worried that they were no longer avoiding human habitations. But, he assured the public, he would track them all night if he had to, and had his dogs to help. He'd take it from there.

The news reporter shivered and asked if Del had advice for the safekeeping of children and pets. Indeed, Del faced the camera with advice for everyone:

Stay indoors. Keep your pets inside. Report sightings. Throw rocks. Do not run or act like prey.

Next the news broke to national promises of what was to come: One mother wasn't allowing the military to bury her son, while a war on drugs exploded into crossfire on the Canadian border, and hurricane season might have a few surprises. Sports in eight, weather in twelve, exclusive on Winter and Lin in fifteen.

CHAPTER 9

During the headline news of war and oil, rising grocery prices and the extension of unemployment benefits, during the jowls of senatorial disapproval, during famine, through the shakeout of the clouds in places already flooded, during water rise and water foul, through Del Brand delivering the local news of cougars, Lin was promised to the viewers. She was always coming up, Winter in her tow. She had just returned from her dramatic visit to the woods with Winter Patent, the wolf man beaten from the underbrush by Lin's bestselling book, which needed no introduction by now. Coming up in ten, in six, in four, in two. Lin Strickland, now in from way out. The spring report on The Winter Wolf Reintroduction. Newly Patented story. Catch it here.

The remote was slippery in Roal's hands. He set it next to him on the bed, then wiped his hands on the sheet. Lin had agreed earlier to tell Roal more about Winter after her nap, but she had left before getting to it. The exclusive he was about to watch should rightfully have been his first. He needed to direct it, needed badly to know where it was headed before it crashed through the picture window of his life.

He wondered how he would get from his house to his office in the morning, from his office to his classroom. Whether his face would flush or drain as he faced his class. Roal watched sickly. Lin sat with Parish Lao, the interviewer leaning forward to find out what the world was waiting to hear. It was from Parish's questions that Roal would have to learn about Winter's project and, by extension, Dina's desires and dissatisfactions. Roal learned that Lin's posture of betrayal was one she held well: straight and even, clear-eyed with a neutral mouth that made her look receptive in her intake, indisputable in what she returned.

Parish was mirthful when Lin admitted the meeting hadn't gone as expected from the beginning. First, Lin confessed to not particularly liking nature, preferring instead to be within a cord's length of the nearest outlet. She'd brought a friend who liked nature. Roal held his breath. Lin worked her way into the story and Parish allowed the warm-up as Lin got settled. But Parish was not there to get Lin's views of nature. Lin was simply the pipeline through which the real subject, Winter Patent, would flow. Turn the right spigot by asking the right question, and he could rush out and flood the waves. Which is what Parish promised, just before the break.

They would be right back. Everyone should stay tuned while the station took a break for ads. Ads for chicken thighs, for alternatives to facial paralysis, and for pudding so rich it could make a family shine with joy. The interruption of the story for the ads felt jarring for how easily the station allowed its important stories to take back seat to the ads which yelled and caressed and intimated. He wanted to know more about *Dina*, and instead learned that the low prices wouldn't last forever, that he should get his soon if he wanted to be happy.

It seemed wrong: how Parish Lao allowed advertisements to separate Roal from the story he needed. With Dina was waiting on the other side, it seemed rude to make Lin's story wait for advertisements of people eating chicken and rubbing lotion under their eyes—all of them looking as though they had not suffered once ever.

Roal looked more closely at the actors to see if he could find any who were acting through their pain, though he could detect no emptiness.

Until then, the smiling people made jubilant by their products were happy lovers of single-serving pudding, Botox alternatives, and always golden chicken thighs. But would this be enough to keep their spouses from leaving them for a tree? Would they arrive home to find a note that it was over—that their partner had left them for a man who sent his wolf kin notes written in urine on the waving grasses? Would their colleagues make national reports about the latest marital collapse in the workplace? Perhaps.

Perhaps he was not alone. Roal found himself sinking into the wide open exaltation of the advertisements, became grateful in their presence. For a moment, he allowed himself to believe he could open a can of cling peaches, smear on some sunblock, sit back, and be okay. The fried chicken thighs looked so blissfully nested in their little boxes. It would be alright. There were twelve thighs, all from the same happy farm, sharing the same golden quality of being Totally Taste-Tastic; such goodness was available to anyone who asked.

And then, Roal was startled back to a shot of Lin, now sharing the screen with a picture of Winter from years prior, a strikingly powerful man whose amber hair and burnished skin became animal extensions of movements that were deliberate and dictated by purpose, nothing wasted. The screen cut to an old interview with Winter. In it, he shifted toward the interviewer, fastening a hungry, interested look on her face and neck. She leaned slightly away and looked around for a little cover from the lights that pinned them to their chairs.

It was an interview Roal had seen years ago, though he couldn't remember the specifics. Winter revealed that the initial difficulty of living with a pack of wolves had not been to become *one* wolf, but to become a *pack* of wolves. It was a species shift of consciousness, he said.

"In our culture humans assume individuality is a given. Although wolves understand the *physical* implications of singularity and can use their individual physical power as a strategic resource for the pack, the idea of a 'single wolf' who is an individual holds no value for the pack. Wolves do not understand identity as being related to individuality. Their identity is the larger organism of the pack." He did not gesture as he spoke, but remained watchfully still. Alert. Gripped. Ready. His eye contact held the interviewer as he explained that the pack had not accepted him until he stopped trying to be a *wolf*. As soon as he became a *function of wolfness*, integration was soon complete.

And then, he laughed, being a function of wolfness became so complete that it was difficult to return to his individual, human self, a model he found deeply flawed. When Winter laughed, he gave his first gesture, a slight wave of his hand to show that the idea occurring to him was enjoyable to him. The gesture released the interviewer, who sank back, relieved and slightly bewildered. The clip faded away, and Parish turned to Lin, slightly amused.

"So, I have to ask. How is it possible for a man who lived with wolves—who identified *as a wolf*—for nearly ten years, how is it possible that after all such a feat entails, the claw-to-tooth challenges over his right to be there, the low temperatures in high elevations, the, the raw-flesh feeding frenzies, the fights over territory with nearby packs—Lin Strickland, how is it possible that after all this, he was, as he put it, 'broken' by your book?"

"Well," said Lin, a slight twitch of mischief on her mouth, "have you read it?"

If Roal had blinked, he would have missed Parish's gawp, the sudden widening of her eyes. She gave a tight smile, gave a slight signal, and then the advertisements muscled in again, seesawing from feast to famine.

Silver cars with plush leather interiors. Women who never had to shave again. Families on matching phones. It hurt him to be on the other side of such existences, where the distance between him and the life he would have to learn to accept was still so vast there was not yet a product that could help him reach it in comfort.

Though he hoped. Though the ease with which the wine opener uncorked the bottle looked amazing. Though the docking station for appliances looked just like an old-fashioned radio. Though the woman in linen pants could now throw balls to her grandchildren and open her own jars. Something for everyone. Almost. But nothing in television's sack of gifts for Roal.

His yearning faded when the ads dropped off and again he faced Lin back from a break and explaining that the meeting with Winter had not been what she expected at all, and had ultimately resulted in embarrassment. The camera zoomed in, sifting her face for the micro-muscular confirmation that it had, indeed, hurt. She straightened up, the camera now her confessional box, the world on the other side a priest who may listen, but is not allowed to forgive.

Lin began again. They drove about three hours, Lin and her friend, the last part of the drive through a skirt of forest that spread into a clear-cut, and then past that to where a vast forest still stood, though it was dead, the trees the color of rust. The driver asked them to get out of the car, which they did, and then he drove away. They waited. It was still early, and the day was clear, so they were happy to wait. Lin walked around to find cell phone reception while Dina stood by a tree and waited.

"Dina?" The interviewer caught the name and interrupted to clarify. Roal froze. Lin stiffened almost imperceptibly.

"Not her real name, obviously," Lin said curtly, before continuing. Anyway, her friend sat against a tree and asked it if it minded their being there. Parish looked impatiently amused: Winter was the subject, not "Dina" the friend who talked to a dead tree. Parish rolled her hand forward, suggesting that Lin get to the point. But Lin went on obliviously—she paced her own stories, leading up, building characters, getting there. She was the expert in this. While Lin made her way back toward her friend they heard a voice. But when Lin looked around, she saw nobody. The voice asked again if they were comfortable, and Dina answered, "Yes, thank you," and Lin said, "Hello? Who's there?"

Lin's friend pointed to a clump of thin trees, their bark flaking and their branches empty. "Right there," she said. Lin said it took her a few moments, but then she saw him, and gasped.

"I'd been staring right at him," she said. "But he was hard to see. And he definitely did not look like that video clip you just showed."

"Are you sure it was Winter Patent?"

"Absolutely. At first it was difficult to spot him because he blended in perfectly. It startled me to realize how close and how invisible he was at the same time."

"What was he doing?"

"Watching us."

"Why was he hiding?" asked Parish.

"That's what was interesting," said Lin. "He wasn't hiding. His clothes blended in, but it was more like he had somehow taken on a tree-like quality. He looked like a tree at one moment and then once I knew he was there, he didn't and I could see him fine. But before I knew what to look for, he blended right in."

Parish asked, "His project is related to blending in with trees? Is this a new camouflage technique? Is he aware of the recent advances in camouflage technologies? Or, perhaps, driving them?"

"It's a bit more complicated than that, but I'll explain."

Parish leaned back and nodded her permission and appreciation, her good nature returning with a promise of clarity.

Lin leaned back as well, relaxing into her story, "Winter Patent is working on a project where he restores ravaged wilderness areas to their natural states, particularly dead forest zones for now. But he approaches it in a radically new way. His method is one that people might find impossible—or at least very hard to believe. It requires using a different kind of consciousness than what we are typically encouraged to make use of. If what he is doing turns out to be possible and reproducible, the implications are huge: it means that far-reaching, inexpensive, sustainable solutions are well within reach to treat all kinds of environmental ills where the environment has stopped responding—oceanic dead zones, clear-cuts, migration patterns, the inexplicable die-offs of forests, lethargic spawning."

Parish still wore a polite smile but seemed disappointed to realize that her interview with Lin had become a call to save trees. Now it was just another interview whose old ideas wanted new fanfare. Eat food you can pronounce. Exercise. Go barefoot. Stop living with people who hit your kids.

But Parish perked up at Lin's next line: "Winter admits that even though his methods would be highly sustainable, they also threaten the notion of what it means to be human. He's working deep undercover for now. He believes it's too dangerous to suggest a consciousness shift of the proportions that would be required for now."

Parish blinked and smiled, then paraphrased what Lin said into a skillfully deliberate misreading, a delay tactic that appears seamless, is appreciated by viewers who also want to be sure they heard it right, and forces the speaker into clarification: "There we have it, Lin Strickland, you say our existence is threatened by a man who looks like a tree and claims that our human selves are in peril—is that right? Sounds like the Winter Wolf Reintroduction is a sequel to the X-Men—are we talking about growing feathers or unlearning gravity? What do you mean by 'threaten the notion of what it means to be human'? Sounds fascinating. Viewers, stay tuned."

The advertisements returned, fighting for their right to redistribute fortunes to the fat, the old, the dry, and the limp. Promises for everyone. The promises came in whispers and shouts. Roal had seen them all before. But now that the promises were pressed up so closely to the arena of his own life he was suddenly implicated by them, related, in-the-context-of. He tried to place himself within the lineup, to see where he might sit at the table next to these new relatives, a table where Dina's face would appear one day too, next to the sunscreen girls and caffeinated boys made high on skateboarding. Which advertisement's family would he inhabit? Had his vision failed him? Did he need a getaway? Were his tools embarrassing? Could he get fresh with a can of diet soda? Did he understand fish-n-chips could harmonize the ages?

The ads had never included him before. But now he saw how they accepted him, open-armed and pitched to the volume best heard by his demographic. He knew they knew he was here, forty-six, full head of mostly dark hair, well trained to sit in chairs and look up at the end-line rise of a voice, his teeth graying, his heart deflated by reality's little piercing.

It would be a matter of time before his own face appeared among these on television. He would be a brief segment, a child in the lineage of this story currently unfolding, ancestor to what would follow, supported by a cast of distant relatives whose barbecue sauce and antacids might turn that frown upside down.

Then Parish was back, turning wide eyes and earnestly to Lin. "Lin, is Winter Patent a threat?"

Lin pinned Parish in a withering stare, annoyed at the obvious attempt to sensationalize the story rather than get to the heart of it. Parish played to the stare by appearing to adore the attention, leaning raptly into it, her hand on her chin as she gazed at Lin.

"Winter Patent is not a threat."

"Is he going to alter the genetics of the human race?"

"That's silly. Really," Lin flared. "What I said was that Winter is able to access tree-consciousness as a way to help support their decision to grow again."

"Their decision to grow?"

"Winter would say yes: their decision. He believes that forests have been traumatized by human actions, so their ability to grow again—their *motivation* to do so—is low. He works on healing that trauma by gaining entry to their consciousness, and then helping to process the will they suppress. Then they can begin again. It's fascinating, but it isn't exactly new. Theories about our ability to communicate with plants have been around for a long time, and are very prevalent in many other cultures. They've even been tested in some of our leading institutions, but Winter is taking it out of the labs and into the woods. He's going much, much further."

"You do realize, Lin Strickland, that this sounds . . . more than questionable, really. It sounds like Winter may be a bit of a fiction writer himself on this."

Lin shifted thoughtfully. "I know," she said gently. "But I believe that what Winter is working on may be as big of a consciousness shift as the earth suddenly going from flat to round. People had to suddenly come to terms with the idea that the sun, not the earth, was the center of our universe. It was shocking for people to even imagine. Think about what it required of people—it must have been terrifying, to suddenly live on a round planet in the middle of space, not knowing if you're going to fall off of it or how the planet stays suspended. What Winter is proposing as possible will be equally hard for people to believe: he is able to reroute consciousness to emotionally access and stabilize traumatized forests so their motivation to heal and grow is at full capacity. Do you see what this means? If he's right, it means we can all do it. And must."

Appearing to believe what Lin was saying would align Parish with the believers in UFOs, yeti, and the race of lizard people—believers whose need for facts was engaged only when a fact arose that directly coincided with the conspiracy theory they sought to support. But if Parish challenged Lin, she might come off looking obtuse and provincial. Or perhaps she hadn't quite understood Lin. What *had* Lin just said?

"Lin, back up. It sounds like Winter may not be home. How would you sum up what you observed?"

"Winter is 'home.' We should note that it's really not a new idea to believe that humans are a projection of energy, and can transform. It might not be common in our culture, but it is not unheard of in other parts of the world. Right now, from what I observed, Winter is becoming a forest, or maybe a tree within that system. Or maybe the system itself. It's hard for me to understand, and harder still to explain, but I'm trying."

Parish laughed, and Lin laughed with her, as did Roal, though it came from a place conspicuously near the sob-region of his chest.

"I know, I know—it sounds farfetched." Lin continued, "But then again, we do live on a round world that revolves around the sun, right? But you know, Parish," Lin leaned forward and nearly whispered, "we didn't always."

After the break, Parish jumped tracks. Convinced that the idea to live-interview Lin had produced nothing but concern that Winter Patent was mentally ill, and that more information about him might be in poor taste, Parish steered the conversation back to Lin. Parish recalled that there was something Lin had promised to reveal: something she was embarrassed about.

"Oh, yes," Lin remembered. "My own pride. You have to understand that Winter has an incredibly large influence on my work. He said he needed to see me because of my book. I was so flattered, and I thought—well, I thought he meant that he needed my ideas, something I could tell him. When I showed up, I assumed we would discuss some of the ways I used physics, neuroscience, and deep psychology to alter my readers' responses. And then. . . ." Lin trailed off, adrift in the memory, vulnerable again to the shadow of Winter. Parish, now softly receptive, gently prompted, "And then?"

"Well, and then I got there, and he dismissed me almost immediately. He sent me home! He let me stay long enough to hear about his project and watch him work a little. But he said he didn't need me there after all."

"Why not?"

Lin coughed a cutting laugh. "You know, he read my book, and we have a few ideas that overlap. But he said the reason he'd wanted to talk with me was because my book left him with serious doubts about his ability to trust the strength of his own imagination, and that unnerved him. He said my ability to deliberately craft literary holography in the mind of the reader was impressive—you know, the way I access the reader's emotions and perceptions through image constructs and language structure?"

Parish nodded yes, but then shook her head no.

Lin continued, "Anyway, he said he found himself susceptible to my ability to do this in ways he didn't entirely understand, and felt used by my manipulation. He hadn't thought he *could* be so susceptible. It shook him to find out that his knowledge of himself was so poor. He felt he had to contact me. That contacting me was the last hunch he would follow, and if it turned out to be wrong, he would give up his project and leave the woods."

The reporter lit up at the prospect of that interview, "And so when is he returning?"

Lin looked at her. "Pardon me?"

"Didn't you say he plans to leave the woods? It sounds like his hunch was wrong."

"No," Lin said. "This is the strange turn of events. His *assumption* of why he thought he needed to contact me was wrong, but his *hunch* in asking me to come was correct. He had assumed that he needed to talk to me so he could address his own concerns. But when I got there, he understood that he had contacted me for a different reason altogether. His hunch had been correct: it turns out he was exactly right to invite me to see him because I had unwittingly brought along the one person he said he needed to be working with. Winter didn't know I'd bring a friend. It just worked out that way. So while his assumption was miscalculated, his hunch was right on: I did indeed provide him with what he needed. My friend."

"Dina."

"He said she was perfect, not me, and sent me home." Lin shook her head indignantly and complained, "He never even asked about my book. The event of my friend's arrival restored Winter's confidence that his 'inner knowing' was still intact. He let me stay to watch a while, and then the driver showed up and I left."

Parish said the time was tight, but she had just a few more questions. Like where the project was located, what the friend's role was, and if Winter needed help.

But Lin replied she had promised not to reveal, imagined the role was related to representing tree consciousness in order to help the dead forest grow again; and, yes, Winter could very likely use some help with the environment—after all, the forests were weakened, the birds kept washing up on shores, cougars were coming into towns to find their prey, people consumed more than the world could support, and entire communities in downstream regions make regular appointments to check their blood for risk.

CHAPTER 10

Roal woke on Monday at four a.m. He had a right to know more. Before the rest of the world heard it on the news. He was sure of it, and allowed it to steam inside him, to build up pressure until it pushed him out of the house into the pre-morning dark. His certainty powered his walk to campus, ready to blister anyone who closed in. And what the hell was meant by assuming tree consciousness—clearly Dina was not okay if that was the goal she shared with Winter Patent. Lin would tell him where Dina was. He would make her. Either on her own or with a court order, she would point to an precise location on a map and be done with it.

Roal had rarely known the force of purpose before, but it felt good as it lengthened his strides and swung his arms with their fisted ends as he cleaved the air with his body.

There was what was before him and what was behind. The world in halves.

There was world to the left and to the right. The world in quarters.

Dina in one of the quadrants. In a dead forest within three hours of his home. In a standing red forest near a clear-cut. Already, the world was becoming manageable by splitting it into parts. The world around Dina shrank with the clues he assembled, and Roal grew larger in it.

On the sidewalks of the early morning, Roal saw no one and was grateful. Since Lin had revealed on television that Dina had stayed behind with Winter, Roal was officially exposed. The hunt to find out more about Dina had probably been assigned to half a dozen journalists already. Eventually, there would be a knock at Roal's door. The knocking would wear a hole in the door until there was an answer. And then the world would look through as the lens zoomed and focused: Dina. Dina gone. Roal threw his lifeboat out in front of him, reminded himself of the cling-worthy details: happy couple, twenty years, Dina simple and sweet, a baker of sheet cakes and stringer of Christmas lights over the plants of the living room. Happy, happy, no regrets, he couldn't imagine, something must be wrong, she needs to come on home.

Roal wanted to be in his office before anyone else arrived. When he was at his own desk, he could close his door. And yet, they would look for him there. Gary and Janet and Felicia and Tony. Especially Tony, who practically attended meetings just to announce the latest divorce or drunk driving incident. At the edge of campus, Roal slowed.

There would be asking. There would be avoidance. He imagined that pity and commiseration might be involved. That people would admit things about themselves he did not want to know. Secret departures of their own early spouses, walk-outs that lasted forever over nothing more than a sock on the floor. Or he would have to endure the silent awkwardness that surrounded Theresa after her husband was arrested with one of her students for public indecency.

It was still too early for others to be up to accost him with their curiosity. The sidewalks were empty. At the pond, he sat on a stone bench nearly hidden by a wall of bamboo. Not a duck in sight or any birds signaling the day yet, which would be, he knew, long and toilsome. Would he rise to it? Roal's steam escaped as he sat there, replaying Lin's interview when she revealed that when Winter found what he had wanted, he was looking at Dina.

He sat for over an hour, watching the cattails as the sky pearled with brightness. Shadows receded from the edges of their leaves and sank into the centers of the long stalks. The water sat still except for where it clung to the edges of the boulders in the middle. It seemed strange that the stones were made alive by the water's clinging when the water itself looked flat. The tree overhead reflected into the pond, a maze of branches falling across the water. It was difficult to separate the layers, to place each thing again in its proper realm. On the surface of the water, it all looked like one world, pressed together as a single dimension. Roal sat at the edge of it. If he moved, the world would shift.

Across the main square a maintenance crew erected signs at the edge of campus. The four of them worked quickly, two standing back to back while the other two posted signs. Each time a sign went up, the crew moved together in a tight group, stopping at sidewalk intersections and buildings to post more signs as they went. Whether it was for the upcoming graduation or the visiting forensics teams, they posted so many signs that Roal knew the campus would be flooded shortly with the sweet, unbearable earnestness of those who turn to signs for help.

Roal watched as a student sprinted from one dorm to the next, holding his tennis racket like a weapon, his face desperate to avoid the risk of having his end-of-the-year sleepover witnessed, which could prematurely seal that night's romance for the entire summer. The crew moved on and disappeared, the sounds of the staple guns fading as the streetlights turned off, giving way to the light of day. Roal felt alone and apart, understanding the sadness of gods who must witness lives they can not enter.

He sat so long the day brightened and felt real, though still he could not find a reason to enter the ghostlike emptiness of the still-quiet campus. Then a squirrel screeched a sudden warning above him and a branch fell. He looked up, but just as he located it, the sun sprang out from behind the Clocktower Offices and by the time he shaded his eyes it was gone. Again, silence. He understood he could wait no more in the cool green of the trees and bamboo. He began to walk within to the sidewalks closest the building to minimize open-campus exposure. He felt he was being watched.

When the night librarian saw Roal from the end of the sidewalk she jumped nervously, but recovered and gave a weak wave. Then she glanced around and altered her path, stepping off the sidewalk and avoiding him as she beelined across the lawn to the parking lot. Next the tech guy came around the corner of Chesterton dorms, but he stopped short as if called back by no one Roal could see or hear, and disappeared.

Roal's faltered for a step, the drag of his foot making a gagging sound against the sidewalk. He reminded himself he had known it would be awful. And that this was his moment, the one he and Chet had been waiting for: the day something happened. He drew up his head and forced himself to become the mountain inhabiting sky.

And still. He trembled. He breathed deeply, and the morning air expanded and settled. He felt it: he had potential. The day might work.

He had always had potential. Through grade school, his teachers noted it, giving him books and puzzles to encourage curiosity. They gave him notes to decode and pressed seeds into his hands and passed along instructions for playhouses that could be built by children. Ms. Phillips gave him a white rabbit, and Mr. Boehnel gave him a collection of old glass lenses. Roal set it all on the dining room table when he arrived home and ate the snack Helen set on the plate.

Later, while Chet decoded, Helen fed the rabbit. While Chet built the playhouse, Helen made a mobile of the glass lenses. And always, the report cards on the thick, yellow paper bore plus marks and checks, with the extra comment section stating that the teachers thought Roal could do so much more. He had potential. They suggested harder classes, questions he should form the habit of asking in order to arrive at more rigorous inquiry, a new language: anything to help Roal give the potential they detected its fair run. Meanwhile, Roal was proud to know they sensed in him something capable of growing unpredictably large.

In college too, his professors commented that he did well when he tried, but he needed to try regularly. Roal found their hope for him somewhat embarrassing, as if it were their own misplaced dreams they saw when they looked at Roal. Nevertheless, Roal showed up on time, handed in papers, raised his hand in class, and enunciated when he spoke. Potential. Roal began to believe that potential was as good as its own fulfillment, and no one exactly said it wasn't.

But in graduate school, his fellow writers were not so patient. When he showed his stories to his classmates, they expected to meet potential's twin brother: evidence. Unpracticed, Roal continued to show up for classes and hand in stories that relied on the same plot each time. His classmates badgered him to give more, to try differently, to open up, to take on. The more he produced, the more he made available for criticism. He needed to produce something of interest. He needed to *be* interesting. He began to write with a Hello Kitty pencil. It had no effect. He carried the black lunchbox of construction crews. Nothing. He grew his hair. The result was terrific.

Just after Roal's hair hit his collarbone, a wobbling undergrad in a thin T-shirt leaned back against him at a party and murmured, "Hey, wanna get native with me?" Roal leaned down and turned his ear toward her mouth to seek out again those words he had almost missed. She put her mouth to his ear and in moist, intimate breath, whispered, "Chief?" and Roal's answer was yes. He urgently wanted to get native with her. Sweat-lodge, stripped-past-the-loincloth native.

The next morning as he walked home a story unfurled: "An Unsettled Territory." The territory, in this case, was the sexual landscape, and it would be settled, claim by claim, by those who made the boldest moves against the natives. While he wrote that the land itself may be spoken for, the desire to dominate all that happened within it persisted. He walked into class and distributed the story. His fellow students read it that night, a horrified shame spreading over them. It clicked: what they had identified as Roal's limitation in developing plot was actually their own error in not having realized the context Roal was writing from. He was Native American. His last name was Bowman—how on earth had they missed it? Their previous negative comments now rang of hegemonic oppression. They should have seen that his characters were symbols. His plot lines were oral history adaptations. They were humbled and at the next class critique they admitted, some bitterly, some apologetically, that they wished they'd had the proper context for reading Roal's work all along.

According to the rules of the workshop, Roal had to remain silent while the class discussed his work. His uncomfortable nods were read by his classmates as the nod of one subculture to the other which has built itself atop it. Not nods of deference, but nods of fearful politeness learned by people who need to survive. Really, it was poignant and humiliating for them all. They noted his potential.

By the end of the class, when he had time to respond to their comments, he didn't know how to tell them it had been a terrible misunderstanding. He said nothing. In that ceremony of silence he became a Native American, tribe unknown. He learned to braid his hair. It made his shoulders ache. He thought of the girl from the bar with the long blond braids—how her shoulders must ripple and flex as she braided, wound, and pinned.

Roal's writing became understood as deeply metaphorical. Roal as a Native American from an undeclared tribe was far more profound that Roal, son of Chet and Helen, who hailed from a three-bedroom rancher in a college town, people who dreamed in English, filed taxes, and assembled the mobiles and playhouses of their child's potential.

When people asked what tribe he was from, he astutely answered, "We're all mutts. It's impossible to escape invasion." He'd hold up his pink pencil as proof. But there was talk in the shadows, of course. One classmate whose mouth was a dark, exciting fruit told Roal they were all waiting for him to welcome himself home again. Another told him more kindly that all acts are eventually impossible to maintain, and he should be careful or he'd have ulcers by the age of thirty. She knew—her sister had tried to be British, and Christmases were awful.

Only with Dina was he free to be uninteresting, and it felt terrific. When he later cut his hair he believed he had severed his connections with that period for good.

It had been a stupid, embarrassing thing for him to allow that story to perpetuate. Obviously. Roal knew it then, and still felt it decades later. But the pressure to become something that matched his potential had been enormous. He had had one moment to let his character rise, but failed despite having been told a hundred times by Chet that character was more important. According to Chet, character studies every day for a test we never know is coming, but personality cheats when it arrives.

As Roal neared his building, people seemed to be avoiding him: no one was outside, but the faces pressed to the windows of the dorms looked both stricken and excited as they watched him cross the grounds. Roal understood this could only mean one thing: everyone knew. He would face it. He would try to wear his height well as he walked, would step long and set his shoulders squarely. Today was the first day, he told himself. The one where they would try hardest to seek out the weakness.

He would construct the suffering and surprise, and therefore control it: *Twenty years—I hope Dina is okay; if only Lin Strickland would reveal the location, I might be able to help.*

Inside, Felicia was detangling her headset. She blanched when he entered, her startled smile expressing the concern of professional remove—as if she knew it were indecent to be in love with the details of his life's fraying but couldn't help herself.

"You're a brave one to show up today," she said. "I'm impressed."

Roal nodded grimly, but said he refused to hide in his house when more information was needed. "Twenty years!" he exclaimed.

Felicia looked puzzled, then asked, "Really? That's quite a lifespan."

Roal commiserated: "Yes. I suppose, in hindsight. But when everything is going well, no one notices time passing."

It was 8:10. Class at nine. That gave Roal time to occupy his space and anchor the story he would need to tell and tell and tell until he believed it too.

At 8:15, Roal was restless. He had prepped his classes ten years ago. At 8:20 he pretended to read, waiting for Lin's key in her door, for Tony at the coffee maker. The silence of the hall threatened him with breakage.

At 8:30, he got up for coffee, though he knew taking a standing position in the kitchen exposed him on all sides, and he had hoped to be in his own chair when the others stopped by, a rhetorical authority, a way to say he saw no reason to rise to their concern. He heard Felicia on her phone working out the details of her children's emergency daycare. She told the person at the other end that she was trying to see these kinds of crises as an opportunity to learn more about her own network of support. She pronounced her esses with a sizzling sound. Roal thought the conversation sounded haunted. Maybe because of the hallway's larger stillness. Maybe because he only heard her half of it, and her responses after long pauses kept shattering the quietude and unnerved him.

Roal walked slowly to the bathroom, passing Tony's office, then Gary's, then Julie's, listening at each for a gather of murmurings or muffled laughter. He passed again on his way back to his desk. The silence felt like a warning. No voices, hushed or otherwise, leaked from the other side.

At 8:50 Roal gathered his books for class and headed out. Felicia called out that Roal didn't need to go today, warning it would be too dangerous, but he needed to follow the line he'd already drawn before him and kept going. If he turned, he might falter. He held his books like a flotation device, rehearsing his lines. He was comforted to believe them: *Twenty years. I can't imagine. Lin knows where she is and says she's fine, but I need to make sure.*

His classroom looked gutted by emptiness when he arrived. Just him and the water stain on the ceiling, a long scrape on the back wall where students tilted their chairs, and a spill like an anemone crusted on the floor. These things disappeared when the room was full. The emptiness made Roal's eyes prickly, his skin chilled. However, Roal reflected, it was the last Monday before finals and graduation. Things often got unusual at the end.

This was about the time when a student he had only seen the first few days of class might show up in his office to ask for an extension and a complete semester's worth of notes in case there was a final. And when the students who steadily missed one class each week might suddenly develop cases of grandparents with exploding hearts, while those of steady attendance might have real panic attacks or freak cases of dehydration that left them hospitalized for a few days. There was always a chance that the graduating class was just now waking up in a field of cows, or had brought one to the soccer field, or was petting one outside the dining hall as a protest of the food service's meat sourcing. An empty classroom might mean anything at this time of year. Plus, Roal was two minutes early.

At exactly nine, one student walked in and sat down, his headphones on and his eyes one can of caffeine away from being jolted fully open. Miller Shiwandu, who never missed a class, rarely spoke, and sat in the front row so Roal could better see him fill pages of his notebook with circles for the first half of class, and color them in during the second. It wasn't until he took out the earbuds, positioned his notebook, and cracked open his can of Rabid that he yawned a greeting in Roal's direction. Then he startled and looked around, recognizing that it was just him and Roal. He fumbled through his bag for his phone.

"Aw. No way." Miller threw his phone back in his bag and looked directly at Roal for the first time. Roal grinned and hoped it wasn't ghastly. Then Miller suddenly grinned back, shaking his head in admiration. He grabbed his bag, saying as he reached the door: "This is crazy, man. Listen, don't let those big cats bring you down. I've got to take care of myself. You do the same—good luck!" And he left. Roal waited ten minutes, unsure of what to do next, then picked up his books and emerged again into the morning light.

The faces of the students gathering to the windows of their dorms floated pale above him as they watched Roal cross the lawn. He made an effort to lift himself into his own height and carry himself across campus. He could hear the grass bend under his shoes as he walked. It sounded like the static of tiny bones. His stomach scooped and dipped, and he went on. He sucked in his stomach, tightening it to leave no room left for the fluttering. A student in the window gave the thumbs-up sign. Others looked on anxiously. He was hugging his books over his heart as if to hide its wild hunt for a smaller, less visible body, so raised one arm and returned the thumbs-up high overhead. It restored him and he kept on.

More faces gathered at the high windows. And cameras. The entire campus seemed to be looking down from the stories and rows of windows enclosing the yard.

He saw the flashes of mini-screens as people pointed their phones at him, and he wondered what those screens would later be used to establish. Exhibit A: a Large Man Walking into the Story He Tells Himself. What would such a man look like?

Roal determined to demonstrate. He slowed his walk, tossed his hair from his eyes, exposed his face to the light, and leaned back into his steps. He was halfway across. He lowered the books and employed the full swing of his arms. It was the deliberate progress of a person who understands the preciousness of daylight, the value of each hour which is impossibly laced by the accumulation of miraculous seconds, each reaching and hooking to the next, gathering and accumulating, pouring themselves into the wide gape of time. He heard knuckles rapping at the glass. Their faces were a blur because they held many things.

Roal breathed and swung, lengthened and straightened. Part by part, he gathered himself until he was a function of walking, a beautiful machine rolling smoothly as it glided slowly, luxuriously across a lawn expansive and wide enough to share with the onlooking world. Roal swelled and floated. He felt the faces of students turned toward him like young suns, and he allowed himself to be wing and wax rising to their heat. He soared. Under the Rally Tree, he made a final turn for them and bowed ridiculously. The rapping against the glass went wild, and he could hear them cheering or yelling. Something was happening, and he was it.

Though as he neared his building's dark foyer, the wings fell away. His damp shirt clung to his back where they had been. Felicia asked sharply if he had a death wish. He managed a shallow chuckle, saying he was just trying to keep going by doing what he knew how to do, and that the students were also doing what they knew how to do, as none of them had shown up in class.

"They're terrified, I'm sure." Felicia said.

"They don't have to be." Roal said. "If I can face it, they can too. It's just life. I'm trying to lead the way."

"I guess you think it's inspiring, but we don't want anyone following in your footsteps," Felicia said, looking at him with apprehension. "I hadn't heard anything about it before I got here. But then I thought, well, I'm here, so I might as well stay."

"Thanks, Felicia. I appreciate that you stayed. That means a lot." Roal rapped her desk twice, softly, and headed to his office.

At his computer, Roal again felt the cold dread when he opened his email. One hundred and thirteen messages? And more sliding in as he read his way into them, his finger poised over the delete key. As he worked his way down the list, Roal saw the all-caps of the email that snapped him into an alarm that made him cold and still: CAMPUS DANGER ALERT: READ ASAP.

Classes canceled. Campus closed. Signs were posted, and the public service announcement auto-calls had gone out early. Multiple cougar sightings. Stay indoors. Watch from the windows. Alert the officials. A large female of nearly two hundred pounds, and two year-old cubs, each approximately seventy to ninety pounds, were sighted on campus and in the vicinity. Young cougars are particularly dangerous, the note stated, because they have not yet learned to fear humans. They take more chances. The female is most likely teaching her cubs to hunt. Stay inside. Keep your dogs and cats with you. Almost all attacks on humans come from young cougars learning to hunt as they establish their own territory. Campus security, the city, and the Department of Fish and Wildlife were working to end the situation.

There were no emails about Dina. Nothing. And nothing about the interview. But a torrent of student emails swirled around the announcement that campus was closed. Or, as they pointed out: it had been closed on them, and they were locked inside their dorms until further notice.

One student demanded to know if the ambiguous "end the situation" meant "kill the cougars." The reply to her, backed by the authority of being from Montana, said that any cougar who enters human territory should be killed because it crossed the line, and the line needs to be clear. He signed off, *Ignorance actually can kill you.*

The emails exploded from there, proliferating and faceting a conversation that seemed to absorb more light than it reflected, hot at the center, each one impassioned by logic or heart, each position so unshakably certain, the conversation devolving and spiraling, protesting and seeking the generosity of understanding:

The conversation must remain civil!

If cougars were people, they'd get the death penalty.

No—humans are the ones in the wrong. We've encroached on cougar territory. They're just trying to live in diminishing nature spaces.

Dear Nature Girl: All territory becomes people territory when it comes to life and death—you wouldn't feel so sure of your position

if you were facing a cougar in person. Then you'd see some
survival of the fittest in action!
Yeah, hot cougar action!

Then, a photo of a majestic cougar with an appeal to spare God's cre-
ations. Followed by dares to see what it feels like to have God's big teeth
ripping your throat out just in time for graduation. Arguments from theol-
ogy majors: God is a human concept and has no teeth.

A mocking claim that God sent the cougar as reckoning, so stay inside.

Practicalists arguing that cougars would probably be the stupidest way
ever for God to send reckoning, as it would likely only claim one person,
whereas driving while texting was far more efficient.

Animal rights students volunteering to drive the cougars to the wilderness
where they could be relocated safely. They were reminded by a lit major of
what happened in Flannery O'Connor's story when granny's cat got loose in
the car and caused the accident that resulted in her death.

And in response to this, a reminder that this was real life, not some fucking lit story.

A reminder from a relativist that all stories are real somewhere, so lighten
up and plus it's a bad idea to transport cougars because what if they're pissed
when you open the cab?

More polemicizing: beauty and destruction, nature and reality, God and
the void.

And romanticizing: cougars kill so quickly they are considered merciful
killers in regions where starvation takes its time.

And hatred: Shoot the fuckers, they're some cold-assed motherfuckers
who don't care whether you're dead or not when they start to eat.

Solutionists advised cutting down all the campus trees and bushes so
cougars would have nowhere to hide. Met with the immediate horror of losing the campus trees. Then cavalier assertions that trees can grow again, but
people are a one-time deal. An ironist stating that people are only a one-time
deal if they believe in the church-speak of the same elders who had left the
student body in debt, out of work, and saturated by media.

Roal deleted seven for every one he read.

They poured in. Roal read and read, though the emails stopped being new, kept spinning back to the same positions—each person more correct and certain than the one before. Roal was about to turn away when he spied one from Lin. He paused, then opened it, but backed his chair away from the close intimacy of the screen:

Roal. Hi. I am sorry I was so angry when I left your house. I gave an interview last night, and I mentioned Dina's name—it just slipped. I am sorry. I didn't give a last name, though, and no one except a few people in the division could even guess who she is. I told them it was not a real name. Plus Dina kept a low profile. Lucky, I guess. I asked other faculty who know her not to say anything, and they said they wouldn't. If you don't want anyone (reporters, etc.) to know, it seems like it can be your call. Neither of you are in the phone book. I'll try to find you later today—we should meet. The fallout of all of this has not been good for me either!
Here's to not becoming prey, Lin.

A nearby email was from the Dean of Faculty:

Roal:
Some things I need to discuss have come up. I would appreciate your insight. Make an appointment to meet at your earliest convenience.
Tagg Larson

Roal walked back Felicia's desk. She was watching a clip of a cougar leaping out of a tree onto a goat. "Terrible," said Roal. Felicia nodded, still watching the four-second clip looping again and again, the cougar leaping onto the goat in a kill so quick the goat never saw it coming.

"Yeah." She said, her eyes on the screen.

"You see the news last night?"

"We're taking a break from news at our house. So depressing. Plus, it comes on after we're all asleep."

"You didn't see Lin?"

"Was she on?" Then Felicia remembered: "Oh—right! Winter Patent! I missed it! I am dying to talk with her! Have you? Is she back? Winter Wolf Reintroduction indeed!" Felicia wiggled her eyebrows and intonated as if the project name was a forest operation for consenting adults only.

Roal stepped away, still watching the video. The loop finally ended and the goat was allowed to lay dead in large and grainy pixels under the cougar's paw. The cougar's shoulders could have hauled a tractor from a sand pit.

The cougars had released him from the task of having to face this day at work, and he accepted the gift with gratitude. As he left, Felicia called out, "Roal, you're not supposed to go out there! There's no word yet on the cougars! They should have locked us in!"

He left campus by the nearest possible route, noting the signs posted at its edges: DANGER: COUGAR SIGHTINGS. YOUR LIFE IS AT RISK. STAY CLEAR OF TREES AND SHRUBS. DO NOT TURN YOUR BACK OR RUN. DO NOT PLAY DEAD. TRY TO APPEAR AS LARGE AS POSSIBLE.

At home, the message light blinked. The auto-message about the cougars gave its warning. Lin's message, left at seven, was the same as her email. A reporter, Kirk Kirkman, called around nine to "follow up on a detail" and left a number but no other information. And Gary had left an awkward invitation.

"Roal, this is Gary. Uhh, Jill insists that you come over to dinner. Because we all have the day off, and . . . (murmur from Jill) and you could probably use the company. I'm guessing you're not much of a cook. Oh—what? (background voice) Okay. Okay, anyway, it will be fun and Jill will pick you up at three thirty. She won't take any excuses, so it's sealed (dry laugh). Just bring your appetite."

And one hang up. *Do you want to know?*

Roal took off his shoes and tried to go back to sleep, almost convincing himself it was possible. But then the metal door of the mailbox clanged, and he knew something had been put into it. He could feel the thickness of the package from where he lay. Do Not Play Dead. Roal brought the mail in, ready to open it despite the name on the return address: Federico Cortinez. There was only one person in all the world with that name who was worth knowing. Do Not Turn Your Back Or Run. Roal nodded, staring at the envelope, and then his hands lunged into it, tearing it open. Inside was a book. Just a book.

Just a slim novel entitled *Under*, about a boy who buries things in the backyards of the families who took him in and later returns as an adult to dig the items up again. Painful and rousing in turns, the blurb stated, but consistently brilliant. Roal opened the book, dedicated to Rachel, always. But the acknowledgments drew Roal's attention: Many thanks to Dina Bowman, whose intuition teaches me about choice.

Roal closed the book gently. He wanted to know what was buried in those yards, if he would recognize anything of Dina's there.

CHAPTER 11

Roal paused at the edge of Dina's room. She'd been gone three and a half days, but her room had already absorbed the absence and held no expectation of her return. The plants resigned themselves against the walls, trailed wearily down ladders, their leaves slumping like wet paper on an abandoned porch. As he watered them, a tired, aching light invited Roal to lie down. The world was blank to him. He didn't know what details to read to get the news he needed.

He curled up in Dina's bed and stared out. Something felt different. He would have to look for clues. The question of where to start was simply his way of prolonging the inevitable. It wouldn't matter where he started. He already knew what to expect: the surprise would be exhausting.

The low bookcase's three narrow shelves were lined with books whose shining spines faced out in tidy rows. The case looked inconspicuous, but Roal stared at it. Something was definitely off. The books were as orderly as ever, as bright and dust-jacket glossy. The little shelf stood sturdily, certainly, its back pushed against the wall as if it were bracing against the slide from its position into the rest of the room's disarray. And yet.

And yet, Roal realized, scanning the room from one side to the other and back, and yet there was no disarray. Not anywhere.

It was not the bookcase that was different, but the room. The case had been the room's dependable anchor, its clean order a declaration that while the rest of the room was in shambles, at its core was the dignified, organized, and steadfast mind of the orderly bookcase. But now the entire room was similarly ordered, the piles of papers with their clutter of wrappers and T-shirts cleared, and the jumble of pens and photographs and postcards gone. Roal could extend his feet from the bed and not tip over a pile of papers. He could, should he choose, put his elbows on Dina's desk without clearing space. He could sit in a chair without first needing to set aside the papers it held. The room was not expecting Dina back for a reason. She had already told it she was leaving. The bookcase waited undeterred. Roal began there.

He removed the first five books, setting them carefully on Dina's desk, a card table with a soft, brown rubbery top. Roal pulled out five more, and five more. He looked at the pile of books for a moment, and then tested one of the books in his hand as though it might be hot. He opened it. He found her there. He was surprised to know with such certainty that he had known already he would find her name in that book, and the next. In each of them: Dina Bowman. In one book after another, she was named in the acknowledgments. She was thanked and thanked and thanked. As a sister, a sage, a savior.

In two books, he found her on the dedication page as well: "For Dina" and "For Michael, Dina, Timothy, and other forms of grace." Roal had actually seen the second dedication a few years ago when Dina pointed her name out to him. Roal read the page and her happy, expectant look. He couldn't remember his response, but he thought she was showing him because she enjoyed the coincidence of seeing her name—of seeing someone else's name that was the same as her own—in the book. He thought he said something about coincidence.

Roal was staggered by the range of authorial presence on the shelves—names that towered: Marshall Plennish; Tahlia Nebezzur; Christophe L. Laberge; Kate Just. And names he'd never heard of.

In each of them, Dina, Dina, Dina—her name a bell of praise. When Roal opened the books where she lived, the white shine of the pages brightened the room.

With the page opened to Dina's name, she was there in a dimension Roal wasn't sure how to access, but he knew she was more fully present than he had seen her for the years they had sat together each night, half-hour increments at a time, to eat the evening meal. There, Dina had recounted the day she had lived, while Roal convinced himself that after his own day all he needed was silence. He placed the books back on their shelves. Touched their spines like their inner pages were dreams, and turned away because he was finally too much awake.

At Dina's reading chair was a thick, lone stack of paper waiting for help: the manuscript from Matthew Ulysses Chafee. Roal leafed through the work, taking in Dina's system of notes and marks. They seemed decisive, swift, and focused, pressed in by a hand that worked the page with authority. It was far different from the first and only time Roal had seen Dina's comments when they had been written on his own story. When he had handed her the story at Kenner's Bar she turned away as she took it from him. When he explained that she had inspired it and he wanted her to read it, she turned back to him, her eyes trapped somewhere between panic and amazement.

"It was actually your braids," he said, "that got me thinking about this story. Anyway, your hair inspired me." His own hair hung, braided, like exclamation points of authenticity.

Dina thanked him, read his name on the upper left of the page and said it aloud: Roal Bowman. Then she slid the pages under the bar, brought out a rag, and wiped down the long plank between them, the conversation over. Though later she told Roal she went back to her room and named a plant after him. They still had the plant: Roal. It was Roal's story, she told him later, that got her started. Though she hadn't been specific, and it was only now that Roal realized what exactly had been started.

The week after Roal gave the story to Dina, she returned it. The pages were crisp and immaculate, as if she had ironed each page instead of reading it. She had attached a list of questions and comments about the main character. Any one of the comments, if addressed, would demand an exhaustive reworking of the contents. She had clearly paid attention. Perhaps too much. But he was also relieved—he'd worried it had been a bad idea, arrogant, perhaps too demanding, to hand a story to the girl who had just completed her GED But she did not seem put off. In fact, Dina included a short note about how marvelous it had been to lie in bed at night thinking about a character that so few other people in the world knew about yet. Roal thought about her lying in bed while thinking of his characters, and the butterfly of flirtation slowly flapped its wings.

Whenever she saw him at Kenner's after that, she wanted to know how the next draft was going. But Roal only wanted to unpin her hair, spread some blankets on the floor, and order pizza. His writing class generally liked the story. They were interested in how the woman symbolized nondominant culture. How she had to fight her own family to retain her authenticity. How the family symbolized a hegemonic culture that equated consumerism with dominance. Add a couple of commas, a few more details about the mother, and good to go. Roal gave the mother a cowlick and a flashback about a humiliation suffered on a tennis court, played with commas, and set the story aside. Done.

But Dina wasn't done. She wanted more. More reading, more stories. More to work on. Flattered, Roal said he'd get something to her, but Dina said she had already picked up books of her own to work with and was happily writing comments and questions for Dickens, Proust, and Barnes. He began giving her the books of the still-living writers he was reading, and Dina took them, thanked him, said she owed him beyond measure, and disappeared so she could get to work. It took Roal a long time to reach out and touch one of Dina's braids, to trace the coiling wind of them.

But there in Dina's office, her comments on the work of Matthew Ulysses Chafee showed none of the diffidence of the comments on Roal's work twenty years ago. For Matthew, she devoured pages, connected dots, made sudden lists of details and questions that seemed intent on slitting open the sack of narrative. Matthew's writing was brilliant, though Roal could see what Dina meant when she kept coming back to the main character's reluctance to share the details of a witnessed beating: it led to unnecessary trust issues. Dina urged Matthew to be brave, to trust the truths of a world that can be corroborated by the dust or clouds, to not allow the narrator to hide behind his family's frightened hope for silence.

Roal read the way he might engage a lunch buffet: cautiously at first, but then, trusting the hand that shapes the food, voraciously, appreciatively, wonderingly.

His eyes scanned the story, darting off to the sides to check the notes as he worked his way through the pages: Had Matthew ever heard of a childhood game called Runaround? Were the heart scans still available? Could he find a relatively untouched 1920s brownstone—if so, arrange a tour. Put character in low-contrast outfit, but date it ten years. Look at 1930 Sears catalog—good plate patterns and home furnishings there.

Roal read and stretched, read and sat in Dina's chair, which sagged but held him. Roal leaned back, thinking about who Dina was to these people. To Pilar and Matthew, to the rows of authors on her shelf. Why he hadn't made her that person himself. When Roal and Dina got married, Dina's case worker asked the judge if she could say a few words before they left his chamber. He shrugged—it was a wedding, after all.

Not exactly a wedding toast, Sue's message was directed at Dina: "Dina, I have known you nearly fifteen years. You have learned so much, but you have not yet learned to ask for things. This isn't your fault—it's common for kids in the system. Too often, when you kids ask for what you want, you are denied. So you stop asking for everything, including what you *need*. But now you are in a partnership, and you can make decisions together. There's no more asking. You don't need permission any more for your wants or needs. All you have to do is imagine what you desire and work out a plan together."

And afterwards, when Big Ken brought them back to Kenner's for a drink, he shook Roal's hand and said, "Dina has never really had something all of her own. Thank you." The quote "Imagine what you desire and work out a plan" still hung on a piece of paper taped to the refrigerator.

Roal played the years like a tape until it began to unravel, the thin black strip of it loosening into long coils and settling softly, draping itself in loops. He crossed his arms over the manuscript on his chest, then leaned back and stretched his legs. It felt good to let go of his feet and height. Felt good to disappear and allow the grip of his muscles to soften. Felt wonderful to loosen the hold of the question of how it was possible to meet this new Dina here, this Dina who asked if he wanted to see her life's work. Is it possible, he wondered, that he had said no? Not just that one night, but all the nights? Can time go so fast, cover so many years when we turn away for a moment? He yawned, his head resting on the back of the chair.

From a great distance, Roal heard his name. Somebody calling from the ocean, from across time and water. He awoke. His name still hung in the air, not receding with the rest of the dream. Was it his dream? The voice called again.

"Roal? Are you ready? I have an errand to run on the way and I need your help!" The voice advanced a few feet into the house, and Roal dropped to the floor. He crawled toward the door of Dina's office and peeked through the crack. Wispy red hair, foxhunt pantsuit. Roal remembered Gary's message about dinner: Jill would not take no for an answer.

"Roal—Gary's waiting to fire up the grill! He needs you!" The double *e* of "needs" dragged into multiple syllables. He would have to go, smile, speak to children, chew, try not to ask people if they believed in living with ghosts, and hope they wouldn't guess he meant himself.

In the car, Jill admitted to Roal that she knew everyone was supposed to stay inside until the cougars were relocated, but she figured they would be safe enough barbecuing.

"After all," she said, "we don't have any big trees, and the kids won't be outside without us much anyway. Plus, with you along, we'll be a big group, and I don't think the cougars will bother us. Do you?"

Roal, still unsure of how she had ushered him into the minivan so quickly, speculated that cougars probably roamed through town all the time, but these ones had made the mistake of being spotted. Jill agreed. Too quickly? Too heartily? He shouldn't have come.

Dina's absence was riding along, sitting between them, and he didn't know how to introduce her absence to Jill.

"The hills," Roal repeated, "are probably full of them."

"At any rate," Jill said sincerely, "I, for one, am grateful for the cougars. Otherwise we wouldn't have gotten to invite you over. It really has been too long."

"I don't think it's been ever." Roal remarked.

"Yes, never! I guess it takes a cougar lockdown."

"I guess that's what it takes."

They drove quietly for a while, and then Jill turned toward the small downtown. She had to pick something up on the way, she explained. Roal nodded and looked out the window.

She pulled into the alley of her office building where two giant boxes stood on the loading dock.

"There they are!" she said grandly. Roal watched her struggle to maneuver one of the boxes from the dock so she could stuff it into the side door.

"A little help, please!" Jill commanded.

"Sorry—of course." Roal leapt from his seat, and together they squeezed the boxes through the door, slid it closed, and drove on in silence. The boxes contained T-shirts, Jill explained, for an upcoming charity walk for breast cancer.

"It's the only time of the year I can get the boys to wear hot pink," she said. She ran her thumbnail over the torn manicure of her pointer, a casualty, Roal guessed, of working with huge boxes of T-shirts.

"It's for breast cancer," she repeated.

"The walk, I mean," she said.

"I help organizations fundraise by implementing large-scale events and projects," she said.

"It gives a face to the issues," she continued after a few seconds.

She said, "It's actually pretty interesting work."

And then, "I like it anyway."

Roal's silence was a crumbling mortar between the sentences. But Jill kept her chin thrust forward, a determined smile on her face as her eyes scanned side streets for cars creeping up on stop signs, and her hands gripping on the wheel.

Finally, Jill sighed and said, "Listen, I'm sorry about Dina. I wasn't honest with you." She glanced at Roal and admitted, "The cougar isn't really what prompted us to ask you to dinner. I just can't stand the thought of anyone eating alone."

"I hadn't thought about that yet," Roal said.

"I figured. It just seems sad. I know you'll get used to it, but whenever you need to, you can eat with us. You don't even have to call. If it's six o'clock, we're at the table with extra food."

"My mother died of cancer." Roal's comment caught them both off guard. "What?"

"The charity walk. They didn't used to have those. I think my mother's cancer was a very private, embarrassing thing for her. If she had seen a group of people walking past our house wearing shirts for cancer, who knows? Maybe she wouldn't have decided it was more polite to just give up." He did not see Jill smile of consolation because he was looking out the window, surprised to have said so much.

Things always got confusing when Helen's name came up. It used to be that when Chet or Dina brought her up, Roal would say what he thought, though as soon as he did, it suddenly sounded untrue. So he would try to correct that statement with something else, only then that sounded false too. Each answer he arrived at had a way of reversing itself, discussion negating discussion.

But neither Dina nor Chet seemed bothered when their positions shifted and inverted from minute to minute, day to day. When Roal pointed out the inconsistencies, Dina would say, "Yes, but that was then," as if language were not capable of carving truth and shaping memory. As if language did not shape a person's very palate.

Roal's solution was to maintain that Helen's death had been coming for some time, so there wasn't much to say. But now he was saying something to Jill, and what he was saying didn't seem too late or too simple. Just aware that if Helen had live at a different time when people went on cancer marches, things might have gone differently for her.

Jill slapped the steering wheel, excited, "Roal! You've given me an idea. You're brilliant—a genius. The walks are usually on routes at the edges of towns. We never do walks through actual neighborhoods. But why not?" Roal waited.

"I mean, really—why not, Roal?" She went on to explain that walks at the edges of towns seemed to reinforce the peripheralization of the disease. But for an issue central to so many people's daily lives, the walk should become central to their neighborhoods.

"I mean, why not incentify people in their homes by taking the walks to the heart of where they live? Sure," she continued, mostly to herself, planning, "traffic is a liability, and curbs could be an issue, but it's possible. In fact," she turned to Roal, "it's the only way to go—this is awesome."

And they pulled into the driveway: Roal and Jill and five hundred T-shirts still unsalted from the bodies that would fill them. After they unloaded the boxes, Jill again thanked Roal for his terrific idea, which she said would reinforce the trends toward localism and communitarianism in ways Jill thought would be brilliantly received. It was exactly the edge she needed, she said, then stopped talking suddenly, as though she had said too much. She pushed Roal gently into the backyard, and he entered, feeling tender and appreciated.

Gary was already at the cooker, working the knobs and cleaning the grill with a long wire brush. His fresh haircut revealed a line of pale skin that ran around his hairline. He greeted Roal as if it were common to see him there in the backyard, where Gary held an early afternoon beer and wore sagging shorts. Roal still wore the button-up shirt and pressed slacks of his earlier trip to campus.

Gary grinned, "Did Jill have to pry you out, or did you go gently?"

"I think we were both surprised by how easy it was." Roal rubbed his forehead.

"So, the cougar. I heard you were defying orders on campus, braving it out and walking around like a man with no cares in the world. And don't deny it because I have photos. Students were texting me the play-by-play."

Half the campus had pressed itself to the windows to watch Roal's saunter between buildings, past shrubs and bunched grasses and finally under the Rally Tree, where the cougar had perched just minutes earlier.

"You *owned* it, man!" Gary punched the air. "Cougars on the loose, and you head out to meet them: 'This is *my* campus!' We had to get you over here before you got eaten." He went back to cleaning the grill intently, as if cleaning it enough might remove the moment when he would have to acknowledge Dina.

Roal decided to help. "Jill told me you guys heard about Dina."

Gary nodded, wounded that the thrill of the cougar story was already over. "Yeah. I'm sorry, man. We saw the interview. We already talked to Lin. We won't say a thing. About Dina. I mean, we didn't know! We did not see this coming."

"Neither did I. Neither did I."

Jill stepped onto the patio, now barefoot and trim in a fitted pink T-shirt that read "Stop the War in My Rack!" across the front. She threw a shirt to Gary, who yelled "Incoming!" and caught it, and the kids stepped out of the house. Two boys, soft and freckled, swam in their bright pink shirts. They were distinguishable only by their scowls: one seemed genuine, and one was trying hard to copy, but his eyes were playful and gave him away.

"Nick, Travis, this is Roal." Gary introduced them as he pulled the shirt over his head.

"The cougar guy?"

"Yep. The cougar guy." Gary looked at Roal at shrugged.

"Cool," / "Duh," the boys said, each evaluating the merit of Roal's walk across campus.

Then the twin of the genuine scowl brightened and said, "I saw it on You-Tube! It's you and then it's a cougar in the bushes. But not the cougar from here. That one was in the tree. But still, you should check it out!"

Roal guessed the boys were between seven and ten, the age span he assigned to most children who had huge front teeth their heads hadn't caught up to yet. He was never sure of what to say to children. They always appeared stoically unimpressed by adults' questions, and, in truth, the adults never cared about the answers.

He pulled out the one interesting fact he recalled, "Did you know that cougars usually hunt alone and can bring down an elk by ripping out its throat?"

Jill looked shocked, Gary looked impressed, and the boys whooped and said, "Yeah! I'm a cougar—you be the elk! No, *you* be the elk!" And then they rolled around on the lawn trying to cut off each other's air supply. Jill shook her head and threw a T-shirt to Roal and then went to break up the fight so the pictures wouldn't have grass stains.

Gary turned to Roal and said, "You better put it on. It looks like you're going to be in the picture."

"Pink's not really my style," Roal said, and set the shirt on the picnic table.

"Nice try," Gary said. Then, dropping his voice, he said, "You just wait— you will put that shirt on. We get pictures of all Jill's charity paraphernalia. You won't have a choice—you'll see." Louder, he called, "Jill, honey? Is that shirt for Roal? Will he be in the picture?" He winked innocently at Roal.

Jill came over and picked up the shirt. She smoothed it out tenderly on the table and sighed. Looking at it, she said, "Roal, I was just thinking of what you said about your mother and the neighborhoods. Who knows what we can accomplish if our work honors our greatest hopes?" She lifted the shirt tenderly, then turned and raised it to Roal, who bowed down to her so she could ease it over his head.

"That was too easy!" Gary cried.

"You're lucky everyone isn't as cynical as you," Jill said. "And you're lucky cynicism isn't contagious, or fatal. I doubt anyone would attend a charity walk for cynics."

Jill fixed the sleeves over Roal's shoulders. She smoothed the shirt across his chest so it was clear from a distance that Roal absolutely believed in the importance of stopping the rack war.

"Is that because everyone would want us cynics dead, or because we wouldn't believe that showing up for a walk would make a difference?" Gary teased Jill.

Jill had been right: Roal would be eating alone from now on. He felt it then, keenly, as Jill and Gary moved closer to each other. Jill was also proba-bly right that he would get used to it. He felt loss whittling a shape he was beginning to identify. It had corners. But for that moment, when Jill tipped her face up so Gary could tap her chin with his thumb, Roal didn't believe anyone, ever, should get used to eating alone. He hoped the boys, who were now setting a camera on a tripod, would never forget six o'clock and the sound of chairs and forks at the table as they ate with someone who asked if they wanted to know, and the answer was always yes.

As the five of them stood together for the second picture, arm-encircled and yelling "Fleas!" at the lens, Roal thought he might die from the tug of war between the happiness of the moment and the despair of everything past the edges of the back yard. The camera's time delay began to blink its red warning, telling them to all pay risible, happy attention to its lens. Then, just before the camera collected its image, Lin Strickland burst through the fence gate into the yard, holding up two bottles of wine: one white, one red. The picture snapped, freezing that moment. When Jill went to check the image, she looked up quickly at Roal, startled, though Roal's face had already recovered, the surprise receding as his color came back.

Before Lin joined her to see the picture, Jill had it deleted, and replaced the lens cap. When she looked again at Roal, he was looking back at her with a blankness that held no bias or loyalty in any direction.

"I wasn't sure whether I should bring bad red or good white," Lin was saying, "so . . . "

"So you brought them both." Roal said.

"Yes," Lin said weakly, remembering she had used that line on Roal. At his house. When Dina had been there.

Jill took the wine and then asked Lin if she wanted a T-shirt too. The boys yelled that Lin could have theirs.

"No, thanks—I can't do the walk. I'd hate to take a shirt someone else could put to good use." As Jill tried to persuade Lin into taking one anyway, Lin protested, saying she really couldn't, confessing, besides, she looked terrible in pink. The boys cheered, and Jill turned to them, telling them that in the Middle East pink was considered masculine. They turned their shirts inside out over their heads and wound them into turbans.

"I wish I could do the walk," Lin was saying, "But it's graduation day. Though I have to say that Roal looks quite good in pink." She paused to consider as she eyed him, then continued, assessing him as if he was out of earshot: "You know, I'd never have taken Roal for an activist. It might be a good change—he wears the shirt well enough." She clearly had intended the comment to be playful, but Gary and Jill exchanged tense glances, and Roal felt the caution of the boys behind him as they paid attention.

"Jill gave it to me," Roal said, feeling defensive, though he tried to keep it light. "But maybe it's true that the clothes make the man." Roal turned to Jill, smiling, "You know, I actually feel like an activist when I have this shirt on." Jill winked at him, and Gary's face eased back into its usual expression of a casual willingness to be entertained by small calamities.

But Lin extended the moment. "Oh. Of course. It's all about your 'Practice.'" She said it conspiratorially and laughed at the reference but wasn't joined. So she dug deeper, "Wear the shirt, wear the life?"

Gary coughed and said he'd take a bad red wine over good white any day, and the boys yelled out that they'd take some fruit blood too. Then Jill leapt into action, rushing into the house for glasses with a call to Lin to lend a hand. Roal and Gary stood with their shoulders nearly touching as they surveyed the yard together.

When Jill and Lin returned, they handed juice to the boys and wine to Gary and Roal. When Lin handed the glass to Roal she looked at him longer than she needed to. Roal accepted the wine and her gaze as a peacemaking gesture. In a low voice, she said, "Sorry there, Chief," and then Gary, Jill, and Lin raised their glasses, their faces upturned and pleased to have wine in the early afternoon on the Monday of the last week of classes and on a day made soft by the new leaves and grasses. Roal glowered, still looking at Lin who, after calling him Chief, appeared determined not to make eye contact again. Gary said, "Here's to . . ." and he paused, looking over at Roal. Gary faltered, unsure of how to bring them together in uncertain times.

Roal completed the toast for him, still staring at Lin as he spoke "Here's to wearing the shirt that makes me an activist. Here's to wearing it every day, in fact, until Lin tells me where Dina is or I find out on my own."

He drank to that in one gigantic swallow, lightheaded before the glass was empty. The rest of the group awkwardly clinked their glasses but did not drink from them.

Jill began to speak, "Listen, Roal, I know this is really hard, but—"

Lin interrupted, "Roal, I promised Winter—I promised both of them—not to reveal the location. I have to honor that. I'm sorry, but I have to."

"Well," Roal said, "then I hope you meant it when you said I look good in pink. Because you'll be seeing this shirt until you decide to break that promise."

Then he thanked Gary and Jill for the invitation, but said he really did need to go, insisting he had to learn to eat alone sometime, and now, as an activist, he'd need to get to work on walking.

Jill protested, but Roal was already through the gate and down the drive, then emerged onto the still-empty streets where he strode like an enormous pink cat, hungry for the eradication of breast cancer, ready to offer support one long step at a time, for countless local miles, and for anyone to see from their windows.

CHAPTER 12

The phone was ringing and the light in Dina's room was still on when Roal got home. A half-halo leaked from Dina's open doorway onto the floor of the living room, and Roal, out of breath and sweating, already regretted his T-shirt proclamation. The light from Dina's room did not make him feel less lonely; it was simply soft in the midst of an otherwise hard day. That was all. The light would stay on, he decided. The shirt too.

In the kitchen, Dina's note was still on the counter. He picked it up: *I do love you ever Dina.* His hunger, insistent from the wine and long walk, pushed through to Dina's the last line: *PS: Whatever you'll need is in the freezer.* Roal winced, disquieted to imagine that when he opened the freezer door, he might find that, indeed, his needs could be measured so easily they could fit into sixteen cubic feet of freezer space, food enough to learn to eat alone by.

The news that night was a mess, and Chet kept calling though Roal couldn't bring himself to answer. Everyone wanted to scoop the news on where Winter's project was, and amateurs and news agencies alike were conducting helicopter flyovers of nearby dead forest locations.

The hunt promised to be intense—reporters laid out possibilities, showing remote regions where they suspected they might find anomalous greening in the old stands of dead trees. Other stories focused on the possible identity of Winter's new mysterious assistant, Dina. Roal leaned forward and tensed, ready to catch any sign about where Dina might be. But mention of her passed so quickly it seemed a side note, mere warm-up for the next developing story: the psychological impact of Lin's book.

The story was big and growing larger. Opening like a mushroom cloud, with people running afraid underneath. At question was whether Lin

Strickland should be investigated for allegedly using her publisher as an unwitting mass distributor for her literary mind-control exercises. She'd used techniques that she'd learned about in neuro-physics to alter people's minds. And now her book was everywhere.

It was difficult for Roal to decide which channel to ride. The stories wouldn't settle in. Each time the news got close to content, it backed out again and split off into another tantalizing dangle of what the viewers could expect: theories of The Mystery Woman, The Undisclosed Location, and Mind Games with Lin. Roal watched enough to know that no one yet knew anything. In the meantime they ran with what they had: Winter had not been able to withstand the effects of what Lin called "literary holography," an affect intended to create a new type of reader consciousness as they experienced the book.

And hadn't Lin admitted in interviews that the book was neuro-experimental? It was a fact that she said she had written with the deliberate intention of changing the ways people thought. Of changing the structure of their brains.

And now, after a day of television shows and internet articles that played and analyzed her interview as teams of psychologists were asked to weigh in on the ethics and impact of what Lin had done, the masses were revolting.

They'd been exposed to what Winter Patent could not withstand. Millions of copies had been sold. The damage might be extensive, though it would be hard to know. Lin had tried to change the very structure of people's minds—it was unclear what the effects might be.

Uneasy readers contacted reporters.

Some psychologists disclaimed any concern, while others advised it would be prudent to close the book and set it aside until the impact could be assessed.

And then the Christian bookstore chain pulled Lin's unsold books and sent them back to the publisher. By the truckfulls. And their angry customers voiced their profound concern.

One family protested outside of their town's library, which continued to display the book on its shelf. By the end of the day, the book was missing, but no one had checked it out. The worriers alleged mind control, attributing recent behavioral aberrations to exposure to Lin's book—waking up and no longer liking the family dog, dumping a refrigerator into the pond, speeding late at night with the lights turned off.

Lin had admitted to having used neuro-responsive knowledge to radically alter the ways text and ideas were absorbed into the structure of the brain. And after Winter himself had denounced the irresponsibility of her mental manipulations and the news alleged mind control, uncertain consumers were convinced they were experiencing the powers of a mind-altering substance for which no laws had yet been written. No one had seen such a thing coming, and no one yet knew whether the act should be classified as a form of terrorism or a civil rights invasion, or whether it was legal.

Roal watched the circus build its tent over the book, amazed at how quickly they assembled teams of experts, at how quickly the public had turned on Lin.

One couple claimed their children had begun using the dinner hour to point out the "unsustainable pattern" of their parents' SUVs, and the sanctity of the family was at risk. The parents cited research showing that families who eat dinner together enjoyed greater cohesiveness than those who did not, and they found it unforgivable that their meals now produced only fighting. In addition, their children rejected plastic drinking cups, challenged the source of the milk placed before them, and wanted to know how the workers of the low-priced, store-brand food corporations were treated. They wanted to start a garden of their own, but were worried about the effects that years of pesticide use may have had on the soil. *The lawn!* the mother stormed, *Now it's no longer a place of childhood play! Lin Strickland has turned the grass of their innocence into a biohazard in our children's minds! I hope she's satisfied.*

Another parent railed that Lin's work had powerfully influenced her teenage daughter, who suddenly voiced a desire to opt out of Christmas: she wanted to stay home instead of visiting the grandparents and the other grandparents and the homebound uncle. She wanted instead a quiet day, just hanging out on the couch and watching for snow and eating popcorn. The birthday of the Lord was at risk. Christmas was going to happen. Besides, the mother had already bought all the gifts for next December on sale last January.

Others jumped in, suspecting Lin's book was behind every door of discomfort. One father asking, "What the hell is a vegan boot maker? I mean, Christ, who eats their boots?"

While others accused that their children's choices to forsake college in favor of working on organic farms for free threatened the entire system of capitalism, wage motivation, and work ethic. No one works for free, they insisted, it goes against what our country is founded on. Until now. Until their kids had access to Lin's book and the deep psychological implant had taken root and radically altered the basic wiring and the world became dizzying and new.

Then families found themselves suddenly ripped apart by desires no one had seen coming, much less could understand: a passion for soap making? for tying plastic grocery bags into decorative patio rugs? apprenticing with a woman who specializes in horse massage? It had to be the book. And everything had been going so well.

Lin's editor was on record stating that nowhere in Lin's book could anyone find the words "decorative patio rug" or "plastic grocery bags," "Christmas," "vegan boot" or "simplicity" (though "simple" appeared twelve times, and "simplistic" four, though not in the context of "sustainability," which also did not appear in the book).

One counterprotester hailed Lin's book as a miracle, insisting he no longer needed medication for epilepsy, while others screamed to drown him out: their medications for bipolar disorder and post-traumatic stress disorder no longer worked as well, and they could see the edges fraying.

The clinicians weighed in, too: suicidal tendencies on the rise. Cutting, scarification. Perplexing, disconcerting. Girls with new breasts were convinced that the uncontrollable urges compelling them to unbutton their clothes for neighbors and boys in the back seats of buses might be the result of the book, and they came forward to confess to their parents. The parents made some calls, found others were struggling too, and made signs to picket the bookstore, demanding the world to Protect the Children.

However, the pediatricians entered to offered a different view. While they confirmed that clinic visits were up for sexually transmitted diseases among girls between the ages of twelve and sixteen, the trend was merely a continuation begun over three decades ago, and they suggested Lin's book had probably not caused promiscuous behavior. However, they were relieved that concerned families might now be able to more directly address sexuality—they were always happy for any awareness that might lead to testing for diseases and a frank talk about birth control. The doctors soon found their homes picketed and their children harassed. They might have to move to protect themselves.

There were serious problems to contend with. Lin's book hid was at the root of all of them in absence of any other explanation.

Lead was found in children's toys. Baby formula was made of chalk. Unthinkable, unnatural. Rural postal offices were closing. Pensions were scammed from the elderly, and female teachers slept with teams of their younger male students. Lesbians wore tuxedos to prom. The term "obese" replaced "hospitable" among respondents asked to describe the south. Inexplicable, incomprehensible. Mines collapsed because someone had purposely deactivated methane alarms. Mental illness terms were extended to zoo animals. Evangelists, uncertain of whether Lin's book had altered the language spoken by tongues, stayed away from services, fearful their proclamations in a language they could not account for might lead them to the valley of the unchosen.

The world was changing in a hurricane's turning. In its eye, Lin's book. In multiple languages, the book was now hailed as the next most possible vehicle for worldwide pandemonium, though other countries seemed less affected. It was the translation, a panel asserted. The translations had somehow broken the code of language devised by Lin to create its effects.

Each interviewee had a panel, each panel had a detractor, and each detractor had a dismissor. The book was a culprit, a scapegoat, a threat to values, a masterpiece—and, finally, a bargain, now that it could not be returned fast enough. Grainy store footage revealed that Lin had last been seen shopping for wine and looking indecisive.

At the center of the controversy was whether what Winter claimed Lin had done was indeed possible: "deliberately craft literary holography in the mind of the reader using neuro-physics to directly access the reader's emotions and perceptions."

Psychiatrists believed it was. "Ideas are planted all the time," they claimed. "Anyone with even relatively simple psychological and neurologic understanding can plant an idea. People do it every day. Think of advertising."

One panelist used the example of food scarcity to show how easy it is to affect human behavior: when people sense shortage, whether the shortage is real or not, they rush to stock up—it's not hard to influence the human mind if you can convince it that survival is at stake. The panelists nodded, then pointed out that advertisements specialize in psychological subterfuge by subverting reason in favor of emotion.

"It's certainly not a new phenomenon," the panel claimed. "If Ms. Strickland knows what she wants to affect, and she has the skill to do so, then yes, it is possible she could radically alter people's responses and perceptions." But one lone panelist sputtered that she was less concerned about Lin's book than she was about how the general public seemed to have a double standard when it came to advertisements.

"After all," she asked, "why isn't the public enraged that children are exposed to over 3,000 discreet advertisements a day—most of them completely age-inappropriate? Why are they instead enraged about this book?"

"Because this book," explained a respondent overscrubbed by earnestness, "is literature. Literature is culture. We have the option to not take ads seriously, though we can hardly say the same for our national literature."

The station then cut to the advertisements, and when they returned, a panel expressed particular concern that, if Lin's book had indeed accomplished what people feared it had, then the most vulnerable populations—children, the elderly, the feeble-minded—would be most at risk. Even Winter

Patent, they noted, who is as mentally tough as a person can get, said he found himself susceptible. The anchor jumped in to remind the panel that Lin herself had reported these facts, and had not refuted Winter's charge. The panel nodded, looking grave and ill at ease. A few of them disclosed that they owned the book, and admitted they had considered recusing themselves from the conversation.

Roal's mouth hung open. He could not fathom how the giant machinery of teams and panels, experts and interviewees, protesters and supporters, trucks full of books and hands clenched to protest signs had been assembled, programmed and launched with such swiftness and targeted specificity. All this, he wondered, in less than twenty hours? Somehow a switch had been flipped, and a complete made-for-media presto-pack was assembled and activated, replicated and multiplied. It was bigger than swine flu. When Lin had said that none of the fallout was easy for her either, it was a massive understatement. He smiled. She would break faster. She would reveal the location.

Roal surfed the news, but the quest to fix Dina's identity had already ended for the evening. She would not be news again until there was an answer. Roal suspected that if her identity were discovered, they would have to contact him for confirmation, but he would deny it, and they would move on to the next Dina lead.

The phone rang again, and now Roal answered, holding it away from his ear. Chet nearly exploded into the phone. "Where is she? I knew it! I knew it! What the hell is going on?"

"She's fine, Dad. Dina's fine."

"Fine? What, is she there? I want to talk with her."

"No, Dad, she's not here. She's working on a project. I can't talk now." Roal looked around for an excuse to hang up the phone. There was nothing.

"Oh, really? Why? Is someone else there? Is that what this is about?"

"No. It's just, it's just. I don't know. I'm exhausted." When he said it, it was true. Roal felt his shoulders slump, and his arm trembled to keep the phone pressed to his ear.

Chet would make this real. If Roal had been hoping before that doing nothing would help things return to normal, he now understood the size of the reality Chet would introduce him to. It would press him flat.

"Roal, don't tell me you're tired. Are you in bed? Dina's in the woods with a guy who howls when the sun sets, Roal. You better not be in bed." Chet's voice evened out, which meant he was about to present a plan, and the plan would involve Roal, and Roal would have to explain why the plan wouldn't work.

Roal preempted Chet, "I'm on top of it, Dad. I have a plan."

"What's that? What plan?"

Roal hesitated. Currently, the plan pretty much consisted of wearing a pink breast cancer shirt until Lin told him where Dina was.

Chet said again, "I want to hear your plan."

"Okay," Roal said. "I am working with some activists." Roal liked how it sounded, and continued: "They have given me something I can use." He paused again, impressed at how the cryptic response sounded so authoritative.

"What do you mean, activists?" Chet sounded suspicious, though intrigued.

"Activists who come together to do things for worthy causes. To make things happen. In big groups. Dad, really, I'm on it." Then Roal tried a new approach, "For example, did you notice they don't even know who Dina is on the news?"

"Yes, lucky for her! She won't know what hit her if they do find out! What a mess."

"Dad—the activists are the reason they don't know. Believe me, I'll find her before the news does. Don't worry." Chet thought it over.

"Well, what can I do?" Chet asked. Chet would need something to do. He was not capable of doing nothing.

Roal assigned, "Umm, how about if you bring over your topo-maps tomorrow?"

"We can look at satellite images for dead zone areas within three hours."

"Yes, and then I go to get her."

"You?" Chet asked.

"Yeah, me."

"What about the activists? Where will they be?"

"Dad, you were the one who said I should fight for something. I'm going to find her. I am an activist too." He couldn't believe how saying things made them suddenly true. Was it that easy for everyone? It took so little to become bigger than the moment before.

"You? You're an activist." Chet's statement was too bare to hide his disbelief.

"Yes."

"Roal?"

"Yes?"

Chet paused. When he spoke again, his voice was miserable, as if the phone might not allow it through. "Why'd she go?"

Roal closed his eyes. The rest of the world was just out there beyond the walls of his house. Waiting for a collapse so it could enter and fill the space. Roal felt like an air pocket in a river. He knew such spaces didn't last forever.

"Dad, did you know that Dina helps authors with their books?"

"Maybe. I know she does some editing, but I didn't know for who. For you, I thought," Chet sounded surprised. "She always has some project going that she's collecting things for. She likes the work."

It was the kind of thing Chet would have known about Helen. Chet knew how to buy the proper inserts for Helen's shoes and remembered to call in her prescriptions when they ran low. Chet knew the pattern of the china he and Helen received for their wedding, and could order new pieces for anniversaries or Christmas. He had known by looking at Helen whether she would need a book or a board game in the evenings, an extra pillow or some hand cream. Such details were in the realm of Chet.

Roal said quietly, "Well, I didn't know that Dina did that work. Until today."

"Oh." said Chet. He sounded sad from a world away. "Sorry to hear that."

They said good night as the regional news moved on to report that grizzlies at Yellowstone were coming down from the hills. Up top, their diet was scarce, so the bears headed to the camps, where they would demolish the coolers, smash car windows like felons of hunger, and slash open the tents to feed on the trembling inhabitants. The people inside were no match for the urgent call of the bears' multiplying cells for calories to prepare them for the onslaught of a spring lumbering toward another mountainous winter.

CHAPTER 13

Again, the phone. Barely five-thirty. Roal gripped the pillow and considered groaning, but with no one to hear, it seemed excessive and useless. The phone fell silent. Roal needed another thirty minutes, minimum. He closed his eyes.

Forty-five minutes later, Chet snapped the blinds open in Roal's bedroom with a crisp, zipping sound, and Roal turned over, confused. The room was bright. Six fifteen.

"Turn it on," Chet said, thrusting the remote at Roal. "You've got to see this. It's a feature!" Roal stared at Chet, whose presence and words were still ungraspable, distant. Chet waved the remote at Roal, and Roal held out his hand for it, then turned on the television and sank back onto his pillow, making the slow, exaggerated blinks of the newly awoken. Chet laid out coffee and donuts on the table next to Roal before sitting down.

"It's from ten years ago. But there might be a clue." Roal started to ask a question, but Chet hissed for silence. The morning news was covering traffic. There was none. It moved onto weather. Clear everywhere. Upcoming stories would cover the sinkhole which swallowed three cars and a burger store in Georgia, oil in the lungs of another whale herd washed up on shore, and transgender shoe outlets that found a retail niche in Utah. Roal wasn't following along. Whenever he looked at Chet, Chet pointed at the television, waiting. And then, there it was: at seven, the morning show would dedicate itself to a recently submitted interview with Winter Patent, the last one he gave before heading off to the exile of his forest project.

Roal had ten minutes before the show, so showered quickly. The pink T-shirt's glow was aggressive and bubble-gum nauseating from atop the bathroom hamper. He regarded it with a sinking feeling. He didn't know how to wear it again. His proclamation from the day before now seemed far away and spiteful in its consequence: the joke would be on him. Roal grabbed the shirt savagely and thrust his arms through.

"Your Lin Strickland is in for some weather!" Chet called, watching another news segment erupt around her story.

Roal stepped into the bedroom, and Chet looked over sharply.

"What's that you're wearing?" Chet asked. Roal thought quickly.

"It's . . . it's part of the plan."

"What—does Dina have breast cancer?" Chet tried to ask this lightly, but his voice hitched with concern.

"No." Roal shook his head. "Not that. The shirt is a sign. A way to easily identify me if someone is looking for me." Chet looked impressed.

"So, is the plan going to get rough?"

"Dad, Winter has a whole section in his book dedicated to keeping the pack strong. No matter what it takes, he says, you know?" Chet looked confused. Roal reminded him, "I'm not in the pack, Dad."

"Right—I know. So what, is the shirt supposed to help them keep track of you?"

"We hope." Roal turned away from Chet. He didn't know how to compose his face so Chet would stop searching it. Thinking of Helen, Roal added, "Plus, the shirt's for a worthy cause. There's a walk coming up, so it won't be unusual to wear the same shirt every day until it happens."

"Every day?"

"Well, for at least a week and a half. Then I might have to keep wearing it."

"A week and a half sounds too long. What kind of a plan is that? We can find Dina sooner than that." Chet nodded to the pile of maps at the foot of Roal's bed. Somewhere on one of them was a thin line that followed the curve of a hill or valley, a ring of peak or a wander of river. Dina was near to one of those lines on the map. Tenderness crested in Roal as he looked at the maps—she was there. With luck, Roal might get there before the helicopters and their cameras started homing in, tightening the sky's distance, and pinning themselves to Dina.

* * *

Winter Patent. Newly discovered footage. An exclusive ten-year-old interview with a then-lean, then-young intern, Mike Kasura, who had since gone on to hybridize bamboo in Hawaii. The older Mike, still lean and looking remarkably hydrated, explained that Winter had not initially been interested in being interviewed by Mike. Or anyone, for that matter. Winter was officially done talking to the media, done with their repetitive, idiotic questions and the endless circuit they'd plugged him into.

Mike reported, "I told Winter I was frustrated by the redundant interviews questions. It seemed senseless. Winter said I could have thirty minutes. It was the scariest and most liberating thirty minutes of my life."

The younger Mike had proposed a different approach that would quickly recap Winter's wolf experience and then move substantively into Winter's next project. "After all," Mike recalled saying to Winter, "you left the life of a wolf for a reason—I'm more interested in where you're at now and, if it's relevant, how the wolf project became a strong point of departure for your current interests."

Mike also revealed, his eyes shining, that it was at that interview that he had received a gift from Winter he was still grateful for to this day. Then the station cut to the ads. In the early morning geared to the sleepless elderly, Roal saw the life of his oncoming years: coffee-stained dentures cleaned by effervescence during a toothless nap; chocolate laxatives so good dessert could be replaced; a wheelchair rated Tops by Tucson. The 800-numbers flashed too quickly, but were repeated and repeated. The act-fast warnings pretended to be about limited quantity, they couldn't hide that acting fast was really about limited-lifetime realities. As in: act now because, let's face it, you're dying, and if we could get even just a few months of better smelling dentures out of you before you go, well, think of how you might regain those picnic privileges.

The sudden appearance of Winter's face to the channel's exclusive was a shocking reminder of another possible world. Winter Patent radiated golden health and sinewed certainties, his facial muscles rippling magnetically under sun-raked skin.

Yes, he quit living with the wolves, he said, a few seasons after he stopped learning from the experience. Winter revealed to Mike that at first—after he had stopped learning—he thought he might gain something from the not-learning, from the discipline of not-expecting, and wondered if having entered a not-wanting phase meant he had reached a higher level of development, similar to when he had matured enough as a wolf to acquire, defend, and retain his own territory. But then he received a message, and the message changed him. And after he had received that message, his pack sensed the difference immediately and was wary about his presence among them.

"What was the message?" Mike asked.

A pretty direct message, according to Winter. One day an enormous treetop cracked off and fell nearly on top of him as he marked a tree within his secondary line of territory—a place not really open for dispute at that time, but still, it had to be maintained. The treetop's fall slammed him into the trunk where he was momentarily stunned. But then, he said, he had a moment of transcendence, of enlightenment, and the tree and branch disappeared while he entered a moment of all-being. When he dropped back into himself, he was standing next to the tree, and had been accepted into the family of trees. Mike began to ask a question, but Winter continued as though he didn't notice.

The transformation shocked Winter. Shocked by the pain, yes; also by how if he'd been standing three inches back the branch would have resulted in a smashed skull. But mostly the startling of Winter resounded in how thoroughly that instant had opened him to the consciousness of trees.

At that moment, Winter stopped being a wolf. He could no longer commit to being just one thing, as he understood that a single-form life focus was restrictive and blinding. There were other lives he could enter. He instead sat at the base of the tree, cradling its enormous top across his lap. As he sat there, he felt within his own body the pull of water running through the roots of the giant tree, water pulled up the long trunk, into the cells, and then pluming vaporously out the leaves in a gorgeous exhalation of offering to the wind.

Winter returned to his den with branches from the treetop, but stopped when the wolves greeted him suspiciously, begrudging his presence. Winter snapped off one long branch, laid the rest of the treetop down, and walked away. He held up a cane to show Mike.

"This is that branch. I carry it with me," he said. "The tree sent me a message. I took this message to an old teacher who urged me to study the teachings of the great master Linji Yixuan's."

"Who is Linji Yixuan?"

"Was. Maybe is. He's a ninth century Chinese Zen master who achieved enlightenment after his master hit him with a stick in response to one of Linji's questions about meaning. After that, Linji Yixuan became a teacher, and his teachings led to an understanding of sudden enlightenment, which today is the Rinzai school of Zen. While some people believe a daily practice will lead to enlightenment, others understand that enlightenment can happen suddenly, in moments of startled awareness. Like Linji, I became enlightened after being struck by a stick, though my master was a tree."

"What is the significance of a stick?"

"What is everywhere and often left unseen?"

"I see." Mike said. Though he didn't. Anyone could see that. Mike Kasura was an intern four months into carrying lights for veteran anchors. This was no starter kitten-in-the-tree story, and Mike's scramble for what to say next was brightly lit: "So, Mr. Patent, a branch fell on you, and you had an epiphany. What was it?"

Winter frowned, thinking: "I didn't *have* an epiphany as much as the tree had *made* the epiphany available, and I answered it. The tree sent a branch down—it didn't fall on me. The invitation of that event opened me up to a new dimension which put me on a new path of discovery.

"Living as a wolf was really all about me," Winter continued. "I didn't do it for altruistic reasons—I just did it to see if I could. I didn't expect it to take more than a few weeks or months. But then, I discovered I could fundamentally change what it meant to inhabit a different kind of self. I learned how arbitrary the human form is once it avails itself to other-consciousness. And I was hooked. Time disappeared, and keeping track of it was meaningless. But then I stopped learning anything new, and I became depressed. Once I understood tree consciousness, though, I realized that my discontent had been necessary. My discontent had returned me to my human self and made me available to receive the message of a more difficult and necessary challenge."

Chet whistled, "Yonder waves of grain! No wonder this footage got lost. What in hell is this guy talking about?"

Roal waved Chet into silence. He was riveted, horrified by the competition presented by Winter, a man who had grown bored by inhabiting wolfdom so completely that he needed to move on. Roal's own job had stopped being new around the time he quit adding new material to his classes, sometime over a decade ago. It had not occurred to Roal that boredom should be problematic, that a lack of learning anything new represented something other than mastery. Winter had become a wolf, and quit because it got old. Despair spread in Roal's lungs. This was not a man he could fight and win.

Winter continued. When the treetop broke over Winter, it was a challenge, an invitation. Winter sat up fiercely. Mike leaned away in the manner instinctive of prey.

"What was the message?"

"Mike, this is always where the interview wraps up. But you said you wanted to hear what comes next, to have the conversation no one else ever gets to. And that's why I'm here. Is this still the conversation you want to have?"

Mike nodded. He actually licked his lips like a child contemplating doors, all of them leading to sugar. Winter looked at him, waiting, his eyes sharp and intent. Weighing something. Mike nodded again, flushed and eager, "Yes, Mr. Patent. Please."

"Okay. Mike, I will tell you." Then Winter leaned forward and looked Mike directly in the eye and stated in a low voice barely smoother than a growl, "But if you change the subject or air this interview with excerpts taken out of context, I will rip you open just above the pelvis. Got it?" Winter traced the slice line in the air just inches away from Mike.

Mike's face shrank. He shifted his legs to one side, prepared to run or collapse at the slightest indication. He nodded unwillingly.

"Mike, the branch awakened me to the fact that I didn't need to mark my territory by peeing on trees. That's an old concept. Territorialism is counterproductive. Each time I marked my territory, I was sending a message to the trees that they were at my bidding—that they were a prop in my own territorial ambitions. Mike, I had been reinforcing a territory of supremacy over nature by seeing it as nothing more than a convenient signpost for my territory."

Winter paused. Mike looked stricken, suddenly aware of why the conversation often stalled at precisely this juncture. He struggled to form the segue that might get him past the territorialism of urine. The pause grew uncomfortable, but Winter eased back to better enjoy it, crossed his arms, and kept his eyes fastened on Mike's face, his smile taut across his teeth. Mike swallowed.

"Your urine. Territory. A branch." Mike's tongue was sticky, and his voice sounded robotic with panic. "Umm . . ." The lights caught the smeared slickness of his face. Mike appeared desperate not to change the subject, but seemed afraid that anything he might say next might miss the point. Would Winter slash him open while the camera's impassive face looked on? Was Winter really past his urges to throw himself at the weakest, the most vulnerable, the one who trips and falters even when running on level ground?

"Come on, Mike." Winter challenged Mike with a smooth and chilling patience, and his body's flex and ripple beneath the black turtleneck was mesmerizing.

Mike finally broke into sound, his voice spilling like a bucket of nails shrill against a concrete floor, "Mr. Patent, I'm sorry—I can't think of what to ask. I'm not changing the subject—I'm sorry, I just, I don't know what to ask. Please, could you please tell me what I should ask next? I want to get it right. I'm sorry." Mike's terror caught Roal in the chest.

When Mike looked away to hide his fear, a giant tear sloshed down his face. Winter sprang quickly toward Mike, holding something blue in his hand, and Mike jerked back so quickly he fell off his chair, but Winter leapt to catch him with a strong, fast arm, and gave him the unfurled blue handkerchief, which Mike accepted and then used while his shoulders hitched and shook, gasping with sobs. The channel promised to show more when they returned.

Chet and Roal sat mute and gaping. Chet appeared deeply moved by what he had seen, but Roal was confused. What *had* he just seen? It made sense that Mike had hidden this interview. Roal had felt Mike's terror. Anyone would have. Roal's gratefulness to be finished with that part of the interview allowed him to unclench his hands. The knuckles throbbed.

"That's who Dina's with?" Chet asked as if he were understanding the gravity on a new level.

Roal nodded. They kept watching.

Winter praised Mike for asking the only question Winter had ever wanted: to be asked what should be asked. Winter knew Mike could do it. In fact, Winter said, the question of what to ask was the same question Master Linji himself had begun with. Mike was on his way.

"It's fear," said Winter, "that awakens us. Fear and love and time running out. Sorry I threatened you. I don't actually practice violence. Though when I was a wolf, it wasn't violence. Just survival."

Mike's nose was puffy, and he sniffled. Winter told Mike how much he admired that Mike had laid himself bare, just plunged right into not-knowing instead of clinging to senseless control of the interview.

"That's what always wrecks it," Winter said sadly, "Everyone tries to hold on to where they hope the conversation will go. But that's just what people do to project who they believe they are and how they want to be seen. They have no sense of what else they could actually be if they threw that projected self away." He paused, then laughed abruptly. Mike joined him, a little too brightly, but willing.

The outcome of Winter's epiphany was that he decided to use his experience as a wolf as the foundation for becoming a tree. Or anything, really. While Winter's genetic code allowed him to physically manifest as human, it also had embedded in it the ability to consciously flex and meld to apprehend tree-being, or water-being—anything with a consciousness. The main message, Winter said, was that the trees were at risk and he could help them. And it was to the trees, Winter said, that he owed his allegiance. It was they, he insisted, who had issued the invitation in a way he understood it. Due to the debt he owed their generosity of inclusion, he determined to find out what they needed from him so he could properly repay the debt.

He would once more abandon human structure to enter the realm of the trees.

"I think they are stuck," Winter concluded.

"On what?" Mike asked.

"Trauma." Mike raised his eyebrows, and Winter explained. "Many parts of the universe are stuck. They can't move because each time they expend productive energy toward their own growth, we harvest it. Therefore, they can't become full extensions of themselves. In short, the trees are traumatized because all the energy they put into their own generation becomes our motivation to destroy them. So in places of repeated devastation, there is no longer a will to be generative." Mike nodded, and looked interested, but was unable to contribute.

"Think of oceanic dead zones," Winter urged. "Think of the tracts of dying Canadian forests, the sterile farm loess, the rain forests where trees go inexplicably hollow, and the factory cows who remain barren unless they are freed from their production expectations."

Winter said he hoped to enter the other-consciousness of the trees, to see if they might transfer their trauma to him so he could process it while they recovered enough to grow again. "It's worth a shot," he said.

"Seems like a long shot—is it even possible?"

"Sure. We're all made of practically the same stuff. I should be able to enter. I don't see why not. Plus, I have had some moderate success." Winter revealed that his efforts to date—which were preliminary and nowhere near to what he believed he could achieve—resulted in robust growth within forest pockets of otherwise dead zone areas.

"Where are these pockets of growth?" Mike asked.

"Obviously I can't allow that to become available," Winter countered. "It would betray the trees. If I tell you, it would result in cutting and measuring them in the name of science, and the project would be over—and right when they need me most."

"Why now especially?"

"I think forests are in a state of advanced shock. We keep cutting them down to make room to plant more so we can cut them down again. They do not understand growth as preparation for slaughter. Who would? The root systems they leave behind are read by the new plantings, who will not grow because they have read the records and don't want to try. Add to that the environmental conditions. In some places it's just hard for them to breathe or get water. It's not a compelling scenario for them."

Mike shifted and leaned in, "Winter, do the trees talk to you?"

Winter let the question hang for a moment before answering. He said, "Mike, the earth is losing forests at a rapid rate. You lose forests, you lose oxygen. So this is not a sidebar issue. And I'm only crazy if insanity means living beyond the limitations of what's currently understood as being possible. In short, no, I do not hear trees talking to me."

Mike cast his eyes down, embarrassed that the assumption of his last question had been read so easily by Winter. When Mike continued, Roal felt embarrassed for him—why did he keep trying?

"So how can you understand their invitation if you can't hear them talking?"

"Trees don't talk, Mike. Don't be absurd. Trees inhabit time. They're a separate dimension available in our own dimension. Why would they talk? It's inefficient. They take on time and space, collecting both as mass. They share experience, which becomes consciousness, but not in a way we understand it. They speak in scent, chat across mycelia, all kinds of ways. That's what makes the project a challenge." Winter spoke calmly, as if what he was saying were old news, covered in dime store coffee shops since the war.

Roal thought Winter needed help. His plan made no sense: to devote his life to trees after accepting an invitation to a different dimension in order to make restitution for the territorial supremacy of peeing.

"So how do you intend to access their consciousness?"

"Exactly!" Winter pounced on this. "That's what I am going to find out. My project is to dedicate myself to learning how to inhabit their dimension so I can help them strengthen."

"What will you do if you fail?"

At that, Winter leapt up, seized the stick he carried with him, and struck Mike on the forehead with it. Mike cried out and fell backward.

Winter strode off screen and was gone before Mike recovered fearfully, brushing himself off carefully as if having hands were new to him. He then turned to the camera. His face glowed tremulously. Mike sized the camera up, bowed to it, and then delivered it a kick that spun the show into grainy darkness.

Chet looked at Roal. Roal smoothed his shirt over his chest. It felt like a blanket he'd had as a child.

"I hope your activists are good backup," Chet said. "That interview was nearly ten years ago. This guy has had nearly an entire decade to get crazier, and he seems efficient."

Roal understood. Really, he got it. It was nearly eight o'clock. Chet pointed to the message light blinking on the phone. "Why not answer your phone? Could be Dina."

"It's not, Dad. It's always you."

"Not anymore. Now I'm just coming right over. You need to answer it. It's easy."

When Roal was five years old, Helen had taught him how to answer the phone. They'd worked on it all morning, and when Chet called Roal answered, and said all in one breath: "Hello, my mother is here just a moment thank you for calling goodbye." And then hung up. Helen laughed so hard she answered the phone with a wheezing, helpless hello when Chet called back.

But now Roal put the phone on speaker so Chet could hear the pleading whine of his own voice as he ordered Roal to call him back. But it wasn't Chet who had left the message. It was the automatic public service announcement. The cougars had been caught. The lockdown was lifted. No need for caution. Buildings and schedules were returned to normal. The cougars were officially relocated.

CHAPTER 14

One look at the reporters pressed to the doors of his office building, and Roal headed straight to class instead. He doubted Lin was in. If she were, he doubted she'd get out.

When he entered his room, Rueben Amado let out a cheer. The class broke into applause, interspersed with raucous, bracing whoops. Roal's surprise upped the mood further, and when Hattie Small called out, "You're here!" Kaylee called back that of course he was—that his arrival was more proof. Of what, Roal didn't know, but he wasn't worried: they were bursting to talk about whatever it was. He would find out.

Roal's plan for the day had been a final lecture: on "The Chrysanthemums." But whatever the students were up to was not related to being ready to discuss the symbolism of the chrysanthemum. They didn't care about the impacted, tangled loneliness of a woman whose gift of her prize flowers had been her first attempt at a step toward the new possibilities of her own life. A step that included the possibility of betraying her husband. Of growing the wet thrill of having her ability to cultivate flowers recognized by a stranger, a stranger who did not know her yet and so might see her as clearly as she believed she existed. The gift of her flower was her signal of the possibility that she might accept the desire of a new man who understood what it meant to cultivate wonder from dirt.

Thinking of all this, Roal felt queasy. He hadn't thought the story would sound so familiar, so specifically kick-to-the-get revealing. And now, in front of the students whose faces said they knew something about him, and that they weren't there for the final lecture but for something bigger, something Roal alone could give to them. He didn't want to discuss the story either. He didn't dare.

It occurred to Roal that all the stories were basically the same: someone betrayed someone else, and things ended poorly for everyone. Sometimes drowning. Sometimes car wrecks. Often illness. Occasional suicide. Defeat, chainsawed furniture, adoptions for motives so misguided no one mentioned them until the dirt was on the grave. Even then the question would be more shadow than body.

The evidence of betrayal was everywhere, available for anyone to read—anyone, anyway, who paid attention. Roal wondered why it was so easy to see it coming when it was written on a page in a story but so difficult when the story was his own. He looked out at his class, wondering if his students could read their own lives, and perhaps the lives of others, maybe his, all of the details a symbol of the inevitable end.

He smiled hesitantly, not sure where he stood in relation to their buzz and uncharacteristic warmth. He cleared his throat, expecting that the next thing he said would somehow make sense of what to do next. But it was the last day. Finals in a week, graduation the weekend after. The students weren't at all fazed by their newfound exuberance. It was a time for anything to happen.

They wanted to talk about Roal's campus bravery as he sauntered from one side of campus to the other and bowed under the Rally Tree. They had seen him cross campus despite the lockdown, watched him walk slowly, drolly, a single person exercising his freedom to take control of his own life regardless of the danger. The students could not have made that choice: they had been locked into their dormitories or prevented from coming to campus for their own safety. Roal alone, they said, gave a performance in an act of classic and brilliant defiance of the lockdown.

They wanted to talk about his walk as if it were the lecture they had prepared: the interpretation of a man who refuses to compromise his own freedom.

Roal sat back on the desk and listened, engrossed by their interpretation, the way they dove into the nuance and micro-gestures of his walk and applied meaning and value to each detail. They unpacked Roal's walk so thoroughly that Roal wondered aloud if literature might not be better off if it became something people could watch from their windows.

"Um, like theater?" Kayden suggested, as if perhaps Roal had not yet heard of theater.

Roal laughed. They all laughed. It felt terrific. He was laughing at himself and felt giddy as his ribs compressed and squeezed his insides until his laughter pressed up against the edge of something darker, a dangerous pressing at the edge of what he could take. He brought the laughter back from that place and it became light and air again.

He agreed happily, "Yes, exactly like theater."

Then Rueben stood up to mimic Roal's slow stroll across campus. What Roal had tried to pull off as nonchalance to cover his feeling of dread, the students had read as a condemnation of college's overbearing rule that campus go into lockdown. Rueben strolled among the desks with exaggerated slowness, posture impossibly erect, leaning far back with the hilarious, incautious gait of a man for whom the rules do not apply and will not be made to exist. The students evaluated Rueben's posture and his style, corrected the way he casually tossed his hair off his forehead so it more closely matched Roal's own habit, and handed him a stack of papers to be held in mock fear to his chest.

They exalted Roal for taking it upon himself to brave both the cougar and the administrative rules that locked them into a building on a fine day. They were all sick of the rules. They'd had it. Limited dining hall hours, mandatory meal plans, curfews, single-sex floors in the coed dorms, download restrictions, library access codes, a list of words not to be uttered on student radio, hot water limitations, parking violations, oppressive feel-good campaigns about best practices in campus environmentalism printed out on glossy, non-recycled paper stock.

And yesterday had pushed it over the top: when the school locked the dorms and no one could leave or enter, the students were officially on lockdown, and the threat for opening a door was a five-hundred-dollar fine. And then they saw Roal. Roal and Roal alone, who braved the presence of cougars. Roal who walked to send a message to the administration about the foolishness of societies made ridiculous under the rule of paternalism and litigiousness. The students asserted that unless such oppression were challenged, it was certain to become the norm.

They railed and stormed—they would never, ever, allow themselves to become desensitized to ridiculous rules, one-upping each other about the signs warning consumers to be careful of hot coffee, plastic bags, and bleach.

"I'm not about to use my hair dryer in my sleep!" Dayton offered.

"What the hell," they said and, "That's what I'm talking about," sometimes looking at Roal to include him, and other times simply forging on ahead. Making it up as they went.

Eventually, they moved on to discuss Roal again. He had surprised them. They hadn't seen it coming. Not from him. They talked about him as if he was already a memory they needed to keep. They wished they had thought to protest, to just pour out of the dorms to join him in support of the clear message he sent that people must be allowed to make their own decisions about how to face life's dangers.

And just like that they determined they had been wrong about Roal.

A day ago, they had one impression of him, and then it changed. It was so easy for them to shift from one belief to the other, so easy for one of them to just say aloud: "We were wrong." Rueben stood to give Roal a high-five, though when Roal missed Rueben ended up hitting Roal's arm instead. Roal laughed, and the sound of it harmonized with the laughter of his students. He felt a ringing in his chest as his laughter blended with theirs, poured from him until he felt their laughter enter him and his own plume back out. There was no end to the circle of goodness they drew from each other.

Roal looked out at his class with an adoration and gratitude that they returned. He was on their side. He was touched by their sudden shift toward him—how easily he was included now that they believed he supported what mattered to them.

Their change of mind about his was charmingly unguarded, leaving him defenseless in the presence of their goodness and certainty. They moved on from the cougar, and began to interpret Roal's classroom habits and assignments: the button-down shirts he wore each day were now seen as a sign of respect to the students, not of being stuck in an outdated hierarchical model; his aged assignments, out of touch and written before most of the students had learned to read, became a bridge Roal was helping to build between generations; his style of delivering lectures evinced his trust in them for having done the reading.

Roal listened, fascinated by his emergent self as they created it. Was it possible that all they saw and assigned to him was really there? Or could be? From where they sat, yes: the bravery, the disdain for overbearing rules, the cutting through hysteria with action, the cavalier disregard for authorities who coddled when they should have challenged. And how fortunate that there was really no way to know otherwise.

If Roal had crossed campus full of bravery and sassy disregard, he wouldn't now feel guilty, but exhilarated that the message had been so clear. But it was not too late to catch the ride of bravery and outrage, to leave behind the old bus of dread and fear that had motored yesterday's walk. He corrected his internal memory so it accorded with the students' version, allowed the actions to stand as they were seen through their eyes. And then, just like that, his guilt shifted to a shy pride that felt soft and luminous. Roal sensed that this idea of revision held potential for him, though could not yet sense its application.

And anyhow, the students were now onto discussing the YouTube sensation of Roal-and-cougar spliced together. It had received over three thousand hits already. "Not exactly viral," gushed Rueben, "but, c'mon, not bad!"

Roal smiled. Gamely? It was hard to know. So many new facial constructions had been required lately. He couldn't keep track of them, their unending succession. How the faces of people whose lives dangled with eternal drama must feel after a lifetime, Roal thought. Exhausted. The students laughed. They were happy to have been so wrong about him. Now, they saw, he just wanted them each to get up and cross whatever metaphorical campus it might be that they faced. To walk through possible lockdown dangers into whatever it was they were supposed to get to on the other side.

Roal agreed, saying that they had basically just explained the heart of every story in the universe.

Then the class began to discuss Roal's shirt, with Rueben channeling the interpretation: "That's the best last word on Cougar-gate ever. No one will miss you in that today. Maybe fear is a kind of cancer."

They interpreted his shirt as a kind of follow-up act. A way to be sure his walk was not overlooked as a one-day thing: Roal's shirt was making an extended point, a line in the sand which would remain—his freedom was not available for lockdown.

When they looked at Roal, they saw a protest. Not about war or oil. Not about the toxins of the ink on cash register receipts leaching into their skin or about lead in the city's drinking water. Roal wasn't protesting homeless veterans or the broken food-chain supply with its *E. coli* outbreaks and its refusal to let small farmers participate. They saw a man who could protest on the very grounds where he lived and worked, a man in charge of his own life: "Yes, there is a cougar. No, do not tell me what to do."

"That protest was pure Gandhi," Rueben asserted. Five minutes to go before the last class was over, and no one looking at their watches. Roal saw the sheen in their eyes: They believed they could learn from this man. Roal fought it for a moment: he would have to become this man. They were still discussing the shirt.

"My stepmom's sister died of breast cancer," posited Kyla. "I don't want to be a downer but I don't think the shirt is a good protest vehicle. It might be like you don't take cancer seriously."

Roal had to make a choice. Having already laughed at himself once, and seen the effects of just confessing to being wrong when you're wrong, he admitted, "You know, I agree. But the shirt actually isn't about the cougar. It's about my wife. But beyond that, there's a walk coming up to raise awareness and funding for breast cancer. It's a good cause to march for."

"Your wife?" The class sat aghast. Their mouths hung slack. "Has cancer?"

"No," Roal said. He couldn't imagine how he had let that slip. He wasn't used to them asking questions about anything he said. "She—well, it's complex. She's just, gone. Um, a few days ago." Roal felt naked speaking of his personal life. He looked down and stared at a speck on the carpet. The class was frozen. He never shared details of his own life with his students, and now they were shirt-deep in the dissolution of his marriage.

"Oh my God. I. Am. So. Sorry. I can't believe you're here!" wailed Dayton.

"I don't mean she died—I mean, she left." Roal went for full disclosure, though it made his chest heave and his eyes sting. "She just wanted to go to a forest to start over. As a tree." Roal laughed fondly, amazedly, surprised at himself for feeling like this was suddenly normal and that he understood it. "She went to the woods so she could become a tree—you know, to give something back."

The class stared at him in absolute dumb silence. Roal couldn't meet their eyes. Their sympathy was crushing, and no one laughed about the tree aspiration. They didn't even ask for more information to be sure they'd heard him right. They just took it in, nodded, accepted.

Finally Eric said it reminded him of Whitman's "Song of Myself": the full life cycle, every atom belonging to me as good belongs to you. How amazing that Roal's wife wanted to live the full circle and come up again as grass, as the uncut hair of graves. Roal swelled with happiness. He had introduced them to that poem weeks ago.

Rueben turned to the class. "Guys, you know what this means. We are going to do that walk. Professor Bowman's wife is doing a cougar-stroll of her own: she decided to make her own way across the field of cancer to get to her final place with the trees. And he still comes to class to honor her choice." He turned back to Roal. "Professor, we had no idea. No wonder you wouldn't allow them to stop you from doing what you love to do. Time is short. We will be there to walk with you."

Roal opened his mouth to protest, to start over so he could get the story right, but instead he surprised them all when he opened up his mouth and a sob burst out of it. Tears followed, uncontrollably, and Roal groped for his briefcase, grabbed its handle as if it were the rudder to steer him past the mess he had made, and fled the room. The students murmured their solidarity of respect and commitment in his wake.

On the way back to his office, Roal was in a panic. Each time he tried to clarify, the story grew more preposterous and entrenched, as well as more beautiful and heartbreaking. Worst, he loved this story. He wanted to write this story: Dina, cancer-ridden, enters the forest to present her last body to the trees, which will accept it and then allow her to become them. Roal, meanwhile, crosses campus as a conscientious objector of the administrative decision to lock up the people it rules. And later, he shows up on campus wearing the shirt which demonstrates his respect for the bravery of his wife's decision to die alone and be recycled as leaf and breath, bark and precipitate.

And yet, much as Roal loved the story, he did not want the life. A beautiful story makes a terrible life. Though Roal also saw that often terrible lives can prompt beautiful stories, and Dina's life, though not terrible, had not been fulfilling enough to overcome the argument of becoming a tree. Which was beautiful.

Teary and torn by how others so readily created the stories of his life that he then felt compelled to live, Roal forgot about the reporters. They had thinned out a bit, but that just gave the ones remaining more room to feed. They were waiting to get an inside word about the accusations against Lin's book of mind control.

A square-jawed woman swept in on Roal, her camera snapping its jaws of aperture. Questions came shooting at Roal as he worked a diagonal plan of one-step forward, one-to-the-left toward his door.

"Will Lin Strickland be removed from the faculty?"

"How has reading the book affected your life? Anything irregular?"

"Campus health center has seen a rise in the date-rape drug—any reason to suspect mind games behind this trend?"

"When is the last time you saw Lin Strickland?"

"Can you explain whether Ms. Strickland's psychological terrorism may have had help from other departments?"

"Is the mind-game data part of a larger agenda that colleges are working on?"

Roal inserted the key, and leapt into his office, slicing it shut behind him. The knocking and questions continued, and eventually Roal stopped calling out that they should go away and let him get to work. He called Felicia, who rang campus security, and though they arrived, they were uncertain of how to conduct themselves in the presence of so many cameras. While campus scuffled outside his door, Roal sank to his cushion and tried to visualize peace. His vision placed him on Dina's bed at home, and he allowed himself to lie there, breathing in her pillow and plants. Roal drew up his knees. The *ohms* he uttered to try to extend his breath and quiet his mind came out from his throat tight and pinched. When his office door suddenly shot open, Roal looked up, startled, and Tagg Larson looked back, then quickly shut the door behind him. Tagg looked down at Roal on the low cushion and still hugging his knees and blinked as if trying to reset the image. But when Tagg opened his eyes, nothing had changed. The dean shrugged, then sat in Roal's large chair and swung to face him, his feet dangling a few inches above the floor.

"What a mess out there."

Roal nodded in agreement.

"I figured you weren't answering your phone because of the press, so I just came over. Listen, Chief, we have a situation, and I could use some insight." Tagg pressed the small tips of his fingers to his eyebrows. The breath he inhaled seemed to sour in his throat.

Roal's nod was cheerless. They had a situation. He watched Tagg with passive, fascinated dread.

"This ordeal with Lin, Roal. Anything to it?" Tagg studied at Roal.

Roal paused. It hadn't occurred to him that the question was one worth asking. He answered truthfully, "I doubt it."

"Have you noticed anything strange yourself?"

"No. Maybe."

Tagg waited.

"I mean," said Roal, "Everything is strange. Life is strange."

Tagg changed tactics, "I hear Dina has cancer. I'm sorry to hear that."

"What?" Roal hastened to correct him, "No. No, Dina doesn't have cancer. The whole thing is a mess. This shirt is for Gary's wife's charity walk. And sort of for Dina, I guess, but not because of cancer. It's complicated."

"Yeah, I heard. You should feel free to take time off."

"Thanks. But it's the end of the year, Tagg. I just finished the last class. I'll be fine."

"I see, okay. Stick it out. Whatever you need," Tagg agreed, dismissing the issue and sitting up straight, his body's rhetoric a signal that the topic had been addressed and checked off. They would move on.

Roal said, "You know, I haven't actually read Lin's book yet, so I'm not a good person to ask about whether there's anything to the claims about mind control."

Tagg looked at him with a nearly euphoric relief, "God, am I glad to hear you say that! I haven't read it either! And now I don't know if I should or shouldn't. It's been on my shelf for months."

"Where is Lin?" Roal asked.

"At her ex–sister-in-law's. She called last night after leaving Gary's. I heard you were there."

"Yes."

"And you walked home, I hear."

"Yes."

"The cougars were still on the loose then." Tagg looked at Roal accusingly.

"I suppose. But I didn't see anything." Roal shrugged.

"Yesterday you crossed campus when we were on lockdown, Chief. That caused some commotion." Tagg's tone was imperious, a little raja who discovers his wish to capture the moon will not be fulfilled.

"Yes. Sorry. I left before the calls went out. I got here before I saw the signs. I actually didn't know anything about it." Tagg looked at Roal curiously, deciding whether to believe him.

"Those cougars were on that same lawn, in the Rally Tree, less than a few minutes before you were."

"I had no idea." Roal's defense sounded careless, his heavy lids offering a challenge to hear something that might make him interested.

"Anyway, I don't want you getting reckless." Tagg took a deep breath, and the next words seemed difficult for him to say, but once he was past them, he relaxed: "Roal, we need you now."

"What do you mean?" Roal let go of his knees and stretched his legs in front of him. Tagg leaned back, as if suddenly aware that the chair he was sitting in belonged to Roal.

"There's always calm in the eye of the storm. You are that calm, Chief. You have always been that calm. We need you to just go on being you. Calm, steady, predictable you. This Lin thing has a lot of people excited, and we need someone to point to who isn't going anywhere, isn't doing anything, isn't rocking any boats or turning over any carts. We have enough of that on our hands now. We really do need. . . ." and here Tagg looked away.

Roal could see that it required effort for Tagg to have to appreciate in Roal the qualities he had grown used to criticizing.

Tagg sighed and then looked at Roal, ". . . we need you to be stable and boring."

Roal smiled without feeling it. "Stable and boring for whom? Why?"

Tagg threw his hands up. "For us. For appearances. Students have been lodging complaints. Their parents too. And the press is catching a lot of what they have to say ahead of us. It looks bad for us, for incoming enrollment—just bad."

"What are the complaints about?"

Tagg leaned back, looked cautiously at the door. Then he leaned forward with his forearms on his knees, his folded hands exquisite as a squirrel in prayer. He spoke low: "Everything, Roal. Absolutely everything. Failed tests, missing keys, binge drinking, group sex, hallucinogenic motorcycle rides, new interests in philosophy, abandonment of medical careers for a viticulture degree, urinating in public, sexting professors, shoplifting adult diapers, pulling fire alarms, night terrors. I don't know. I don't know. I just don't know. You can't imagine. Everything. Parents are arriving in a week to collect their kids, and they're worried. They sent their kids to us, and now they're afraid we've put them in harm's way with this crazy book and this stupid media. Nobody knows how this stuff of Lin's works."

"Does it work?" Roal's doubt seemed pointed.

"Sounds like it can. Hypothetically. One expert said the mind is like wet clay: it can be easily manipulated and holds a shape pretty well." Tagg trailed off, looking adrift in Roal's giant chair. Then he sat back and ran his hand across his face.

"Well it is college," Roal said admiringly, thinking of the class he'd just left. "The kids are going to do stuff that will surprise their parents. And maybe themselves."

"Yeah." Tagg looked reminiscent, probably remembering an all-night road trip toward someone's favorite barbecue or stargazing from the golf course and waking up to sprinklers.

Roal cleared his throat. "What does Lin say?"

"Oh. Lin. Well she says it's nonsense. And it is. It really is. I think. Anyway, academic freedom and free speech should have us covered. Plus, no one *requires* Lin's book for a class, so technically no one has read it because we've asked them to. Lin says the hype is manufactured. She's probably right. It does seem overblown. But people are uneasy. They want answers."

"Or a scapegoat. But maybe she could give an interview to clear the air?"

"That's what I suggested. But she said no." Tagg shook his head, including Roal in a wide-eyed question of what else could possibly be done, "Lin says people are choosing to be irrational, so it won't work for her to take a rational approach. She also thinks denying it will only make it real. I'm guessing if you sit solid—and I mean unsurprisingly solid—and we give it a week, everyone will forget. Remembering the past takes so much energy—it's best if we can just let it all disappear. Within a week people will move on to something else. Maybe a bear will get stuck in a trash can and everyone can forget about Lin's book." He looked hopeful.

Then Tagg's leaned forward and looked directly at Roal, "Listen. All of us should let go of the past, Roal. You and me. I, for one, am willing to let go and move on." Tagg stared intently at Roal, and Roal understood that he was no longer deadwood and was now officially considered an asset. The past would be forgotten and the energy of remembering it would not need to be expended.

"That works for me," Roal conceded.

"Fine, fine." Tagg did not move to leave. There was something else. Tagg looked at Roal squarely, then said, "Also, Gary told me that Lin took

Dina—your Dina—to the woods to meet Winter. And that Dina stayed. But that you don't know where she is."

Roal groaned. He defended Dina, assuring Tagg that Dina had left of her own accord, did not have cancer, and wanted to stay to help Winter with his project. Roal said he didn't agree with everything, but that's how it was. Tagg nodded, hearing Roal out. But there was still more.

"Roal," Tagg said. "Can I talk to you? Can I tell you something?"

"Okay," said Roal, cautiously.

"I mean, if I tell you this, will you keep it to yourself? We need you to stay in the game here, to stay on the court—no fouls or wild shots. Focus on the ball."

Roal sagged, feeling the same annoyance for sports metaphors as he felt for sports themselves, which he hated because they required shorts and sneakers and reminded him that his lungs had a capacity, and the capacity was finite.

"Roal, what if I told you I might know where Dina is?"

"What? You do?" Roal sat up straight.

"What if I did?"

"Well, that would be great. And surprising. Do you know?"

"Maybe. More or less. It would be helpful if you and Dina could patch things up and work it out at home. Then it won't look like things have gotten really strange in your court too. It'd help with the Lin mess."

"You know where Dina is?" Roal repeated, his face a surge of hope.

"Well, Lin borrowed a college car the week before Winter's meeting. She needed to be less visible to the press, and her old truck wasn't exactly under the radar. She drove the car to Winter's location when she backtracked. It has a GPS tracker and we pulled the info."

"Where is she?"

"I can't tell you exactly, but it can't be far from where Lin parked. This is a lead not available to the press, so at least we're ahead of them there, and we want to keep it that way."

Roal nodded excitedly. "So where? Where?"

"I'll send the information over when I get back to my office. But remember, keep it under wraps. This is between you and Dina—a private affair. We want you to get there before the press does and puts a spin on how Lin influenced the most steady man to ever walk among cougars at Braddock College. Keep it low. I'll be in touch."

Tagg Larson hopped down from Roal's chair and the open door sucked him into the hallway where voices paused and then closed in. Roal sat stunned on the cushion. Dina had a road which led to her. Roal would find her and say—something. He would show up and look at her. He would open his mouth, and words would come out. And at that moment he would find out exactly what he had to say. He couldn't wait to hear it.

CHAPTER 15

Gary poked his head in, "Hey, nice shirt! I knew you'd stand by it. So, what have you done?" Gary waggled his finger toward Roal as if in mock warning to a darling brat. "Jill says you nearly crashed her server with all the people you've gotten to sign up for her walk! She's never seen anything like it. Students sticking around on graduation weekend to fundraise? And their families too? What gives?"

Roal shook his head and groaned: "It's a big misunderstanding. They think Dina has cancer and has gone off to die in the woods. When I tried to explain, everything just got worse."

Gary whistled, exulted, "Jill *loves* these kinds of misunderstandings. If she can pull off the kind of fundraiser it looks like this will be, it might be our ticket out of this place."

"Out of here?"

"Certainly out of here. Out of Braddock. Out of this town. Out of this state and side of the country. All of it."

"Out of Braddock? But you have tenure."

"Tenure by default. You know what I mean." Gary's laugh was inclusive, but when Roal looked puzzled, Gary shuffled uncomfortably, as if perhaps Roal did not know what he meant, and it would be indecent to spell it out.

"Anyway, tenure wasn't hard. It just landed on me. Mostly though, we have no family here. We have no museums or theater. We don't even have Indian food. Every Friday night is an action movie in the living room with pizza. My kids are in a cultural wasteland. Jill's got an interview coming up, and when she shows the numbers for this charity walk, she'll be in the running for sure."

"Where?"

"Where what?"

"Where is the interview? The job?"

"Chicago. Where we're from. She's ready—we're all ready. And the pay would be fantastic. She'd be worth nearly two of me."

"What would you do?"

"Don't know. Take a few years off. My next book's coming out. That should buy me time. Or teach at the university. They're interested."

"I didn't know you wanted to move."

"I have kids, Roal. Last week they brought home their year's worth of art projects from school, you know? It was basically coloring book photocopies and a pinwheel. But you know the worst part? They were so proud of it. It killed me. They think Abraham Lincoln is simply a memorial to an honest man. As far as they know, black people were set free, but they don't know what from. Nothing about slavery. Nothing about Native Americans being slaughtered and then herded onto reservations. As if it's rude for education to confront truth. There's not even any science at their school—no visits to a pond to see tadpoles. Hell, we don't even have real water here. Our town's lake is a reservoir, and it's stocked with genetically retarded fish who can't breed. Yeah, man, I'd say we want to move!" Gary cleared his throat and looked fiercely at Roal.

Roal was taken aback. Gary wanted to leave because his kids made pin-wheels in art class? Because the lake's stock fish couldn't reproduce? Gary's ability to flare over small details was nothing new, but this seemed extreme. Roal was thrilled and defensive.

"It's not so bad," Roal said. "I grew up here."

"Yeah, I know. And look." Gary said this sadly, as if Roal were a surgery that hadn't come out right.

"My parents live here."

"That's why we came. Jill's grandmother—we moved here to help her out. Then she died and we were stuck. That was nine years ago. Jill's been looking for work since, but there's nothing in her league here. But now this walk has entrants pouring in. Huge! All of them naming you as the inspiration. This could be the edge Jill needs to compete for the job she's looking at. So, thanks." Gary glowed from the reflection of his next possible life.

"No problem," said Roal. "But it's not really me. It's a misunderstanding—I'll have to explain it at some point."

"Roal, you're a Zen master." Gary turned firm, his words a protest against any desire Roal might have to set the record straight: "There are no misunderstandings. Just interpretations and possibilities. I'm asking you to not wreck this shot for me and Jill. Just go with it. It's for a good cause. And for our family. If there's a misunderstanding, that's a personal issue. For now, it's an opportunity that will help a lot of people out. Don't let them down. Go Zen with it. Let it happen. Accept. It's where we are now. All of us."

Gary trailed off, having run out of Zen-isms. Hearing his own words coming from Gary, Roal flushed. All in one morning, he was a hero of cancer acceptance to his students, a rebellious statement of anti-lockdown sentiment, an asset of stability to the college, last chance for a family's escape, and a pariah to the study of Zen. He could hear how it must have sounded to others when he spoke of his practice: the empty righteousness, the desperate superiority, the obvious leveraging of a belief system to avoid the responsibility of an action system. Zen. The sound of it servile and slick when rung by the wrong intention.

"Is that how it sounds?" Roal's voice was hollow, directed to no one in particular. Gary looked away.

From his desk, Roal looked miserably up at Gary, and said, "Gary, I have never understood what it is that people want. Or why they want it from me. Good luck to you and Jill. I hope she gets it."

Gary slid backward out the door. Roal's arms folded under his head, and he rested within them, declaring himself dead to Zen. Even the *ohm*s had diminished over the last few days, and no longer clapped against the bell of his need. When Angela stopped by, she found him like that: cradling his head, letting go of his practice, terrified by what might fill that space next, and wishing to the god of black holes that the information about Dina's location would arrive so he could head to the forest, find the dot on the map, and return home with his life in order.

"Mr. Bowman?" Angela stepped back when Roal looked at her. His eyes were bloodshot, and his drawn face was dark contrast to his shirt.

"Angela."

"Yeah. Sorry. I sent a bunch of emails? I didn't mean to. I just got angry? Because I hadn't heard back. But then I figured you were busy? And you were. Your wife I mean. So I wanted to say I was sorry."

Thank you, Angela. Everything is fine."

"Okay. Just that you seem overwhelmed . . ." Angela texted as she spoke, "I saw the dean and that other guy coming out of your office. They must have been bad . . . you look bad anyway. I didn't know about your wife. I'm going to do that walk. . . . no wonder you couldn't meet last Friday. Sorry. . . ." Angela looked up from her phone and raised her eyebrows, expecting Roal's answer.

Roal hesitated, replaying Angela's skipstone path through the conversation. He thanked her for stopping by, but Angela put him on pause by holding up her finger, indicating that Roal should wait while she texted, but Roal turned his face away, lay his head down on his arms, and closed his eyes. A few seconds later, he heard the door click when she left.

When the GPS readout arrived, Roal called Chet and told him to get ready, then pulled the contents from the envelope, and there it was: a highlighted line leading slightly south and then decidedly east, dotted along the way by the names of towns. Places Roal had heard of but had never visited. Wheaton, Pastine, Voyage, Malva, Petition. Names that sounded homespun and sleepy all the way to Idaho.

Roal was buoyant. He packed his briefcase, locked his office, and slipped away from the reporters who called after him but did not follow.

As he crossed the campus, students hailed and waved. They called *Yo* and *Dude* and *Hey*. They gave him peace signs and raised fists of solidarity. He was among them, included importantly. As he walked, they were texting and receiving, watchful and exuberant. Roal did not know most of them, but they recognized him and snapped into alertness at his coming. They called out that they'd be walking, that they had signed on, that they were on their way to signing up. They wished him luck, wished him well, said *Hang in there, man*, and *Be well*, and *Take care*, and *Right on*.

Roal smiled and floated past them, trembling within at how precariously their beliefs were pinned to reality. Carrying the envelope made Roal feel hopeful and proud, as if it contained the answers to the question of his footfalls: what next? what next? what next?

He understood that the students were reading his face and finding themselves in it: headed toward the unknown with a purpose, hoping that whatever they carried with them would be enough to build their futures from.

When Roal arrived home, Chet yanked him inside, then gingerly took the envelope from Roal's hands as if it were made of cobwebs, a fragile, irreproducible thing. Chet swiped his hand over the table, clearing it of crumbs and wrappers, so he could arrange the maps on the kitchen table. He lined them up so the highlighted trail connected one piece of paper to the next. Roal looked around the kitchen. It appeared Chet had been though the cupboards and sampled most of the food. Crackers, dates, nuts, chips, dried apple rings, cereal, and olive spreads, all of it half eaten and still open. It looked like the party was over.

Roal felt a twinge of loyalty to Dina: the invasion, the knives still smeared with cheese and jam, the litter of wrappers and crusts on the countertops, the crumbs and burned coffee she would have to clean when she came back. But then—he remembered.

Roal was becoming familiar with the feeling of shock when he remembered she would not be back. He did not yet accept the feeling, but he understood what it meant, and he understood by this that departure happens gradually, that one gets used to the stages of the feelings a little at a time. Dina would not be coming back. Was definitely not, Lin had said, coming back.

Chet studied the maps, bringing out his own detailed topographical maps of the extended regions. What would Roal do if he did find Dina first? Ask her to return, certainly. He had to do that. It was required to at least ask. It yet that seemed sad, somehow, really, to tell her to come home.

If Roal didn't find her, Dina would get to continue doing what she wanted to be doing. But if Roal found her, it was expected that he would bring her home. Maybe she would come if he told her he hadn't known that there was so much they might have talked about. Maybe she would believe him and return. But Roal wasn't sure it was fair to make promises he didn't know how to keep just to win her away from her own emergent life.

Chet sniffed the air, then reached out without looking and switched off the coffee maker. He wrinkled his nose and looked at Roal apologetically.

"I let that pot get away from me," he said. "And don't worry about all this—I'll clean it up." Chet indicated the counters, and Roal studied the man he knew he too might become: a man who made his own food, cleaned his own counters, saw to it that the kitchen was in order. Roal turned back to the maps.

"Where?" he asked.

"I'm guessing, I'm going to say . . . just a minute. It's not far." Chet took the map and headed into Roal's study, then turned on the computer. Together, they watched the satellite image home in on their continent, spin and tip the globe as it turned it to expose their western region, zoom in on their state, and then whiz east past gray towns, green forests dotted with clear-cuts and red trees of the standing dead, until it zoomed over the Idaho border and bore down on one specific swath of red-brown forest. A dead zone. Their dead zone. Chet closed in until they could make out individual trees, sent the screen to the printer.

"Here. Right here, I think." He circled a small area on the GPS map with his finger, and tapped it. "Yes, start here. It's less than three hours, right at the edge of a paper company's forest, not far from a logging town, shows a dead patch that matches the GPS. This is it. Start by circling the area a few hundred yards in from where Lin parked the car."

"Are you sure?" Roal was still in awe of how seamlessly Chet had integrated himself into their house.

Chet snorted, "No, I'm not sure! But this is a really good start."

"Dad?"

"What?"

"I'm not sure how to say this, but I want to prepare you. Dina might not come back. I mean, with me. She might not want to." Roal said this gently, as if to protect Chet from a truth he hadn't already considered. But Chet waved him off, annoyed by the extra, unasked-for information.

"I guess I know that. It's her life, Roal. But you have to at least go after her."

"I don't know how. I don't know if I should."

"Of course you should." Chet frowned at Roal.

"I don't have anything to offer her that she didn't already leave."

"You could try offering her a little bit more. You haven't really tried that yet." Chet looked away when he spoke, but Roal could see he was angry from how he pointed his chin at the wall.

"Lin said Dina's doing something she really believes in. That it's the most important thing she has ever done, and she wants to stay. And if she wants to stay, I can't force her to come back. It might not be up to me."

"Stay, go, whatever she decides isn't really what matters." Chet looked at Roal, his eyes narrow but pleading, "I hope she comes back. She's the best thing in my life. But she'll have to decide. Who cares what the answer is? Just do it because it's right." Roal returned to the map, tapping the same area Chet had indicated.

"Okay. I start here."

"You'll need a tent."

"Do you have one I can borrow?"

"You'll need a pair of boots."

"What size are you?"

"Oh, crickets. Haven't you ever gone camping? No, of course not. I have half a mind to burn your giant stack of paper and board your office up while you're gone."

"Please. Dad, please." Roal leaned on the table, his weight pressing into his arms. If Chet's voice had been at all playful, Roal might have thought that he was enjoying making things difficult. But Chet's voice was singed and annoyed, and it alarmed Roal that Chet was not trying to make it easier. Finally, Chet sighed, and with that sigh Roal relaxed and eased off his arms.

"Fine. We'll get you ready. It'll take a few hours, so you can leave first thing in the morning. And the weather," Chet remembered. "We've got to check the weather."

Chet strode into Roal's room and Roal followed. Chet picked up the remote and began jabbing his thumb into the channel button. He found what he wanted, and they watched storms gathering in the south, rain breathing over the east, humidity rubbing itself against the Midwest. But in the inland northwest, the weather promised to be clear but windy, warm and perfect for finding a wife amidst the dead trees. Roal headed in to pack his kit bag when Chet called him back.

"You've gotta see this!" And Roal went back.

Chet had flipped to the news. Another drug bust was being reported in Idaho, following the explosion of a helicopter whose passengers had been seeking Winter Patent. The pilot and two amateur documentarians were dead. There were no survivors.

A somber looking reporter, Drew Klein, reported that sources had indicated that the amateur reporters had thought they found the Green Winter site, but had instead discovered a hidden marijuana farm hanging within the trees. Local tips indicated that the leader of an international marijuana plantation operation had recently appeared near the Canadian border to "deal with" the rash of reports exposing his grow farms. Each report had been made by people out searching for an intensity of green among the trees of their regions as they vied to be first to reveal Winter's location. And each of the grow-farm discoveries resulted in the seizure of thousands of acres of crops, but not one clue to Winter's project.

Drew Klein described the vast hidden networks of marijuana farms hanging within trees across the US. And now three men were dead, their helicopter shot from the sky as they'd hovered above, snapped pictures, and called their wives and parents to say that they had done it—discovered the Green Winter site. And then, one wife said, her breath catching, the phone went silent. Terribly silent. She knew something awful had happened.

The sheriff who found the wreckage confirmed the pot farm growing over eighty feet up in the canopy. The sheriff sounded impressed, describing the nearly invisible irrigation system that ran up into the trees and grew plants three times the size he'd ever seen on the ground. He wanted the world to know that the men had died as heroes. Their discovery might save children. The shooter was at large, as was the leader who had given the order. His photograph revealed a man with light brown hair parted on the side, a banker's haircut, a discordant fey smile that revealed a rakish, chipped tooth, and a collar shirt unbuttoned to reveal a softly creased neck.

The story's angle then shifted to the role that drug production plays in depressed economic regions, particularly those without access to larger urban areas and with vast areas of land not accessible to law enforcement. And apparently this latest search for the Green Winter site had called attention to the fact that Idaho was not immune to this trend, despite its proximity to Washington where pot was legal, which made the farms all the more confusing—access was already so easy. At any rate, already strapped police forces would no longer have the luxury of pretending not to notice.

Klein theorized that no one had more to gain from finding Winter Patent than the area's drug operations, and they certainly had the resources to do so. Air traffic could get thick. The search would be dangerous.

"Everyone wants to find Dina!" whistled Chet, looking impressed. Roal felt sick.

"They want to find Winter." Roal corrected. "Dina hasn't been mentioned. That's good."

"They're all looking in the wrong area anyway. They're up north. This is good for you. But still, it's just a matter of time."

Roal headed back to the bathroom. Chet called after him, "What do your activists say about all this danger?"

"What?"

"Your activists. What do they say?"

"Oh. The activists." Roal answered, "They're kind of undecided."

"What?" Chet appeared in the bathroom door, watching Roal pack antacids and toothpaste.

"I told them to back off, Dad. I have this one. It's my fight."

"Did they believe you?"

"It doesn't matter. It's what I want." Roal debated the allergy pills, then added them to the bag.

Chet clutched Roal's arm, "They're not real. Are they?"

"Dad. Stop it. We have what we need now." Roal brushed Chet's hand away, but felt sympathy when he saw how easily Chet's hand fell to his side and hung there, loose and open as a slit promise.

"You said there were activists," Chet complained. "That you were one. What don't you want to tell me? Does Dina have cancer? Is that what this is about?" Chet indicated Roal's shirt. "Is that what you're not telling me?" Roal, exhausted by the effort of keeping the one true story of his life free of tangles, snapped at Chet, glowering over him in the small bathroom.

"What don't I want to tell you? Seriously, Dad? Where do I start?" Chet blinked, and Roal went on.

"How about not wanting to tell you that I'm alone because Dina left me for Winter, and that's a story national television will cover? Or that becoming a goddamn tree is a better future than staying with me? Or that I was just given a future at Braddock today based on my agreement to be boring? Or— or maybe should I not tell you that my colleagues think I'm a joke? I don't want any of this. No, Dina does not have cancer. And I don't even know if I really want her to come home. Maybe she . . . if she—forget it. I'm just not good with people." Roal deflated and trailed off, his last words a plea for forgiveness, which he expected to find when he looked again at Chet. But Chet did not look concerned. He looked appalled.

Chet spun from the bathroom to storm into the kitchen. Roal put his face against the bathroom mirror. It felt like water and invited him to stay. His breath haloed out around his face, and when he opened his eyes and stood up again, Chet was already back, thrusting a backpack into Roal's chest.

"You got food, water, a knife, and the maps," Chet snarled. "You don't know *if* you want her back. If! If! *As if* is more like it! Get out of here now. Go and do it right. Go!"

Chet's voice was sharp, but one cheek trembled. Roal grabbed the back-pack and kit bag and squeezed fearfully past Chet as Chet railed after him: "You don't know. You don't know. Poor you. Why Dina would want to come back, who knows? But you had better ask her!"

Roal said nothing, his head low and shamed to hear Chet say it out loud: he didn't know why Dina would want to come back either.

Not yet stated was that Roal feared that if he asked her to return, she might do as he asked. And that led to the next unutterable thing: Roal could survive her leaving, but he would not survive her return if it meant he had to earn it. And failed.

His chest tightened. Chet pushed him out the door and threw the keys into the driveway. Then he slammed the door watched from a window as Roal picked up the keys, entered the garage, and backed the car out. At the last minute Chet softened and waved. But Roal didn't see him. His eyes had teared up and, lest he start to cry and Chet would see, he was staring desperately at the nose of the car, which he turned and then straightened in the most likely direction of an answer.

CHAPTER 16

After fifteen miles, Roal pulled over to adjust the radio and pull the maps from the bag. The inside of the backpack was a litter of loose snacks, a half-full water bottle, napkins, and a butter knife still smeared with olive spread. Roal recognized it as the remains of the food from the countertops.

As he assessed what he had, he noted that he would need to fill up the water bottle and load up on more food, which immediately made him feel purposeful. Needing to do these things meant he officially had a plan: water. Beyond that, he was three hours from Malva, and would have to see what happened next. He drove, in love with what the road did to people, leading them from one unanticipated internal place to another. He allowed himself to keep a small part of his Zen practice intact by enjoying the moment of right then: the moment of being on the road in his car heading southeast toward a calling. He had a mission and a next step, and beyond that, was open to the whatever of what may come.

He liked the way the road placed him into an exact place and time. There was no other. Not for him, and not for anyone else. Only the specific time-space convergence of where the time of day, speed of travel, and point on the road placed him. He pulled over to the side for a handful of almonds from the bottom of the bag. His radio streamed Creedence, and he tilted back the seat for a better view of the sky. The almonds tasted sweet and broke apart in long, smooth halves in his mouth.

An officer tapped on Roal's window, startling Roal. He grasped the steering wheel, hauling himself up, then vacillating between first unrolling the window or turning down the volume on the radio. When he addressed the officer whose crisp shirt disagreed with his long sideburns, Roal's indecision about what to do made him feel guilty, his voice turning obsequious in an attempt to appear normal.

"Afternoon, Officer."

"Afternoon, sir. May I see your registration?" Roal handed it over. His license too. He stopped himself from trying to find other things to give to the officer. And he then stopped himself from making an observation about spring, the road conditions, from saying he'd always wanted to grow his own sideburns long like the officer's, stopped himself from admitting that he hadn't taken a road trip for years and now here he was on the last day of school driving toward a purpose without a promise. He suppressed all these things with his hands gripping the steering wheel in an unnecessary effort to keep them where the officer could see them.

"You're pulled over to the side of the highway, sir," the officer observed.

"Yes, Officer." Roal waited. The officer waited, and Roal asked, "Is that okay?"

"No, it isn't. This is a highway, sir. You need to move on." The officer leaned down and in, looking into the open backpack. Roal moved back and away so the officer could look past him uninhibited. The officer scanned the maps, then looked back at Roal again.

"Are you traveling far?"

"Not too far. Just a few hours."

"This is an old car."

"Yes. I've had it since college. It was my mother's before that. I almost never drive."

"Where are you headed?"

"To Malva. To see my wife. In Malva. Just past it actually. I hope. If she's still there." Roal tried to stop talking, but more kept trickling out. Roal admitted he had not yet been to Malva, but had always intended to go. That he hoped Malva would have a place to stay for the night, and that his wife was not exactly expecting him, but it was the right thing to do. "Anyway, anyway," Roal finally concluded, his voice tapering off. The officer kept his eyes fastened to Roal. And then he snapped his fingers.

"Got it! You're Roal Bowman. Car registered to Roal and Dina. Aren't you the cougar guy? That's right." The officer repeated, "You're the cougar guy."

The officer pointed to Roal's shirt. Roal nearly explained it, but the officer stopped him, and continued, "Yeah, you know, my son is doing your cancer walk. Kai Sparks? Your walk is the first community service he's signed up for on his own. I'm Terry Sparks. I'm happy to meet you—you know, you're an inspiration for all of us. So sorry to hear about your wife. I hope she's still there for you, sir. Best of luck." Officer Sparks offered his hand, and Roal shook it awkwardly in the tight space of the window. The handshake, he knew, again allowed the story to gather mass, each new believer creating a reality that was going on without him, a story of his making, but beyond his control.

As they exchanged the simple goodness of a handshake, Roal nearly recanted, nearly confessed it all to the officer. Roal wanted to confess that his wife had made a choice that did not include him and he did not feel qualified to argue with her, that Dina did not have cancer but had something far more difficult to know how to help her through: a passion that carried her beyond him and revealed that the gray siding of their house was a symbol of the interior apathy which had leached to the exterior and dulled it. He wanted to say it wasn't cancer, but passion, that was spreading inside of her, though the spread could not be measured by a machine that could target the area, radiate her cells, and send her home. He thought of Matthew Ulysses Chafee's manuscript and Dina's comments. He wanted to tell the officer that Dina had a fine mind, was a person he'd have liked to talk to at a party, but that—if he had to admit it, and he was in a confessional mood because the officer was still standing there—he wouldn't feel right about taking her home from that party because it would remind him of the terrible geese at the park, their wings clipped, their flight over, leaving them to the dogs and the children riding past on bikes with rocks in their fists. So much to confess that held a mirror up to a life that was at last of Roal's own making. There was no one who could make it work, who could slide in and erect the future of his potential in hopes that he would grow into it. He was exactly here, in this car, on this highway, now.

Roal's breath in was ragged and deep, his exhalation at the edge of telling the officer all of it, and Officer Sparks bent in closely to ask whether Roal was okay to drive. Roal shook his head. He needed to start over. He thought of Gary and Jill who wanted to begin again in Chicago, and of the students who would do a walk because Roal allowed them to see him as they wished to. They would do the walk together, adding it to the experiences that would one day allow them to tell a story that was beautiful because it was true. So many people now depended on him to ensure that the story was true, and it seemed like such an easy, generous thing to allow. He was okay to drive. He nodded certainly, thanked Officer Sparks, who checked Roal's maps and gas tank, and said it looked like Roal was good to go.

"But stop on the way and get some food into yourself. Look for Lookout's in Voyage. It's the best place between here and Malva. Their burgers will anchor your belly. Believe me, it's the best way to make sure you don't drift as you roll." The officer tapped on the top of Roal's car as he went back to his own car and then waited until Roal pulled back onto the road and away.

The road slid smoothly under the tires. The Buick's tan hood gleamed cleanly, moved silently through the countryside. The houses became sparse, while the land became expansive, oceans of barely emergent wheat sprouts like green velvet softening the dark brown underlayer of earth. Each house along the way was a place where Roal saw that someone had one day thought to build a life. He wondered if they were still living that life now or if it had moved on past what they knew to expect from it. Lives with clusters of shade trees just outside the houses, and barns downwind of the house. Bright tractors in the front yards and dull ones under the tree at the side. A forsythia's yellow shower spilling onto a wheelbarrow. Was that the plan? Forsythia, a horse in the barn, a breeze riding the tire swing, a pile of rocks, and a tablecloth on the taut clothesline? Was it all the master vision of how the whole story was to work out in the end?

I should eat, Roal thought as he drove and drove. Past fences and smashed rabbits, over the cracked asphalt of aging roads and under the swoop and dip of swallows. The houses began to group to themselves again, squeezing out the stretches of land until Roal reached the town of Voyage, where Lookout's

Lounge swore a neon oath to BEST FOOD HERE. Roal drove by to check out his other options but soon turned back: Main Street ended just a block later without another choice in sight.

Inside, the bartender turned away from the television when Roal entered, nodded to acknowledge him, then turned back to the television. The three men at the center table watched as Roal slid into a booth. Roal felt the primness of his pressed pants and pink shirt against the men's stained cowboy hats and muddy boots which looked like declarative statements of that day's work. Roal was relieved he hadn't taken Chet's advice and worn a pair of boots—the new cleanliness of them would have announced his fraudulence, especially in front of this group who understood that work leaves evidence. Roal's leather shoes were all the confession he needed that he could make no claim to their world. Roal did not fit in, and it pleased him to decide that this was okay, as he would not have to pretend to know anything about whatever it was that clung to their boots or had made their hands ropy with veins.

The men turned back to their food, talking low or lapsing into silence. When Roal figured out that the bartender wasn't going to come out to get his order, he went up to order a beer and a burger, yes on a pickle, sure on the extra fries. He sat back down with his beer and the bartender turned to the grill and began to cook.

"Order's up!" The bartender called. He set the red basket on the bar and Roal could see the pile of thick fries heaped over the burger. "Ketchup's on the bar. Help yourself."

"I will." Roal got up to collect his food. When he turned around the men were looking at him.

"I guess you're from out of town," one of the younger two said.

"I am. It looks like my shoes gave me away." Roal tried to assess the man's tone, but their faces were inscrutable.

"I suppose they did. That and your shirt. And your pants. But mostly that none of us have never seen you before. What city are you from?" The two younger men grinned small, shy grins and leaned back in their chairs. The older man sipped a soda.

"It's not quite a city, but we have a college there, so it seems big. Bigger than it really is."

"Which one?"

"Braddock." The two younger men looked at each other, and the one who did the talking looked back at Roal.

"Where the cougars came from." Roal's surprise made them chuckle. "We know Braddock. They export their cougars to our woods."

"Here?" Roal's surprise made them laugh again.

"Right here. The three of them. And we have livestock. If they'd of left them where they were, they coulda cleaned out your feral cat population. But now they'll go for our calves and sheep."

"And my pony. And my old reindeer." The old man spoke. "They should of put those cats down when they could of."

Roal turned the idea over, "Interesting. I actually thought they did. I thought 'relocate' was just a code for kill—so the students wouldn't get upset. I guess they really did mean relocate. I hadn't expected that."

"Don't get too cozy in your hometown, though," the older man spoke. "They'll be back. A couple of hours of territory won't keep them away if they liked where they were. Their territories cover over 140 miles, and there are three of them. That's a lot of math to spread them over. They'll be back."

"After they clean up here, you mean. Thank your mayor for us if you would," the young one said.

The three of them agreed grimly, still looking at Roal as he held the ketchup. Roal moved to head back to his booth, but the old man spoke again.

"So what brings you here?"

"It's complicated. I'm headed to Malva."

"You don't look dressed for complicated." The old man's eyes swept over Roal.

"I know. But that makes it more complicated, so it will have to work."

"Is that shirt about the walk in a couple of weeks?" The quieter young man spoke for the first time. Roal looked at him, again surprised.

"Yes. The walk for cancer."

"Breast cancer, on graduation weekend." The young man corrected, and Roal agreed.

"Exactly. How did you hear about it?" Now Roal's surprise seemed to make the young men draw themselves up proudly, and Roal could see there was something at stake in the answer.

"I'm headed over for graduation because of my girlfriend. Becka said she signed me up for that walk in the afternoon." Then the young man mulled it over: "You know, I thought she made the walk up because she was planning some kind of surprise for me—but it really is a walk." He sounded forlorn, and his companions burst into laughter.

"No, it's alright." The quiet man sat back to assure them. "I don't mind. Whatever she's interested in is fine. I don't mind walking." Then he addressed Roal, "Will you be there?"

"It's no longer a choice. I'll be there."

"Yeah. Her whole sorority signed up for a teacher whose wife is dying. You know him?"

"I'm starting to." Roal felt drained. The steam from his burger had probably wilted his fries already. He made another move to sit down.

"Do you know that lady whose book is doing the mind control?"

"I know her. She's a friend of my wife's. But I don't know about the mind control."

"Can that really happen? Becka gave me a copy and I read most of it, but I didn't notice anything."

"Oh, it's all manufactured griping," protested the talkative companion. "Most of the people complaining about problems seemed like they were waiting for someone else to pin their trouble on."

The old man flared, "That's what I say! A bunch of stories made up by people who can't clean their own traps. There was no problem with that book until Winter Patent said there was. And why did anyone listen? Didn't he say on TV in front of everyone that he's crazy? Didn't he? Talking to trees. And they answer! He ruined that poor lady's book. She didn't deserve that." The men's conversation moved back to themselves, releasing Roal from its expectation.

He headed back to his booth and brushed the fries aside, then grasped the burger and began. He poured the ketchup, dipped and gorged, bit and tore, set his elbows on the table, licked his fingers, and raised his glass to the bartender, who watched Roal feed his hunger with an amused satisfaction, his back to the television, which showed an entire town jumping off a dock into a frigid lake, and then flashed to Lin's face, which glowed out, looking breakable and strained. Roal's mouth fell open. *The Evening Highlight with Pete Meissner.* Roal lowered his glass and leaned in, then carried his meal to the bar for a better view.

According to the Meissner Report, Braddock campus was now in what appeared to be a waning uproar. Some students claimed a fear of failed finals because of Lin's book. Others worried that the long-term effects might unwittingly compromise their futures. One young man said he had only read the first two chapters, but began suffering from headaches and a gag reflex every time he brushed his teeth. His doctor thought it could be end-of-the-year anxiety, but the young man said he'd never had this happen before. He was worried. His parents were worried: they owned the book. Pete Meissner wanted to know if Lin had a response to their worries, and she said she certainly did: if she were the parents she would be worried too, but not about the book. In fact, Lin went on, if their son had read the first two chapters, he had covered only the first three pages of the book. In fact, Lin said, she was having a hard time finding anyone who had actually read her novel from cover to cover.

Pete stepped in to report that Braddock had conducted interviews with the people who had lodged complaints. He told Lin that their interviews seemed to confirm Lin's own suspicion: only a handful of the complainants had actually read the entire book. Eighty-two people owned it or had borrowed it, but had not read more than a few dozen chapters. The remaining twenty eight had not even opened the book in their own hands, though at least sixteen of them had a roommate who owned it and so had spent a considerable amount of time in its presence. One of the young women who had actually completed the book filed a suit because afterwards, she became depressed and isolated from her family. She no longer wished to return to the

Alaskan island where she had been raised, and her decision to not return would jeopardize the family fishing business. It was a terrible situation to be placed in. It constituted emotional distress.

"Somehow," she snuffled while looking earnestly at the camera with blinking innocence, "The book is anti-family, even though it isn't about a family. I don't know why the college would hire someone who's interested in tearing apart the family unit, which is our primary source of health and wealth and knowledge."

Pete Meissner's associate, Chandler, followed up. Chandler had located the young woman's ex-roommate. The ex-roommate revealed that earlier in the year, the complainant had sued her because whenever the roommate returned from the dining hall, the complainant claimed to feel sickened by the smells which clung to her roommate's clothing. When the roommate tried to make things better by lighting scented candles, the complainant had an asthma attack and missed the deadlines on several assignments. The roommate moved out following the lawsuit, which cost the roommate's parents over twenty thousand dollars in lawyer fees. The roommate was the other person who had read the entire book, but she had not filed a complaint and did not feel threatened by the book. She said that after she read it, she mailed it to her parents as a thank-you gift, and they had read it too. They sent it back to have Lin sign it, which Lin had done, and the book now sat on display in their living room.

"Reading that book was a remarkable experience," said the roommate. "And since my family is out about twenty thousand dollars, we've decided to savor it like the family vacation we can't afford this year."

The three men were now standing at the bar near Roal. When Lin reappeared with Pete Meissner, the younger one said, "There she is." And the other two nodded. The bartender moved slightly aside to improve their view.

An old interview with Lin was aired, in which Lin explained that she had written her book to tell a strong story, but also to play with an idea she had about eliciting specific emotions.

"Complex emotions," Lin said. "Not just happiness or fear or anger, but emotions that are more complex—emotions like vulnerable, frightfully overjoyed, abandoned, wounded pride, cloudy thinking, disgust, yearning, profoundly deep unrequited love. These are all emotions we have the capacity to experience, and yet few of us are able to identify them. I wanted my book to elicit specific bursts of isolated emotional realities that allowed the full range to be experienced. Once they are experienced, then the body does not need to store them. I sought to make the book a kind of emotional palate cleanser, though in the context of a strong narrative."

The reporter then turned from that interview to Lin live at his side and asked her, "Do you stand by these words?"

Lin nodded, "Yes. But it's important for people to recognize that feeling an emotion is not going to create the kinds of issues they are assigning to the book. For example, feeling repressed or galled—both emotions elicited in different ways in the book—would not lead to destructive or negative behavior. Experiencing them may sound uncomfortable, but it actually leads to greater self-awareness, as well as a feeling of peace."

But Pete interjected, "However, Lin, in some cases, this self-awareness has led people to wonder if they weren't better off before they read your book. Many of the allegations are pretty convincing." The reporter tried to sound threatening, but Roal could see that a deal had been struck: Lin granted the interview because the reporter who tracked her down had an angle, and the angle was sympathy.

She responded as though her answer were just occurring to her, "I think that what the allegations reveal is that our culture is terrified of emotions— our own and those of others. Instead we are looking for ways to minimize difficult conversations or situations. For example, my ex-husband divorced me via text messaging. Many of my students equate having sex with being drunk and not with intimacy. I would say that if people become suddenly irrational because they are avoiding their feelings while reading the book, then the issue is not with the book, but with the culture reading it."

"What do you mean, the problem is with the culture?"

"Okay." Lin smoothed her hair behind her ear, "Our culture is not a reflective culture, but it is reactive. And reactions negate a deep internal dialogue. For example, elective surgeries are up because people would rather literally take on an altered ego than just accept their own faces. With texting, it's easier to change plans than to make one and keep it. When a child is teased at school, the first thing parents do is try to improve the child's wardrobe. In a consumer culture, the answer is not to get to know yourself better. It is to figure out how to better channel yourself though the lens of product-currency. We assume that if something feels uncomfortable it should be avoided, and if it needs to be avoided then it's bad, and if it's bad it can be fixed with a product. What this means is that our discomfort never leads to internal reflection. It leads to an external product solution. My book is an attempt to get people to sit with the beauty and potential of discomfort which could lead to inner peace."

Pete Meissner broke for a fresh round of ads, which the bartender turned away from. He cleared Roal's basket and empty glass, looked at the clock, and turned back to the television.

"Interesting," said the young man whose girlfriend signed him up for the walk.

The other young man said, "Yeah." Then added, "From when she was here before, you wouldn't of known she had all this on her mind. She seemed so regular and laid-back, not so nervous."

Roal turned to the men: "She was here? When?"

The old man thought about it. "Last year sometime. Had to be the spring. She and some of Becka's friends came out for a couple days during calving. They wanted to see the new calves. They were here, what, two nights?"

"Two nights," Becka's boyfriend agreed.

"Nice gal. You oughta read her book." Lin had been everywhere. This town had sat just where it was for over a hundred years, calling out to nobody, and Lin had reached it before Roal. Had seen its new calves and had stayed two nights and been remembered. And Roal was here now, his life spinning forward into a future unclear with the newness of it because of Lin, the catalyst. Roal was surprised to find he did not mind that he was behind her, following the yellow path of her recent blaze through town. He would make his own trail at some point, but would see first where this one led and where it broke off from Lin's.

As the three men were leaving, the older one tipped his hat and said, "Good luck with complicated!" Roal gave them a wave, then settled his bill and headed to the bathroom.

Chandler's next story expanded on the other whirlwind that had taken over Braddock College. "As if the story of Lin and Winter isn't enough," she laughed, "here we meet a story of courage and inspiration: Braddock's own cougar walker. Last week the usually mild author and writing professor Roal Bowman braved a walk across a campus swarming with cougars as a protest against the campus lockdown. This week, he has set off an all-campus race to sign up for a breast cancer charity walk. While he could not be reached for an interview, students say they have been galvanized by his amazing support for his dying wife's unusual decision to spend her last days in a forest. In honor of Professor Bowman, the students are banding together, turning out, and walking for the cure following their graduation ceremony."

Next to Chandler, a video of Roal aired: his YouTube stride across campus, books pressed to his chest as if in resolute determination to prove the heart's capacity to experience ravage and loss. The following advertisement left him there, midstride and inspiring. The bartender looked at the name on Roal's receipt: Roal Bowman. He flicked off the television and straightened quickly, tucking the receipt into the register when Roal emerged from the bathroom.

"Off to Malva, then?"

"Right."

"Where are you staying?"

"I hadn't gotten that far. This road trip takes me back to my college days—I might sleep in my car. I just might." The bartender eyed Roal from toe to head and whistled.

"Got a big car, I hope."

"It's a boat. 1974 Buick LeSabre." The bartender considered this, and warmed to Roal.

"That must mean you don't have people in Malva."

"No. Nobody. Just one person I need to talk to, but she's just outside of Malva."

"You made a long trip for a conversation—you could of used a phone." The bartender indicated the one behind the bar, but Roal's smile looked patient and faraway sad.

"No—no phone where she is. But it is a long trip for a conversation," he reflected. "I guess that's what happens when there hasn't been enough conversation in the past. You end up driving to a forest for a last effort just to see what happens."

Roal pushed the door open. When he turned to look back, the bartender was already on the phone. But when the bartender caught Roal's eye, he hung up without completing the dial. Roal gave a last wave before turning back to the parked car of his evening.

From there, Roal saw the bartender reach for the phone again and then dial hastily, gesturing as he spoke, looking out to the parking lot and, seeing Roal's car, confirming something. Roal had a cold feeling the conversation included him. There wasn't much he could do to hide himself: traveling alone, tall and heavy and framed in a bright pink shirt, a man whose quietness could be interpreted as dangerousness for those who didn't know better, a man not afraid to get into a scrape with cougars, a man, perhaps, used to using his hands for dirty work—he had, after all, barehandedly torn his food apart at the table and swallowed the fries without chewing. He was headed to Malva, and would be impossible to miss.

CHAPTER 17

A soft night enfolded Roal's car as he pushed through to Malva, its cheerless, empty streets where shops displayed their austerities scattered on bare boards, as if the window displays doubled as storage space.

Roal looped back, struck by the thin-spiritedness of the stores which seemed, in their naming, too aware of how imagination led to dreams, and dreams led to disappointment. The names offered only literal explanations of the goods or services they offered: The G'Night Motel, The Dress Shop, The Coffee Bean, Grocery Store, Bottle Shop & Upholstery, Family Hair, Custom Meats.

And yet, even as they proclaimed their goods, they were careful not to overpromise. The five-foot-tall iron cleaver propped next to the butcher shop had For Sale painted on the rusted blade. The library was for sale. The courthouse had become a theater, though that too was for lease. All over town, houses and tractors and bicycles for sale, each with a number to call. Parked trucks bore their sale signs in the windows, and the scrap metal heaps in the front yards had signs sticking out of them: For Sale. All of it. Fork-lifts, stock tanks, wheelbarrows, wagons, backhoes, and iron fencing. A few lights seeped from a curtainless house, but Roal didn't have the heart to peer in as he drove by—so much was already on display. It looked like the rest of town had gone to bed early, hoping to wake up and find itself with a choice.

At the G'Night Motel the night-glazed clerk told him to wait while she went to make up a bed for him.

"Would have had it done if I'd of known you were coming!" she called as she left, letting Roal know that things weren't always so last minute. The neon light over the parking lot flickered a tepid yellow moon in its last phase of wane.

"We have coffee in the morning and free local," the clerk announced as she handed Roal his key.

"Great. Free local what?"

The clerk shrugged, "You know. Phone calls. TV. But the reception doesn't come in."

In the morning, Roal stood by himself in the cramped lobby, drinking the coffee before heading down the block for groceries. He walked against the wind and the line of trucks rumbling toward work. Roal felt he should be driving something larger than himself.

In the store, Roal remembered water. And toothpaste. And a toothbrush. Roal remembered that he used to love Little Debbie Snack Cakes with milk. Potato chips and sweet roasted peanuts in a jar. Beef jerky and frozen pound cake and sesame seed candies. It had been years since he had shopped for groceries. He had forgotten how much fun it was to discover the small, important artifacts of his childhood, how road trips allowed certain food privileges regular life could not endure.

When Roal emerged from the store, the line of trucks had mysteriously vanished, and the town's sleepy shuffle toward another day seemed less dire. It was spring after all. The bleak swinging of all the half-hinged FOR SALE signs might not go on forever. Someone might yet come to Malva and recognize a dream.

Back in his room, Roal felt an urge to touch the smoothness of the phone, to press its buttons and hear a voice at its other end, for the voice to tell him that the day was off to a good start, and by nightfall it would all be over. Roal pushed the numbers for Chet's house, but Chet did not answer. Roal called his own home, and Chet picked up on the first ring, his *Hello? Hello?* agitated and expectant, as if he had been waiting for Roal to deliver whatever bad news Chet knew well enough to wait for.

"Dad, it's Roal."

"Roal! How are you? Where are you? No—don't answer that! Are you okay?" Then Chet dropped his voice and asked meaningfully, "Are you . . . alone?"

When Roal answered, he could feel Chet's impatience.

"Roal, now they're calling. They know. The reporters. They say Dina has cancer and is in the woods. They want to do a feature on you for your support and get an update on her health. But another one, Drew Klein—look out for him—he says he believes our Dina is the same one working with Winter. He wants to know where you are. He'll find out, he said." Roal tried to break in, but Chet rushed on.

"And it's worse," Chet continued, "Last night, late, a guy came looking for you. He said he knows where you are but he wants to do it peacefully. He said it's better if he finds Winter first so no one will get hurt. He said he has investments to protect. What does he mean? What does he mean, investments?"

Roal's mind groped, unnerved to hear Chet sound rattled. It was a relief when Roal heard his own voice, its steadiness, a voice that could get to the bottom of things. Roal asked what the man looked like, if Drew Klein had stopped by or just called, if anyone else knew where Roal was headed.

"No. Except your dean. He gave you the map."

"But he wants to make sure no one finds Dina before I do, so he wouldn't have said anything. His secretary would know, though, and so would whoever pulled the GPS info from the car." Roal ticked off the people who might know anything. "And then there was the officer who stopped for me yesterday—he knows where I'm headed. Oh, and the cowboys, but they cared more about the cougars—and maybe the bartender."

"How many cowboys?"

"Three. Only three."

"But that's already almost a dozen people! Don't tell anyone else what you're up to. Drew Klein makes it sound like Dina has a secret romance that needs to go public. But this guy last night—he seemed dangerous. He wasn't messing around."

"Tell me again what he wanted?" Roal peeked out the window at the town's stillness. The sun had lit the broad faces of the storefronts, the reflections glaring at Roal.

Chet said, "He said he needs to find Winter. He wants to reveal the location peacefully. His investments are suffering, he said."

"What investments?"

"He wouldn't say. He's about five-nine, brown hair. Conservative looking, but cold. Razor cold. He said to give you the message that he knows where you are, and he knows you are going to find Dina, and that Dina is probably with Winter. All he wants is to take some pictures so he can reveal the location and get back to business. He's going to call me this morning to get your answer."

"So he doesn't know for sure that Dina is with Winter?"

"He suspects."

"Okay. Fine. If he knows where I am, I can't stop him from following me. Plus, I don't care if he reveals the location. So what? I just want to find Dina. It'd probably be a good idea if Winter is brought in to get some help anyway. Why is this guy even asking? He could just follow me. And you know, it's just a matter of time before he or some other reporter finds the location."

Chet hesitated.

"What?" Roal hated the silence. "What else?"

Roal felt an old gnawing inside him, recalling Chet's hesitancy years ago when he called to report that Helen wasn't feeling well, his voice distant and disquieted. When Roal asked to speak with Helen, Chet had paused and hesitated, then trembled at the end of the line before finally admitting to Roal: *She's not breathing. They say she's gone. What do you think?* Roal said he thought it sounded like she had probably died, and Chet said, *That's what I think too, but I don't mind being wrong.*

Now Roal heard the same kind of withholding and asked again, "Dad, what is it?"

"Roal, this guy is not a reporter. Believe me. He was very comfortable making threats. He's up to something bad. Said it's crucial I don't talk to the police. And he does plan to follow you. But he says that if you see him, that if you see anything, you better not say anything to Winter. He says Winter will fight to the death to keep his place a secret, and that he'd be happy enough to oblige him. All this guy wants is to get in, take a few pictures, and get out so the world will stop looking for Winter and he can get back to his own private business. That's what he said. But he's talking about killing. And

I can't tell anyone or you might get hurt. Or Dina." Roal let this sink in, sharp anchor to the tender depths.

"But if he knows where I am, why is he asking permission?"

"Well," Chet said. "He needs you to expose Winter. To keep him in the open so he can get good pictures as definitive proof." Chet said the last part softly, as though he had failed Roal by passing the information along.

"Who is this guy, Dad?"

"I don't know. Brown hair, dresses like an guy who might sell boats, average everything but a chipped tooth. Normal looking, but chilly. Just look after yourself. If he follows you, don't tell Winter. And if he doesn't follow you, don't look for him. Stay in the open. With Winter. Whatever you do, be careful."

"Okay. I'll be careful." Roal sat on the bed and smoothed the pillow cover next to him. He knew he did not know what it meant to be careful in this man's world. In his own world, to be careful meant to say little, follow a routine, show up on time, moderate your voice, express doubt thoughtfully, cut back on red meat, and keep your laces tied. He doubted the rules of his life would come in handy for the man Chet described.

"Roal. I want you to know something. I do love you."

Roal set the phone back on its cradle. There it was again: *I do love you*. The phrase passed from one intimate to another when the goodbye may have to last forever.

I do love you: I will not see you again.

I do love you: we are already apart.

I do love you: what I am leaving you with will make you doubt that I mean it.

I do love you: I insist on this because it was real and I claim that.

Roal understood Dina's note. She loved him. He was on his own. And now Chet, asking Roal to enter the woods, a madman at his back, Winter at his face, Dina somewhere in between.

Roal stood up and looked around the room. He smoothed the bed sheets. He wanted to leave it neat because he because he would be leaving it forever: the unassuming, overburdened dresser, sagging mattress, crisp sheets, folded hand towels above the sink. When he left, whatever he left behind would be cleaned and thrown away. His footprints disappeared beneath him as he walked to return his room key to a still vacant office.

Then he dawdled in town, practicing a look of unawareness as he tried not to reveal that he thought he was being watched: he filled his gas tank, washed his windshield, organized the food and water in his backpack, mindlessly studied again the last stretch of maps he had already memorized. When he at last aimed the car east toward the mountain rise and forest stretch, his heart hesitated each time he looked in his rear view mirror, then it caught up quickly and tumbled, its beating a kind of companion to the rattling of the car as Roal drove over the faded, potholed, weedy streets of Malva. He saw no one coming after him.

At the edge of the patched town, Roal passed an expansive parking lot where rows of trucks were parked on blacktop smooth and expertly marked with crisp yellow lines. Culler Paper. The lumber mill. The lawn around the mill's yard and buildings was plush and thickly, deeply green, a gift of color for the dust-cracked town behind him. Roal wondered if the lumber company used a formula to calculate how long it should promise prosperity to the town in order to populate its workforce and take its trees. Maybe it would provide jobs for years. Months. But eventually it would cinch its belt and tighten the promises it made to a single day. Just enough to get by. That would happen just before the town was ruined and its forest was gone. And then the mill could start again somewhere else and single-wides would self-assemble overnight.

Geysers of water sprayed out across the giant stacks of logs in the lumberyard. It looked like the only rain Malva would get all season.

Roal drove on. Because he had to. Because he was close and closing. Because a thin cord pulled his stomach forward. Because Malva would keep for itself anything that didn't get out fast enough. The road coiled as he climbed. He saw a silver truck, a white minivan, a gray Jeep in his rearview at different times. They peeled away one by one, and on he drove alone.

CHAPTER 18

Roal followed the map. When the road's pavement gave out and turned to washboard gravel, the car climbed in a jarring rattle. Roal hung on and kept going. His tires stirred up a dust cloud that rose and hung as a fine, loose sift in the air. When he passed the signs that read: PRIVATE LAND: NO TRESPASSING, Roal continued. He answered only to the yellow line of the map and an impatience to end the uneasiness of not knowing how the story would find its climax and resolution.

The not-knowing unnerved him. Before he'd spoken with Chet that morning, he had seen three options: Dina would come home with him. Dina would stay. Dina would not be found and he would have to start again as more and more people gathered around and cheered for his false life to work out according to their own desires. But now that the man had shown up with a threat and a warning at Chet's house, there were other options: Winter could die, Winter could kill, Dina could be harmed, Roal could run away when the shooting started and be eaten by cougars who thought he smelled like the last town they'd liked so much.

As Roal topped the next hill, a giant stretch of rust orange forest blazed in front of him like a wrecking yard of corroded iron. The dead zone. It was in utter shambles: trees lay upon each other like a dropped game of pickup sticks. spilled onto the ground, leaning against each other in piles, some of them caught in the arms of the still standing trees who themselves were the same dry-needle orange as those that had fallen. His heart again tumbled and fetched, though on he followed the yellow path of his map until he at last found a turnout. There he parked the car, rocking it back and forth in the cradle of gravel and dust before it settled at the side of the road. The dust he'd raised was quickly carried off. When he pushed the door open, the wind yanked the door open and swirled the wrappers around the car. Roal lunged to catch them before they were sucked outside and stuffed them in his backpack.

He did not know what to do next. The map had taken him this far, but only this far. He was alone to face what would happen next. Then he saw another cloud of dust, far away down the side of the mountain. Roal's heart contracted. He had to get away from his car. He grabbed the backpack, stood up, and tried to work out a plan.

Chet would have had a plan. He would have plotted as he drove. Roal tried to think like Chet: *You get some legs and run. You get into the forest and get looking. Spiral out.* Chet's plans involved action. Not thinking or wondering. Just getting on with it. Chet would mark the trees so he could find his way back out again. Roal remembered what Winter had said about marking territory and how it proclaimed superiority over what was being marked. Though Roal did not feel superior as he looked through the withered apron of roadside bushes and into the forest that had died standing up. The forest held Dina and now included him. He did not want to offend it, but he had to go in, and he wanted to make it out.

Roal tore the wrappers into strips and crammed them into his pockets. Then he turned to the forest and leapt over the ditch, urgency lofting him as he sailed through the air and then landed on the other side: he was in. Officially there, in the forest.

Roal hurried in deeper, putting distance between himself and his car. When he almost couldn't see it any more, he began wedging strips of wrappers into the bases of trees or tying them to branches. The forest groaned in the wind. Roal worked his way quickly, deeply into the forest and looked back: his car had disappeared an it seemed he'd gone further than he could remember walking, but his shining, foiled trail twinkled back at him like candied promises. He listened for the sound of other car's approach, heard nothing. He breathed a slow full breath and plunged in further.

The sound of the air moving through the dead trees was different than when it swept the green and limber trees of Roal's back yard and campus.

Here, it sounded higher, more reedy and dry, scratched by the terrible limbs: some broken and dangling, others jutting form the ground where they'd fallen, and still other entire trees that had begun to topple but were caught in the arms of neighboring trees who held onto them like an offering of mercy to the sky.

The smooth bottoms of Roal's shoes were slippery and he picked a path carefully through the ruin, scrambling over or skirting around fallen trees and branches. He wanted to be in and out of the forest quickly. He was anxious to be wandering in a forest where even the slightest wind sent branches to the ground. And the wind varied from slight to extreme in turns.

He fought the urge to call out for Dina, reminding himself that the louder he called the better it would attract the man avowed to follow him. He listened again, but heard no footfalls, no evidence of anyone behind him.

He walked until he felt certain he was deep enough in. Then he circled back and worked his way like a giant thresher across the space he'd gone: back and forth, looking for something that would give him cause to stop: Dina in the distance, a piece of fabric, a pot next to a firepit. The wind pressed down and a tree groaned nearby; in the distance a loud crack echoed through the forest. A tree falling over, a gunshot. Roal didn't know which, He froze, listening. When Roal turned in the direction of the sound, he saw nothing, and the forest returned to the whine of wind through the brittle branches.

He stepped around a small shrub that had shy green leaves trembling at its edges. In a few more steps, he skirted a fallen branch which arched over a fern not yet uncurled. The wind snarled, and another loud crack registered through the woods, a falling tree, though when Roal turned he was again surrounded by stillness. The dead trees gave no breath, took nothing from Roal. He was alone. When Roal turned back, his eye was caught by something else: more green. And then he remembered.

He was going about it wrong by looking for Dina and the remnants of her life at home: cooking pot, sweater, skirt. Dina and Winter were here for another purpose altogether, and that purpose was green. Roal should be looking for green.

He looked from the fern to the first trembling bush he had come across, then scanned the ground beyond them. More dots of green. They were sparse and tiny, but glowed defiantly, newly, against their rusted backdrop. When he turned the other direction, he saw that in the distance the green began to concentrate, connecting green to more green, then disappearing over a small hill. Roal followed the dot-to-dot of new growth to the hill's rise, and when he crested the top, he stood astonished as he looked down into a meadow of old stumps and fallen firs, all of it covered by shrubs, vines, rose bushes, and seedlings: green on green on green. Tiny spring orchids spotted the ground, their lavender so electric and neon-thin they looked like they hovered above the ground in a glass aura. A liquid pour of bird song traveled from the far side of the clearing to Roal's ears.

Then Roal sensed a movement and turned his head quickly, his focus landing on any perch it could find, a tree, a fallen branch, a broken trunk, the spaces between. Nothing. The world held its breath and went still in the sweep of his gaze. When he moved again the moist air of the clearing let go and enveloped him, reminding Roal of his house with its close, green air and the exhalation of plants. The air that rose up from the meadow overrode the powdery smell of the beetles burrowing under the dead bark of the trees in the forest behind him, and the sun on the vegetal life made the air feel thick and spongy, possible and laden.

But then, what had he expected? Lin had said that the results were impressive. Then Roal shook his head—to begin feeling impressed meant believing that the project was real. He corrected himself: since the project was improbable, the results were too. The meadow, Roal thought, is just a meadow.

Again the wind rose and Roal felt a movement—a flickering or a flash—closer this time, but again when he looked at the landscape it seemed to have snapped into a frozen, expectant hush. It waited. Roal felt his heartbeat pulsing in his wrists, heard it in his ears. Something watched him. Perhaps a trick of the wind, Roal thought. It was whistling through the treetops, shaking the branches, which clattered and rasped. His watch ticked loudly, each second a pause of consequence before the door of its thin hand slammed into the next position. Something was moving, a sift of needles lifted by the air and then settled to the ground. A suspension of a branch, wavering. Breath through Roal's lungs. He remained watchful, but then remembered he was not supposed to let on that he knew he was being followed. He was to appear natural, nonchalant, as he roamed the dead forest in search of his wife.

He forced himself to appear casual. He took off his backpack and shuffled through the snacks. He turned his face to the sky as he took a long, slow drink of water. He chewed his snack cake with carelessness, just a man alone in the woods without suspicion. He made a point to examine his peanuts, to hold the fruit leather up to the light with a thoughtfulness usually reserved for palimpsests. All the while trying not to appear as though felt the eyes upon him. He packed the food back into the bag and zipped it. The bag caught against something as he hitched it up, and when he turned to see what it was, he leapt back, a terrified cry curdled in his throat. The pack was held by Winter Patent, who stood less than a foot from Roal. Winter stared up at Roal looking amused, if not slightly bored, as though he'd been waiting all day at that very spot for Roal to appear exactly there beside him.

CHAPTER 19

Winter motioned with a hand for Roal to be quiet, but in Roal's unsettled alarm, Roal mistook Winter's sign of caution for a handshake and so grasped Winter's hand in his own, pumping it according to the muscle response trained by years of social habit: the offering of one's hand as a ritual to assert that there is no threat, that the person will accept what the hands invite into them. Winter took the offering, and each man shook the hand of the other without speaking, each crushing the other's hand and finding its challenge equally strong, and each staring into the face of the other for some kind of landing.

Roal studied the solid goodness of Winter's face, handsome and surrounded by fine, auburn curls interlaced with gray. Winter's clothes, a thin wool the color of the red forest, clung to his shoulders and chest, but hung loosely from his arms and torso. The wind caught the fabric, and Winter seemed to sway and quaver as his clothing rippled over him. Winter's nose twitched slightly toward Roal's bag of food.

"Winter Patent," Roal finally whispered. He looked past Winter for a sign of Dina, though saw only distance through the trees.

"Roal," Winter answered in a low voice. "You came. We wondered."

Roal recognized Winter's unwavering eyes, the alert, deliberate flex of his body as he turned away from Roal without breaking his hold on the handshake. Roal recognized the square shoulders and the compact stance. The thick neck and the taut lips pulled back over the blaze of even white teeth. And yet, Winter looked like a strange inhabitant who had taken up residence in the previous body of his younger self, as if he had pulled this new self on hastily, before he was able to smooth out the wrinkles or rinse it with clean water. Roal thought of a wet foot after it is finally pulled from its soaked through boot and sock. However, Winter's grip on Roal's hand was amazing: Roal wondered how much longer he would have to hang on or if he it would be alright to admit defeat and let go. Abruptly, Winter released Roal's hand, though he then grasped Roal's forearm and led him quickly from the meadow, back over the hill's rise and into the red forest. Once there, Winter stopped to listen, cocking his ear in all directions. Then he began to speak, his voice intimate and low.

"Three things, Roal. First, it's good you're here. Welcome. Second, don't go into that meadow. It's on its way to recovery and it doesn't need me anymore, and I want to give it space. Undisturbed. Third, Dina's not in that meadow. I finished with that space over two years ago. She's working on an area that's much harder—the area of the falling trees you heard as you walked this way. I'll take you there, but we'll need to talk first." Winter held up his finger and waited, smiling, as though he was a conductor for the breeze as it picked up and began to surge.

Roal waited, and then heard it again: another giant cracking in the distance, followed by the crashing of one tree through the branches of others. Winter nodded and looked at Roal again, sharing his pleasure.

"She's really good," Winter said. "I am amazed by what she can do."

Roal nodded as though he agreed. Then he shook his head. He was in another man's land, and the words were of his language but did not mean the same. The air seemed charged around Winter.

"I'm here for Dina. Where is she?"

Winter nodded, "First we'll get some food. Then eat and talk. Then I'll take you to Dina." Roal stopped walking.

"No," Roal said, "I didn't come to talk with you. I came for her. I want to see her now." Winter frowned at that.

"Not possible. She's not available, technically speaking. First we'll talk, but not here. We can talk once we get to my place."

"What is Dina doing?"

"Trees. Consciousness. She's helping to make way for growth."

"But I want to see her now." Roal heard his voice insist, heard the petulance under it, and knew before Winter spoke that the answer would be no—Roal's voice had lost control, so he would not get what he wanted.

"I know you want to see her," Winter said evenly, "But we weren't expecting you for a few days. She's not yet available. It'll take some doing to get to her. But we can try in a bit."

Roal accepted this glumly, stomping along through the woods as Winter guided him by the arm. Like a captor, Roal thought. Winter's feet were wrapped in dark buckskin and made no sound, though he seemed to step without watching where he placed his feet. When Roal tried to place his feet carefully, his steps snapped sticks and kicked apart mounds of red needles. He wondered if a walking stick would help, then remembered the stick of Winter's interview, the stick Winter had always carried.

"Where's your walking stick?" Roal asked.

"My walking stick?"

"The one from the treetop that fell on you when you discovered you were done being a wolf."

"I'm sorry?" Winter looked at Roal expectantly. "I have no idea what you mean."

Roal insisted, "The stick. From ten years ago? The one that feel on you and that you hit an intern reporter with—Mike something who raises bamboo? You said you always carried it with you."

Winter thought about it, and then he gave a snort of sudden recollection and began to laugh. He let go of Roal's arm and beckoned with his hands for Roal to join him. But Roal felt uneasy and looked around to catch his bearings. Winter laughed harder, then reached into a pouch at his waist and drew out a handful of plastic and foil: Roal's markers that led back to the car. Roal's face twisted, and Winter's mirth increased. He waved the strips at Roal, and Roal took them, then looked around for the road, a clearing, the car. Winter's laughter boomed in his chest and then ran slowly out.

"Don't worry. Your car's just over there. No need for litter here. About the stick—so funny. That was a prop. People can see ideas better when you give them a specific shape. Mike Kasura. That was his name. Did they air that interview?" Winter laughed again, then continued, "I bet that was something. I was getting deep into this work by then. Did you say Mike is working with bamboo?"

"Yes. In Hawaii."

"I heard from him a few days after that interview—he said he was making a change, that everything came to him the moment I struck him: lucky blow. So he actually did it and is working with bamboo. Good for him."

"What stick did you hit him with?"

"Just a stick. A prop. For television. To make it real to the viewers."

"Oh." Roal was quiet. It had been real to him. Winter looked at him intently.

"Roal, if I made a habit of carrying the original stick around, then I would have just turned it into a prop. I don't believe in memorabilia. Instead, I try to let experience inform me. It helps me stay adaptive. Anyway, I'm glad Mike decided to air that dreadful interview. He was so embarrassed of it, but I thought he did well. Well enough." Winter seemed to be recalling the interview, grimacing and chuckling both.

"Maybe Mike was protecting you by not airing it earlier—the interview was a little . . . inventive," Roal suggested cautiously. Winter chortled again, enjoying the thought of being protected by Mike Kasura. Roal heard the heartiness in Winter's laugh, the sensual appetite for pleasure, and shrank from it.

Winter pondered, "But why air it now? That seems strange."

"Because of Lin," Roal answered. "And the letter you wrote her. Everyone wants to be the first to find your new project. They're calling it the Green Winter site." Winter stopped walking and again held up his hand for silence. Roal waited, and another distant tree echoed its fall, the sound carried on a strip of wind wending past. Winter did not move. He faced the wind and continued to listen, his lips slightly open and his eyes far away.

"What?" Roal asked. "I don't hear anything." Then a second tree fell. The forest floor rippled. Winter looked at Roal, shaking his head and shrugging in open marvel. He continued to walk and picked up the conversation.

"Lin. Good writer. And a good friend to Dina," said Winter. Roal grunted.

"No?" Winter asked. "Not a good friend? Or you don't like her writing?"

"Well, she left Dina here. I've never been left in the woods by a good friend."

"No. But maybe you didn't want to be left whereas Dina did, so that's a different thing. Hearing what someone asks for. Wait, now—just a minute." Again Winter held up a hand for Roal to be silent. And again Roal waited for the sound of a falling tree, but nothing happened. Winter slipped forward slowly, his body a rippling series of tiny movements that made him look like light filtering through the trees. Roal watched him, mesmerized and frozen, his own body inhabited by a heavy silence that spread and stretched between himself and Winter. He wanted to run, to break away and find Dina. To call her name and have her answer. To have Winter chase him in the open while Roal ran, calling loudly enough to attract the man with the camera so he could get a good shot and the project would be revealed.

Roal looked around to locate a path through the trees that could take him toward the sound of the falling trees, toward Dina. He began to edge away slightly, keeping his eyes on Winter. As he prepared to turn, a sudden explosion of beating wings burst from the ground, a blinding scatter of needles erupting from the forest floor as a grouse shot up from its hiding place. Winter sprang forward and batted the bird from the air with one hand, then landed over it in a crouch where he snapped its neck and stuffed it into the pouch at his waist. Flight to bag, not quite two seconds. Roal felt a thin sweat cool his lip. He abandoned his plan to make a run for it. When Winter turned to Roal so they could continue, Roal backed away. Winter looked surprised, but then he smiled kindly.

"It's lunch. I told you, we'd get something to eat."

"I brought food. I have plenty to share. You didn't have to, to. . . ." Roal indicated his backpack, unsure of how to finish. Something about what he had just seen—the speed or the knowing, perhaps the everyday casualness with which Winter stuffed the still-warm bird, its feathers not yet settled to the ground, into his bag—unsettled him deeply.

"Thank you for offering," Winter said. "But I can't eat what you brought. It's not really food, you know. It's just substances people assembled in factories and then packaged in plastic. Then someone else who probably won't touch the stuff thought of a marketing campaign to establish a suggestion of edibility to consumers. Real food, by the way, does not rename its ingredients to make it sound edible—it has a single name of identification for both the living and the dead entity. Like 'grouse'. Or 'marmot'. Or 'carrots'. Not 'Little Debbie' or 'Mr. Salty'. But I appreciate the offer."

"I thought you said you stopped being a wolf," Roal mumbled. "And gave up violence." Winter thought about what Roal said and then nodded.

"I see," he said. "Yes, I did give those up, you're right. But that doesn't mean I have to abandon what I learned. Imagine if you quit being a writing professor. You wouldn't suddenly declare that you were no longer able to recognize written language. You would use your previous knowledge to get yourself to whatever the next level would be. As a wolf, I learned about survival. It would be foolish to abandon that."

Roal understood Winter's answer, but he needed to have Winter concede something so that there might be a chance against him.

"What about violence?" Roal asked pointedly.

"Oh, that," Winter chuckled. "Yes. I believe in eradicating it."

"Then what about the bird?" Roal felt he was getting somewhere, and his voice was filled with a teacherly caution, a gentle tone of reminder that there was more to be considered, that the answer would be self evident once the path to it became clear. But when Winter turned his face to Roal, his expression encompassed such awareness and concern that Roal felt ashamed for insisting that hunger should come without consequences.

"Roal. Hunger is violence. I confront it directly and am grateful I don't need to rely on others to address it. But I honor your concern for the grouse."

They walked on in silence. Just as Roal thought his footsteps were becoming more muted, Winter stopped him and gestured, saying, "Well, here we are." A broad sweep of Winter's arm indicated a mound of branches and dirt heaped about four feet high. Roal looked at it, confused.

"We are where?"

"Home." Winter dropped to his hands and knees and disappeared through a small opening in the tangle of branches that looked like they had fallen from above. Winter popped his head back out and said, "Come in, Roal. It's bigger than it looks. We can talk in here." Winter's look to Roal was a command. Roal sank to the ground and crawled through, half expecting Dina to be in a kitchen on the other side, her hands full of the work of making everything Roal might need.

CHAPTER 20

As Roal crawled through, he cursed that he had failed to keep Winter exposed in open spaces. But once inside, that idea disappeared, replaced by the kind of glee usually reserved for runaway cub scouts who discover a hidden shelter. The dugout was exactly like the one Roal had wished to come upon when he was a boy. Its ceiling of sticks and roots rose well over his head when he was seated, the interior roomy compared to the childhood shelters he'd fashioned out of boards, sheets, and abandoned crates and then stocked with household surplus he hoped nobody would miss. In Winter's hut, earthen shelves carved into the walls were stocked with books, jugs of water, a few rolls of fabric and leather, a small cookstove, a pan, and two bowls. A pillow and blankets were rolled up against one side of the dugout. The roots that formed the back wall of the dugout were hung with a pair of reading glasses, two pairs of socks laid out to dry, and a collection of leather pouches which bulged or sagged in their various states of fulfillment.

"Welcome to this summer's home," Winter said. Roal looked at him happily.

"This is great. I could live here." Roal did not care that he was gushing. The tidy space felt snug and exemplary in its stern loneliness. "It reminds me of that book about the boy who lives in a giant burned out oak tree. Did you make this?"

"Yes. I make them wherever I work. But I've had company lately, so this one feels a bit tighter than usual."

Roal's joyful nostalgia popped. Dina. Here in tight quarters. Roal looked again at the two bowls: she and Winter ate in this small space. Slept in it. Got dressed. Undressed. Roal stared disconsolately at the bedding and counted two distinct rolls. He counted them again, repeating to himself that there were two, not one, two not one. A feeling of gratitude to Winter for having two separate rolls rose up in him, though he tried to suppress it because the gratitude felt like a betrayal—Roal did not need to give Winter gratitude, the emotion of suppliants; instead, he would need to summon wariness, cunning, anger, reserve, and determination. Gratitude for the bedrolls in Winter's small hollow of shared earth should not be counted among Roal's inventory.

Meanwhile, Winter opened the pouch he wore around his waist and removed the bird. Its head lolled on the floor when Winter set it down. Winter opened the bird with a small knife, then gutted it and stuffed the small cavity with a handful of greens. He set the bird in a pan and set a clay bowl over it, then poured a thin trail of water around the bowl, and set the pan on the cookstove. Roal took it as a good sign that Winter used a stove and allowed himself to read the stove as a sign of weakness that Winter did not use fire in the old way, could perhaps no longer coax a flame from sticks and control the blaze. It also meant that Winter did not eat his food raw, and so was perhaps a man with a softness for comforts, a man with a weakness.

Roal looked around for other signs of Winter's waning powers: blankets, books, reading glasses, a flashlight. It was unlikely that in his twenties as a wolf Winter would have been caught reading with his glasses on as he curled up in a pile of wolves. Roal did an inventory of the assets he had with him, anything he could use should he need to fight with Winter. The only thing that came to mind was the butter knife Chet had swept into his backpack. Beyond that, he had about three pounds of junk food, a bright pink shirt he might be able to wave as a flag to attract attention, and his car keys. It didn't seem like enough.

However, Roal counted among his assets one thing he had which Winter did not: knowledge that the man with a camera was coming, and soon this would all be over. Someone would show up and take control, and then Roal could find Dina and he would say something to her, and she would say something back to him, and he would listen, and then something would happen next. But for that plan to work, he had to get Winter back into the open.

"Should we go outside while this is cooking?" Roal asked the question, and immediately regretted the tactical error. He should not have asked. He should have asserted that now they would go outside. Or he simply should have gone outside and waited for Winter to scramble out after. But he had asked, assuming that the implication of the answer he wanted to hear would carry itself to the yes he wanted, as it most often did. However, Winter was also a man who was used to people saying yes, was also used to heading in the direction of his own desires, and was not accustomed to answering according to the answer the other person hoped to hear. Winter's answer, like Roal's, would always be exactly what he wanted to have happen for himself, and Roal knew it. Questions work only on those who believe there is value in the contract of agreeability.

"No." Winter waved Roal's suggestion away. "I need to tell you about the project first. So you'll understand when you see Dina." Roal bristled at Winter's implication that the project took precedence over Dina.

"I'm not here because of your project. I don't want to be rude but I don't care about the project. I'm only here for Dina." Roal made as though he were about to crawl back up and into the open, but the look on Winter's face stopped him. Winter looked genuinely distressed, and Roal sensed that the distress was for Roal. Winter reached to the tangle of roots behind him and took down one of the pouches that hung there. He held it, weighing it in his hands, balancing the decision of whatever it held between himself and Roal. Finally, he spoke, though slowly and with frequent pauses to give Roal room to interrupt.

"Roal, you will see Dina soon. But she isn't able to see you now. I mean that literally. She isn't able to use her eyes to perceive right now. When we work, we can't fully inhabit two worlds at once. It's like a trance, I think you would say. Our senses leave this dimension—the one you and I are in right now—but our bodies remain. But in the other dimension we can stretch our perception and consciousness with the extended body of all that we enter."

Roal's low-lidded eyes remained motionless with thinly checked irritation as he stared at a root over Winter's head. Chet's warning repeated itself in his mind: Winter was efficient. And not well. And he'd had ten years to craft the language of his purpose. A decade after that last interview, and Winter still believed he was present in the stars but could answer for the trees. Roal waited.

Winter continued, "Right now Dina's body is not far from here, but Dina herself is spread out among the root systems and mycelia and whatever is preparing to grow above them. She's dispersed and expanding. We might be able to call her back in a while. It's hard to explain because it's not exactly the way we're used to experiencing ourselves. Or what we're truly capable of. And I should mention for the record that Dina isn't here to have a relationship with me. She's here because she can become, infinite—and be received. It's . . . it's hard to explain."

Roal rolled his eyes at the understatement.

"So she's close?" Roal clarified.

"Her body, yes." Winter's voice was patient. Even generous. "But Dina herself is spread out, is proliferative. That's not exactly the word, but the concept seems fitting. But for our purposes it is best to keep in mind that form is emptiness, and emptiness is form. We will not find Dina when we reach her body because she herself is otherwise."

A chill ran its thumb down Roal's back, and for the first time, it occurred to him that Dina might not be alive. What Winter was describing was what they might expect to find in some shallow grave in the woods. Dina's body: *We will not find Dina when we reach her body. She is spread out among the root systems.* Roal ran his hand over his face as if to steady it in the company of horror. He heard the wind shift above them, and a small gust of needles swirled from the forest floor and rained against the shelter. The wind was picking up.

"So," Roal asked, "so I could go to see her body, then? And know for certain that she's, she's unharmed?" Winter looked at Roal with another sympathetic look, which Roal was beginning to understand as a condition of Winter's madness, the look awarded to Most Likely to Become the Saint of Butchers.

"Yes, of course." Winter assured. "I can take you to look at her body. But it might cause her to regather faster than might be prudent, to leave her current state before she's ready. If that happens, things could get unpredictable. Maybe unstable. But maybe not. I really don't know." Winter looked contemplative as he played through the possibilities of what might happen when they found Dina. As if he hadn't yet thought about the consequences, or he was suddenly aware that things could become less clear once the story was seen through someone else's eyes. Roal tread carefully.

"Listen, Winter, I traveled all the way here to find her, and I appreciate that you're being so . . . mindful. Thank you for that. But I don't really know you, and so far all I've had to go on is Lin's word that Dina was fine when she left. I need to be sure Dina's here by her own choice. I am counting on you to help me find her so we can talk." Roal's implication did not ask permission, but left the grace of its suggestion intact.

"And I will, Roal. I will. But the timing is important." Winter again weighed the pouch in his hands, thinking. He set it in his lap, and then looked at Roal with unfathomable kindness.

"Dina says you have studied Zen in your own way," Winter began, "So you should understand that when Dina is not available, it is because she is beyond—she is not gone, but has gone into the gone, into a gone which is beyond. Her form is emptiness without sensation or perception. What can be seen is not seeing, and what can be heard is not hearing. Right now, Dina is seeing and hearing, but not according to what can be seen or heard, and if you see her now, you would not be looking at her. She no longer resides in her awareness."

"Okay, that's fine. Let's go have a look." Roal did not try to appear impressed by Winter's explanation. He wanted to see Dina. That was all. But Winter's seated stillness suggested no move toward the small opening. Instead, Winter watched Roal, and then began to speak once he seemed to have determined that Roal was ready to hear what he would say.

"Roal," he said, "Dina no longer considers herself in your service. When she decided to stay here, she was clear: she considered her debt to you paid." Roal began to protest, but Winter continued, holding up his hand to silence Roal.

"I know. There was no debt. At least, not one you were aware of. But Dina felt you gave her a great gift, and she honored it until she felt it was complete. It's this awareness of freedom that has released her from relating one causality of loyalty to another. She has allowed the walls to disappear, which has affected the range of her generative abilities. That's what you hear when the trees fall: that the forest has accepted that new growth is a life-giving possibility rather than something which promises their destruction. The forest is allowing its old self to fall away so there will be room for new growth. It is important to recognize that Dina is not the same person as a week ago. Or even a day ago."

Roal shivered in the cave. He heard what Winter was saying, but his mind replayed years of his marriage, looking for evidence that he had expected to be owed. He found nothing specific and didn't know what to say into the sound of the wind tearing through the branches above them. The forest overhead was dead and only dead, though Winter spoke of it as though the life was evident. The meadow Roal had seen was not evidence of anything except a meadow. Whatever Winter had done with Dina, it seemed clear to Roal that Winter was trying to prolong the discussion, to put off going to look for her.

Winter's explanations about Dina increasingly rang the high-pitched bell of Roal's skepticism. As a professor, he had heard hundreds of excuses that asked him to believe or not believe one thing in order to explain another, and what he had learned was that true stories didn't include many details, though the false ones did as a matter of habit: *I was gone last week because my mother booked a surprise flight for our whole family to go to Tobago to celebrate my sister's recovery from cancer and there was no internet there so I couldn't contact you.* True stories did not build themselves on elaborate defenses that implicated others: *My paper was impounded in my friend's car, and I didn't save it on computer, and the copy in the car is my only copy and impound can't release the car until next week.* And true stories did not gather more stories to themselves to corroborate the first one: *I couldn't read the book because my roommate loaned it to his girlfriend—who really loved it, you should ask her—but she loaned it to her manager, but can't ask for it back yet because she doesn't want to look like a flake and lose her job—you can call her boss if you need to, but she thinks she can get the book back in a week.*

Winter's efforts to keep Roal from seeing Dina were suspicious: Dina is not present in her body; Dina no longer owes you a debt; Dina is not the same person—and all of it under the pretext of Roal's old Zen philosophy, lifted as if to convince him to accept her new form as emptiness, her new perception as uncoupled from awareness. He found Winter's knowledge that Roal had practiced Zen unsettling, Winter's pathology now including the fact that he had gleaned information from Dina about Roal so he could better fashion his arguments when Roal showed up. Though Dina could not yet know that Roal had abandoned Zen, which made Roal feel a sudden warmth of gratitude to Lin. He now understood that Lin had done him a favor by accusing him of being an imposter. If she hadn't, Winter's strategy might have worked. Roal held this information to himself: it made him feel hopeful to know another thing that Winter did not.

Roal backed toward the opening. He was ready to work a search that spiraled out from the mouth of the dugout, calling in a loud voice again and again for Dina, a tactic that, if the man with the camera was real and present, would certainly attract attention. Then the man with the camera would get his evidence. Roal would need those pictures to exist in case he did not escape to tell the world. As long as that man was in the woods Roal was not abandoned. He turned to crawl out.

"One last thing, Roal." Winter called. Roal paused and listened without turning around. "Here—you should have these. Dina left them behind when she made her choice. I think they will be useful to your understanding. She has cut her ties to the world that held her bound before." Roal turned around to see Winter tip the leather pouch, which spilled out long loops of bright, coiling gold into Winter's open hand: braids, Dina's braids, which now hung from Winter's fingers like a ruined offering, a late song of severed loss.

CHAPTER 21

When Roal launched himself at Winter, he aimed the entire focus of his body at the neck, where he tried to squeeze from Winter anything that could explain why Winter had poured Dina's hair into his hands as though any man could touch it and not weep.

Roal pinned Winter with his weight, but Winter's body neither answered nor resisted. He lay under Roal with his eyes closed, his body slack, allowing the breath Roal pressed from his lungs to be replaced by the force of Roal's weight. He lay still as Roal demanded an answer, a location, a reason why and why and why. He would squeeze it from Winter's throat, get an answer from the last breath. He pressed and pressed and watched as the expression on Winter's face faded from surprise to surrender, and then to something Roal could not read: an emptiness or sadness without end. Roal pressed still more, afraid of letting go because he knew that if he allowed Winter to recover enough to stand, Roal would lose.

Winter sagged under Roal's hands, his body a sack that emptied itself into the ground below. His eyes were closed, his mouth open with an awful darkness. Roal loosened his hands, suddenly afraid of what was too late, of what had happened by his own hands. He stared at his hands, then at Winter, wondering what to do next. Over him, the air breathed heavily, the forest groaning in unison as it moved through faster than it could flex and adjust. Roal's heart thudded so hard it seemed to ripple the ground under him, the air around him, and he understood that in the valley of guilt and reckoning there was also the desperation of choices made tight and impossible by a single moment that threatened to become the entire story.

Roal held his head in his hands for a moment. He would need to find Dina, if he could. If she was able to answer. Otherwise he would need to mark a path out of the woods and return later with authorities and dogs. He could do it. He would have to. Again the ground stirred as if it were taking in a giant breath, though this time Roal knew the sensation did not correlate to the pounding of his heart. It resided outside of him, and then he heard a deep breath, Winter's breath. Roal yanked his hands from his face, prepared to defend himself, though there was no threat from Winter. Instead, Winter remained lying in front of him, relaxed and enjoying a deep breath which seemed to allow him to open his eyes. Roal trembled in the territory of his gaze: he could not try to kill Winter twice.

Winter turned his head to seek out Roal's face and smiled. It was a smile of unendurable forgiveness and apology, the sweet ache of which Roal did not have time to appreciate as the ground around them began to warp and quake, the dirt walls of the dugout shifting apart as the giant tree whose roots tangled near Roal and Winter's heads tipped over, pulling its roots with it like a tablecloth trick gone horribly wrong, a trick that reveals the tablecloth was attached to the building's only buttress. The dugout's shambled roof of sticks and fir needles lifted like a lid, then dropped down in a thick sift of dirt while the walls caved in and Roal and Winter were swept up over the edge by the massive thrust of roots as the giant tree above them groaned and crashed through the surrounding trees, their dry branches snapping as the tree's dreadful fall scraped the limbs from their trunks.

When the tree hit the ground, Roal felt the echo of its body against the earth fill his chest, then pull itself back into a grain-sized fist, taking the air from his lungs with it before the waves of its falling again rippled out, rippled from his heart to his lungs, and from there to his arms and legs, to his head which throbbed with the rise and scatter of each speck of dust, which he understood to be as necessary as each cell of his own body, all of it charged with and saturated by treefall, the enormity of its haul dragging a heavy undertow which swept through and over him.

When he at last opened his mouth to breathe deeply, he coughed and gagged on the still-sifting dirt he sucked into his mouth and lungs. When he was finally able to drag himself onto his hands and knees, he shook the dirt from his hair and face, watching as it sifted down past his face where the sun caught and held the dust, lighting it briefly before it filtered out of light's reach. Roal too felt himself held by the sun and wondered if he was like the dust: an object shaken free into the sun, where the sun might hold him for some time before he was given back to the ground. His pink shirt glowed like sunrise.

He still had one of Dina's braids wound around his hand, and when he went to wipe his face, the braid was cool and soft against his skin, like a chord played by water, though more distant. He would find her.

He stood up and bellowed Dina's name, calling again as he rubbed the dust from his face, and again as he blinked and coughed, and still again after he pressed his forehead into his hands and held it there, the braid against his brow. How often he had wanted to hold Dina's braids in his hands again. He remembered the last time he had taken the pins out of her hair, the time she was shivering with the flu and wanted to go to bed, but couldn't undo her braids because it hurt her arms to raise them. Roal had eased the hairpins out one by one and set them on the dresser in her room. If she'd been standing, the braids would have nearly reached her knees. He helped her into bed, and she rolled onto her side and curled up, her cheeks feverbright. Roal backed out of the room. That had been over seven years ago. He lifted Dina's braid to his face again and tried to remember what they had smelled like before they had been stored in a leather bag and covered with forest silt.

Winter was watching him from a few yards away. Roal called Dina's name again, his eyes on Winter as he allowed his voice to open up and expand into the echoless woods.

"Trust me," Winter stated. "It is unlikely she will hear you, despite what just happened." Winter's smile was gentle and expectant, as though he understood that it would hurt Roal to hear what Winter intended for him to understand. Roal did not know how to answer that smile, did not know what to do now that they were both standing where the wind seemed to threaten the branches overhead. The dead forest was falling to the wind's surges and gusts.

"Despite what just happened?" Roal repeated. Then asked, "What did just happen?"

Roal tried to replay the events for himself, but they had happened too quickly for him to know which details were central to the story and which were peripheral: was the image of his hands around Winter's throat major or minor? Did the feeling of his heart surging into his own throat matter as much as the dirt beginning to tremble before it crumbled from the walls?

He recalled the slow motion of the walls caving in, of his hands on Winter's throat, of Winter's vacant slackness beneath him as Roal pressed his weight down. Of Winter's unspeakable smile. Of the roots sweeping the ground out from under him as they churned him onto the surface. Dust flecks a filtered glitter, the backpack sinking into the ground. He saw it all, but did not know how to assemble it whole, which details should be included.

"What happened. What happened." Winter deliberated as he thought it over while tapping his thigh. "Well," Winter decided, "I'd say that what happened is either that you received a warning or I received assistance. It's hard to know which. Maybe both."

"There was wind," Roal said.

"There is always wind," Winter replied.

Roal looked around, dazed but determined. "I want to see her."

"Okay. Let's go." Winter stood up, ready.

"Where?"

"That way." Winter looked Roal over carefully. "Are you okay?"

"I'm, I'm sorry. I thought I . . . I thought you were dead. When you weren't moving. I didn't mean to kill you." Roal spoke down to the ground, imagining what would happen if he had killed Winter Patent.

"No. I wasn't dead. I just wasn't present. I was in the across, the beyond. When I become consciousness, I am not separate from the entering. I don't think you could kill me here. And I don't think you should try—for your own sake. This is where I live." Winter gestured to include the trees and the forest floor, then looked back at Roal with as expression of a helpless host.

"But where did you get Dina's braids?" Roal asked. "She would never cut them off."

"But she did. She did cut them off. She used a knife."

"But why would she? She's never cut her hair in her life." Roal's insistence felt right. He insisted because Dina herself had insisted that she could never cut her hair—it connected her to those gentle, unrushed hands of her mother, hands that brushed and braided Dina's hair as the yellow sun broke over the horizon of their mornings.

Roal insisted because other women cut their hair, shook their heads to show how the new cut made shining waves that lit their necks and gave them back their girlhood smiles: shy, flirtatious, aware, but Dina was not like other women and they held her slightly outside of their spheres as they compared hairdressers and styles and what they might try next.

He insisted because he would now have to do this task without Dina's hair, and he was suddenly terrified that he might not know her, had never known her, would not know how to engage her if she was not the same person she had been before.

He had thought his life without Dina could become manageable, had believed it for a moment, though now that Dina was new and unimaginable, the idea of life without her was something else altogether. It would now be a life without a person he had never known but had been within reach, and it was the promise of that other person which called to him sharply and seemed to suggest that the loss of her—the person he had not yet met—was to be felt more deeply than the loss of the person he had known for so long.

Roal searched Winter's face as if waiting for Winter to admit that Roal must be right after all, Dina would never cut her hair. Though Winter said nothing.

"Are you ready, then?" Winter finally asked. He sounded tired, and his face looked dimmed though he sat in the light. Roal hoped it wasn't an effect from nearly choking to death. Or not a permanent one, anyway.

"Is she 'available'?" Roal asked, immediately regretting his tone. Why challenge Winter just as he was about to deliver the very thing Roal most desired?

"I don't know," Winter answered. "But you seem intent to find out, and it seems foolish to convince you when you are intent on attaching your understanding to yourself. And, really," Winter warned, "don't try anything aggressive—everything is on alert right now. We don't want a repeat of that." Winter looked as if he were on a stage and the audience was clapping. The trees remained quiet, doing apparently nothing to earn such regard. Roal was afraid.

"What made that tree fall?" Roal asked as Winter began walking. "I mean, I know it's dead and the roots are old, so it probably broke off in the wind?" Winter's weathered face brightened. Roal hustled to catch up.

"No. That tree didn't break off at the roots. The roots came too. They practically pulled us from that hole. You were there—you saw." Winter guided Roal around a mound of scratched up forest floor.

"Cougar sign there. Fresh, too. Look," Winter pointed to a recent scrape, a pile of needles and bark, a wet odor Winter read with his nose. Winter reflected to himself, "Strange. There's nothing here for them. No deer in this forest for years. Maybe for squirrels?" Winter scanned the area. Roal shrugged. He needed to get back to what happened to the tree, to what had made it happen so he could identify it next time before he got too close to the roots of a tree that was about to go.

"But maybe the root base wasn't wide enough to support it anymore? Or the tree was too top heavy. Or, or. . . ." Roal looked to Winter, who seemed to sift and flicker through the trees as he walked, his shifts into disappearance and back like an attitude of movement.

". . . Or maybe," Winter suggested coolly, "the tree was faced with the choice of you or me, which for the trees is the same choice of giving up their will to live or defending it. And the tree chose me. It decided on growth."

Roal thought about this, tried to enter into the way Winter saw the world, though understood mainly that Winter was suggesting that the tree had fallen over because it willed itself to do so.

"You think the tree did it on purpose?"

"That's what we're here for!" Winter exclaimed, relieved that Roal finally understood. "To help the forest express its will, to make a choice about its own life without fearing that life is just a precursor to a future harvest."

"So," Roal said slowly, "if you mean that the tree chose to save you, and Dina is controlling the trees, then that means Dina chose you over me."

"Not at all," Winter assured. "Dina is not here to exercise her will. The trees are not a tool for our will. Dina is merely within and among, indistinguishable from all else. She is available to the trauma that the forest is blocking and can help to clear those blockages, but only if that is the true will of the forest. As long as blockage remains, the forest will be stuck in the tragedy of its own demise."

Roal found Winter's calm certainties more unsettling than the pitched and delirious accusations Lin had leveled at him.

"But what if you're wrong, Winter? What if none of it's true? What will Dina be left with when she finds out it's all empty—all some crazy promise you're telling yourself because you don't know how to fit in any more?" *Like Zen*, Roal thought. What did he have now?

"Think about it." Winter paused, waiting for Roal to think, though Roal did not know what to think about. "You were there—why would that specific tree fall at that exact moment unless it made a decision? Prior to you trying to choke me, it had no signs of instability. From my point of view, it's a very good sign that these trees are falling—it means the forest understands that a future of growth will not be a form of suicide for it. I know. I have lived in forests for years. I know. That tree fell to clear a way for new growth. It is understanding growth as a condition of what is necessary, of intrinsic expression which is not negating. One that needs me. And Dina."

Winter's piercing look challenged Roal, though Roal only nodded stiffly, the old scuttling crawl of disbelief and fear back on his belly. Dina alive. Dina dead. Roal had heard of parents who knew without having to be told that their child had died. They felt it in their guts that a cord between them was severed by death. Roal wondered if that was what his feeling of horror was: that empty feeling of Dina no longer be in the world. If Winter took Roal to her body, Roal would have to play along, to allow himself to enter the madness of seeing what Winter saw until he could find his car and escape. He did not ask Winter to clarify. He did not challenge the logic. There was no point. Winter walked and Roal walked next to him.

Even if Roal did challenge Winter, whatever Winter said would reinforce the validity of his mind's madness. No different, Roal reflected, than the story Roal had told himself of his adequate marriage, his wife's unremarkable life, his devotion to Zen. Winter was doing it too—telling the story he needed to believe so he could continue being the person he had created. There was no answer Winter could give that would be sensible in the woods. Winter and Roal picked a winding route through clear patches of forest floor. They were officially in the open. Roal felt hopeful that the man with the camera might be somewhere close, the focus tightening. Just as Roal thought this, Winter looked around again, sniffing the air, and Roal nearly gasped in fear that Winter smelled his thoughts of betrayal.

"Do you smell that?" Winter asked. Roal breathed in attentively, but smelled nothing. Winter grunted and walked on, looking about alertly.

From where Roal stood, the world of Winter was fragile and thin, a reality that depended on Winter living alone lest it crumble in the company of others who would contradict that vision by not being able to see it too. Though Dina was with Winter. She had stayed.

They stopped walking and Winter sighed.

"Well, here we are. But we will have to wait." Roal followed Winter's gaze: on the ground just ten feet away at the edge of a clearing, barely visible in her bark-colored clothing, lay Dina, unmoving, her face distant as a stone in shadow. Roal cried out and rushed to her, kneeling next to her and pressing his head to her chest. He sat back in amazement.

In a relief that shook him, his heart gave a consolatory heave. Dina's chest was a slight rise and fall of breath, and her hands lay at her sides. She was asleep, a shadow across her face. And so small within the large house of the woods. Without her hair she looked boyish and playful, her face unaware that time leaves tracks. The muscles of the person she had projected herself as had let go, revealing a face underneath that seemed to hold a more accurate self. Those muscles did not seem held by who the world saw her as, but the truer fact of who Dina was. Patient, alert, abandoned.

CHAPTER 22

"Dina?" Roal's whisper trembled in his chest before he spoke it. He reached to wake her, to feel her bones to make sure she was whole and unbroken. Winter placed his hand on Roal's shoulder.

"Please, don't. She isn't really there yet." Roal shrugged Winter's hand away roughly and leaned close to Dina.

"Dina? It's me, Roal. Are you there? Can you hear me?" Dina's breath pulled in and out, an easy exchange between herself and the world. Roal smoothed a chopped strand of hair from her forehead.

"Please, don't touch her. It might disturb the process. She's just not there right now. You're not touching Dina—you're just touching your own recognition of Dina. But now you know she's fine. We can come back later." Winter backed up, gesturing for Roal to follow.

Roal dismissed Winter, "You go. This is Dina. I know. But she's not answering. She needs water or something. Dina, I'm here. Everything will be okay." But still she did not answer: not a flutter of eyelid, not a quickened breath. Roal felt a panic rising. She could not hear him, and the trail of wrapper strips leading back to the car had been collected and handed to him. He did not know how to leave to bring her help, if he could find her again if he did get out. Roal placed his hand on her forehead. It did not feel hot. Roal realized that the darkness of her face was not a shadowed darkness. Her face was a clayish gray, and her hair shone silverbright against it. A gust of wind riffled through, and Roal cleared dust from his eyes.

"Her face is gray. What's wrong with her?" Roal's question was offered over his shoulder, though he didn't take his eyes off Dina. Winter walked over and looked down at Dina, nodding in an unconcerned, scholarly agreement.

"I don't know for sure. I suspect it has to do with making ourselves available to other dimensions, other forms of being. When our basic capacities for understanding what it means to inhabit space and time radically shift, I think there are consequences for our outer forms. I mean, by shifting how we inhabit dimension, we must also be shifting a base level of our composition. But there's no need to worry."

"I'll decide." Roal put one arm under Dina and began to lift her onto his lap. A tremor passed under him, and in the distance he heard the groaning fall of a tree, then another. He froze, waiting to see if the same heaving wrench of earth would happen nearby as it had in Winter's shelter. The ground smoothed itself again, and the forest returned to windy silence.

"Put her down, Roal. This is a serious warning. You have to understand this or it could get you killed. If the forest wants to live, it will not let her go—not when she has committed herself to it. The decision to wake has to be hers. She must be free to come and go from that world. If you remove her body you will be removing her choice to return. The forest will not allow it." The wind pushed trough the forest as a wall, and branches snapped fell in its wake. Winter nodded as if to indicate his point had been proven.

"It's just wind, Winter. It's just a crazy story you're telling yourself about coincidence to make you feel important. This forest looks like shit. You're not helping it. It's just wind!" Roal held Dina in his lap. He'd forgotten how small she was. Winter didn't appear to be listening.

Winter was sniffing the air intently. He caught a scent and suddenly his eyes narrowed and his body was rigid and alert. He smiled with what Roal found a chilling anticipation, then slowly turned his head until he was looking in the opposite direction. He scanned the woods beyond, his nose twitching.

"Something is happening, Roal." Winter cautioned, "I'm not sure what yet. But put her down." The wind pitched its tent of agreement over them.

Roal cradled Dina in one arm as he smoothed her hair and brushed flecks of dirt from her face. He felt it: he loved her. Right then, he loved her and knew it. He cupped her face with his hand and pressed her to his chest as one of her arms dangled and her impassive face revealed nothing except dismissal from the world he held her to. When he loosened his hold on her, she took a deep breath to fill the air he had pressed from her in his embrace. The forest again trembled at the edge of his vision, seemed to retract and waver slightly, and then began to rumble. Though this time he felt a low breeze, a warmer one that seemed to run under the cooler wind that scraped at the branches above. He could not determine the agency of the forest's grumbling. Bark and small branches began to rain from the branch tips of the trees, and then the branch snaps of falling limbs. And then, silence, deep and thorough as a cliff drop of darkness in the ear.

"That's a warning, Roal. You have to put her down. If you give her time, she'll be back. Just wait—please. For your own good." Winter was pleading. Roal looked at Dina. She was not there. He laid her back on the ground, but stayed next to her, his arm across her so he could stroke her arm, keep dirt off her face.

"I want to talk to her, Winter. Alone. Leave me alone so I can talk."

"She can't hear you."

"I don't care. I probably need to say more than she needs to hear anyway. Give me a few minutes." Winter nodded and faded into the forest in the direction of the scent he had located. When Roal sensed they were alone, he cleared his throat gently, and began. His voice was a stranger to his throat.

"Dina. Can you hear me?" Roal tested in a whisper, then looked around to make sure they were alone. "Dina, Winter isn't here now—let me know if you're in danger." Nothing. "Dina, can you hear me?" Again nothing. "Okay. It's okay if you can't. I didn't hear you either. I'm sorry." Roal wiped his eyes, looked around to see if Winter was lurking anywhere nearby, but saw nothing. "Dina, did you tell Winter you paid your debt to me? What debt? I never said you owed me. You didn't owe me. I love you. I'm sorry." The skin over Dina's forehead was so thin and pale Roal could see a blue vein pulse in her forehead. He couldn't remember if her skin had always looked so translucent in the half-light of flickering shadows.

He watched her lie there. The still standing red trees swayed stiffly for as far as he could see or hear. Their groaning reminded Roal of leather saddles and he imagined the trees being ridden by the wind. Dina's breaths were steady. Not labored, not sharp. Roal watched her, uncertain of what should happen next. He began to talk.

He admitted to Dina he didn't know what would happen next. He told her he didn't know how much he could trust Winter, though suspected not much. His voice felt notched and rough, unsteady. But the more he talked the more it smoothed itself out. He lay back and kept talking, telling her whatever he could think of just to keep saying something.

The falling trees had left him shaken and scared. He was afraid of the forest, afraid a wind might come up and bury them all or, worse, if he left Dina there, might fall on her when he could have prevented it. He was afraid he might not find his way back to the car, though was happy at least to still have the keys in his pocket. His clothes were a wreck. He was afraid of her without her hair and wondered what she would be like without it. Now that she was unable to hear him, unable to respond, he talked into her absence with the part of himself he had withheld from her. He admitted that he understood the irony, but he would go ahead anyway. He wanted to tell her everything.

He wanted to go get help, but didn't think Winter would let him go unless he pretended to believe the story. He said he wasn't sure he could be convincing. Before, he would have thought he could convince Winter, but he understood now that others saw through him more easily than he saw through himself. He found himself enjoying lying next to Dina as he talked into the air. He opened himself into it.

He told her what had happened on campus with the cougar, the story that had spiraled out of control about Dina being ill and Roal's support of her decision to die alone in the woods. He told her he was wearing the shirt Jill gave him, pink and clever about stopping the war, and he meandered on to wondering what the walk for a cure would be like with the entire campus spilled out over the sidewalks just after graduation and Roal as a false hero. He wondered how much of anyone's life is available for anyone else to under-stand, and speculated that maybe each person's life is nothing more than the story they tell themselves about how life is supposed to work. Roal admitted his story had been too simple. He had allowed himself to be too simple and had also allowed himself to see Dina that way. Worse, he had needed her to be that way for him. He understood it was too late. He would need to start over and Dina wouldn't be back. He couldn't ask that of her. He wanted her to know that.

He went on. There was so much to say, now that he was talking to the air and the trees were standing up reliably the way they should. He talked until he understood he was just talking in order not to have to stop because he knew that when he did stop, that would be the end. There would be nothing more to say and no reason left to start.

He wondered aloud what it would be like to eat alone, shared with her the happiness of Gary and Jill's boys as they wore shirts they detested and jumped into the picture glad to be a part of it. He told her Chet seemed unsurprised by it all, as if it was good to finally see that things were taking their natural course. Roal wondered who else had seen it when he could not. He told her about going through her office, the dedications and acknowledgments to her, how embarrassed he was to not want that part of her to exist so he wouldn't have to apologize for having denied it. He explained how he had tried to imagine her in a room alone and how he had failed to summon her whole unless he too was present. He understood. He got it. He trailed off.

He wanted to know what it was like to disappear from the body. He had carried his body in front of him like a permission slip his entire life. To disappear from it would be to stop existing. He closed his eyes and saw the tendril roots of his eyelids' veins. Dina flickered next to him, her arm against his. The trees seemed to release warm air, and it poured in over Roal. Dina shifted her weight. She rolled her body to the side, away from him, and Roal turned as well, toward her, and swung his arm over her and held her to him, her back pressed to him as he held his breath and allowed it to be the last time. Knowing it was made him wish it could be forever.

"Roal." Dina named him, and he felt received. He wanted to thank her for knowing his name first.

"Dina—you're back."

"You came." Dina rolled onto her back and looked at him, their faces nearly pressed together.

"Yes." Roal glanced over his shoulder to see if Winter was nearby. He saw nothing and lowered his voice. "Yes. Are you okay? Please, tell me if you're in danger—Winter can't hear you. It will be okay." Dina smiled from a distance.

"No. There's no danger, just possibility. I think I'm . . . happy." Her calm gaze held him.

"Then tell me—did you make a tree fall over to protect Winter?"

Dina looked curiously at Roal. "Why did Winter need protection?"

"We had a misunderstanding. He showed me your braids and I thought something was wrong. But mostly, mostly, I'm here, and I'm sorry." They breathed in and out, their breaths matched and close in the midst of much to say.

"Thank you for coming." Dina looked up into the trees. "When I came with Lin, I hadn't known it would be to stay. I hadn't on planned it. I mean, I was planning something. I thought something would come up, I just hadn't expected it would be so soon. Or this. But then I came here, and this is it. This is for me."

"I love you." Roal said. It had just slipped out. "I mean, I know you won't be back. That I won't ask for that." Roal lamented, "I don't know what I mean. I haven't earned my life. Until now—I think this new life is probably one I've earned."

Dina sat up. She reached up to pat her braids the way he always did, but her surprised hands ended up sweeping through her short hair and shaking out the fir needles and bark flecks. "I have to get used to that—my hands remind me of what my habit forgets."

"Did you really cut them off?"

"I did."

"I didn't know if you were still alive when Winter showed me your braids. I thought something terrible had happened."

"No. Just something new. I stopped missing my mother. I missed her my whole life. People used to tell me I missed the idea of her because I had been too young to know her, but I missed her. All the time. And you—I missed you when we were together. But not now. It's okay now." Dina's smile for

Roal did not hide anything inside of it. It was content and whole. And that was all. Roal felt himself receding. In the distance a tree crashed to the ground.

"Was that you? Are you making that happen?" he asked. "I don't understand the project."

"No. I never make it happen. I just help to process blockages. Then they sort of decide. I think. It's hard to explain." She looked puzzled, as if it hadn't occurred to her before that what she was doing required a language. "You know, the forest itself already has momentum, so it could be that trees are falling because a larger decision has been made. Or Winter. Or the wind. I don't know. Winter might be in there now. I'll need to go back soon too. There is a lot to do."

The comment reminded Roal of Dina's other work, the work he had discovered in her office. He confessed to opening her mail and going through her office. He flinched when another tree began to moan and splinter, and waited for the fall. "Are you angry? Did you do that?"

Dina's laugh was gentle, a mother's laugh for a child when explaining that she did not make the world. "No—I'm fully here. With you. And I can't 'make' anything happen. I just make myself available without perception, without limitation. I can't use the forest as a vehicle for my own will. It doesn't work that way."

"Winter said you work with trauma. You help process it. Doesn't it hurt? It sounds . . . painful. I guess. If it's even real. I don't know, Dina. Does it affect you?"

"I suppose. But it isn't painful. Without judgment, the framework of the past disappears. And so does causality," Dina explained. Roal waited to see if there was more, something to work with to get to the next place. Dina continued, "Anyway, it's not like I have to relive the events that caused the trauma. But the trees do until it's resolved. So that's what I do." Then she added, "And I don't mind that you went through my office. I cleaned up everything before I left. There's only one thing left."

"Matthew Ulysses Chafee?"

"That's it," she said, surprised.

"His letter said he wants you to help him with his book after all. What should I tell him?"

"Just send him back his manuscript. It's already done." Now Dina's smile did hide something. Perhaps that she was pleased to see Roal was perplexed at this.

"But you hadn't gotten his package yet."

"I know. But they don't gather all that information for me. They do it for themselves. They have to send it into the world to practice letting go of it. I finished my comments on his book months ago. But he wasn't really ready to release his secrets. He wouldn't be able to make it better until he could reveal whatever it will take to improve it. Just return the manuscript to him with my comments on it. No letter, no fee. Give it a week and mail it back. And thank you. It is good to be done with that." Another tree fell, but Dina continued through the branch-stripping noise of its descent, "Be sure to send it, okay? It's terrible to be kept waiting for something that never arrives."

Roal considered this, but could not meet her eyes. The air seemed cooler, the bite of the breeze a bit sharper than before.

The trees groaned in their rigid swaying, branches rasping at the sky.

Dina fretted, "This is strange."

"The wind?" Roal asked.

"No. Though this wind is unpredictable. Just that the trees are letting go differently. I don't know how to explain it. " She looked at Roal, alarmed, as another tree fell. "I am going now, Roal. And you need to let me, for yourself. I thank you for the story you wrote for me all those years ago. It changed my life. I love you."

Roal reached out to hold her, afraid to speak, afraid that if he opened his mouth it would be to ask her to come back, though he also knew he would only be asking because he did not know what else to say, not because he wanted to be responsible for the answer. But he did open his mouth. He had to say something.

"Dina, I made it here." And he held her the last time as another tree fell in on the others, taking their branches with it.

Winter came running back into the clearing, hissing at Roal, "I told you. Let go of her. Let go! Don't you see?"

Dina held up her hand to Winter, then settled back onto the ground at the base of a tree. "It's not him, Winter," she called. "It's something else. We thought it was you. I'm going in. There might be something else going on. Roal, as long as you carry me in yourself, you will not be empty, and you will not be filled. Thank you for coming. And for letting it just be that." Dina closed her eyes and her face settled, and she was gone.

Roal watched, astounded. She had been in front of him, her eyes expressive, her face animated and generous, and then, a vacancy so blank it was like she had fallen through the trapdoor of herself.

The air overhead throbbed slightly. Roal held his heart to see if the throbbing came from inside. Winter looked to the distance, sniffing. His face turned from side to side, then snapped to face a single, sudden direction, as if caught by a hook at the end of a tightening line.

"Find cover," he growled, his eyes narrow. He turned to Roal, "Someone else is here. I'll see if anything needs to be done." Winter took two leaping steps and disappeared.

Roal stood alone in the forest. Dina was gone, having dived down into whatever system would return her complete to the broken world around her. She stirred briefly on the ground, fluttered her eyelids.

"There is a man. He is staying close to the trees. He seems near." And again she disappeared, back inside of the world that would not allow her release until she sought it.

Roal hesitated: the man with the camera. He was there in the forest with them. Roal had hoped for the man to appear, though that was before he had found Dina alive and determined to complete her own project. All the man had wanted was a picture, a betrayal of one person from another. Roal believed he could have arranged for this if it had involved only Winter. But now that he knew Dina was unharmed, the man was a threat. He would expose the forest and Winter, bring in the scientists who would cut and measure. Dina's project would be over, and she might return home, knowing it was Roal who had seen to it that the project should fail. Roal couldn't believe he had bellowed for Dina like a bull signaling its rut. Winter was nowhere to be seen. Dina's eyes flickered, aware again on Roal's side of the world. Roal wanted to hide, but that would leave Dina alone on the clearing. She moved again, then took a deep breath as if heaving herself over the edge of Roal's world.

"Something is following the man. Get a branch. But move slowly. It is moving stealthily—stalking him, getting ready to pounce. I can feel it." And again she dove back under.

Roal heard, then saw, in the distance another tree fall, then another, like a terrible game of dominos, while the push and pull of Roal's heart pulsed in his fingertips and across his forehead. Roal considered moving slowly toward cover, toward a thick branch that lay at the edge of Dina's clearing, though he felt compelled to stay close to Dina, to keep his eyes on her as she lay exposed in a falling forest.

He cautiously circled the area and picked up a stick, then returned to Dina and waited. He did not know for what. The throbbing of his heart swallowed the sounds of his footsteps, the sounds of the breeze. Winter was gone and would not be back to save him from whatever kept pulling Dina from her world within. Roal looked again at Dina, and hoped Winter could save himself. Dina needed him.

At the place of the falling trees, a trembling anticipation rose like heat waves, and his heart's noise receded until he could hear through it to the forest's held breath of silence. It felt like it too was waiting. He stood over Dina, stick raised and ready to strike. The wind chilled his wet shirt. He realized he was sweating and breathing hard. He would need to stay calm. An image of the campus signs came to him: STAY CLEAR OF TREES AND SHRUBS. DO NOT TURN YOUR BACK OR RUN. TRY TO APPEAR AS LARGE AS POSSIBLE.

The next time the trees began to sway and creak, they were close enough that Roal could watch as their branches trembled, then the shaking accelerated as the wind whipped through snapping branches. One tree began to tilt and pivot from its position in the ground. Roal craned for a better view, but froze when he saw a person scuttle out from the base of the falling tree and then try to disappear behind another tree which, Roal could see even from the distance, was far too small to obscure the man.

The forest held its breath again. Silence, followed by the man's next shambling run to find cover behind a large tree. Roal stood transfixed, staring at the man, though he knew he was supposed to look away. Roal stepped quickly behind a nearby tree, his eyes moving from Dina to the man in the distance. The wind circled through the trees, kicking up dust and playing the branches like a broken instrument. In the distance, the wind seemed to shift the landscape until parts of it went sideways, one tree shedding its branches while the top of another sheared and dropped to the ground.

Roal looked down at Dina, impassive, nearly invisible on the forest floor, when another movement flickered just at the corner of his vision. When he tried to look at it directly, there was nothing. It had been a low something slinking along the ground. He strained to see the flicker of movement better, craning cautiously as he held his stick swing-ready, scanning the distances between himself and the tree he wanted to move to next. He moved from tree to tree clumsily but slowly, relieved the noise of his footfalls was swallowed by the forest noises as the wind raged overhead. He could feel it: something was going to happen. Was happening. He felt it as a throbbing against his chest, a throbbing that pressed in on his ears, that vibrated against his skin.

Again Roal pressed one hand to his chest, as if to quiet its rapid beating against him, though his hand felt only the steady, rhythm of a solid heart at work. There was no commotion there. The air pulsated with throbbing. And then Roal understood. It was not his chest. It was a helicopter.

So distant that he could not determine which direction it came from, but close enough that he could feel how the spinning of its blades changed the air, competed with the currents that blew through the trees. Roal heard the low thrumming of the chopper's wings recede. The sound of it seemed to be dipping in and backing off in a lazy pattern of back and forth. When Roal looked to the sky, he heard a shuffling sound along the forest floor and scanned the distance to find its source.

The man had crawled out from behind the tree, his body ducked low as if to shield it from the rain of branches he had begun to expect. But the trees remained still. Stooping low and ducking through open spaces, the man began to make his slow way toward Dina's clearing, so cautious in the open spaces it appeared he was afraid of being betrayed by the air. Though Roal still wore his bright shirt, he wasn't sure whether the man could see him from where Roal stood behind a screen of thin trees that had been pressed together by a fallen giant.

Still a few hundred feet away, the man slunk toward Dina's clearing. He moved awkwardly, like an injured animal, crawling on two legs and first the left arm then the right, as he passed the camera he carried from hand to hand. He stopped to hold the camera up, and Roal caught the lens glint as it swept methodically over the clearing, pausing each time the shutter clicked. Then suddenly the camera made a wide swing and pointed straight at Roal, aggressively pinning him in its view. Roal closed his eyes to erase the world, opened them again and the world was still there, though sneaking closer, the man now within easy calling distance, close enough that Roal could see to which side he parted his hair. The man's face was a moon shining at Roal, only Roal as he crept forward.

Shadows played at the edges of where Roal knew to focus. He debated waving, thought perhaps he should try to intercept the man halfway, perhaps to lead him in another direction, but then Roal saw another form and froze, his hands gripping the stick and eyes widening in horror. A golden cat with wide paws, huge, silent, ready, had stepped from behind the last tree the man had passed. It flicked its tail, lowered its shoulders, its golden eyes fixed on the man's hobbled, lurching crawl. The man kept scuttling forward, unaware as the cougar allowed a space to widen between them, allowed the man a bit of distance as the cougar's body sank low and measured the gap. And then it began to move, its trot accelerating until it became a lean ripple of muscle flowing like an amber purr over the forest floor. Roal's breath hitched and caught in his throat and he nearly had time to think about waving the man back, warning him, but the cougar was faster. It leapt clear of the ground and the front claws, bared and spread, fastened into the man's shoulder, gripped it, while its teeth buried themselves in the neck. And held. The back end of the cougar continued to swing through the air, the man becoming a toppling pivot point around which the cougar's body turned, and they spun once, the cougar's long dark tail whipping through the air, pulling the man off his feet, turning him all the way around easily as spinning a bottle toward a question. And then the man dropped down, the cougar atop him, and not another sound.

The camera was still flying its slow-motion arc through the air as they fell. Roal couldn't believe it had been so quiet, the transition into finality so silent and complete. There hadn't been so much as a cry of surprise or pain, or even a heavy thud as they dropped to the forest floor. If Roal had been looking the other way, he never would have known a man's life had just ended. It seemed like there should have been more to it—a shift in the light, a father running out from the edge of somewhere to cry and protest, an ambulance that pulled up and got to work. But it was just silence and the golden head of the cat bobbing back and forth as it licked the face and neck of its kill with a concentration that seemed both chillingly casual and incredibly tender. The body never moved again.

Roal backed closer to Dina, trying to appear large, though the cat paid no attention to him. Roal knew that the cat knew he was there. That it watched the entire area with every hair of its body attuned to the possibility of threat and fulfillment. Roal was nothing to the cougar. For now, anyway.

For now, Roal would stand over Dina until he could do so no longer, he would keep his eyes on the cougar until light or his wakefulness failed him. He would have to watch it eat, he realized. His skin buzzed and ached from the charge of what he had seen and continued to see. He felt a tingling in his hands and brain and his eyes didn't seem to be tracking right. He was suddenly exhausted and agitated, overwrought and starving. Dina lay whole and breathing easily near him and he settled into her breathing, his eyes on the cat.

The cat tilted its head, paused, and looked up. Roal heard it too: the chopper's blades were distant, but cutting closer to the clearing where Roal stood. The cougar rose warily and circled its kill. Then it swung its head to look directly at Roal, stopping with a stillness that pinned Roal to the air behind him. Then, its eyes still on Roal, it reached its head down and took the man's shoulder in its teeth. It dragged the body a few feet, then a few feet more until the cougar stood near a fallen tree's upturned roots where a giant hole of earth had been churned up at the base.

The beating of the chopper's wings on the air grew louder. Roal knew he was supposed to hide from the helicopter, hide Winter's site at any cost, but could not move from where he stood over Dina. If he ran, the cougar might follow. If he left Dina, the cougar might kill her next.

The air throbbed harder over him, the sound of the wings growing sharper. The cougar pressed itself to the ground, throwing looks in all directions, unable to detect the direction of the threat, and Roal raised his arms over his head. The cougar's attention snapped to Roal with a mere flicker of its eyes. Its gaze tightened a cord between them. It watched as if it sat on a throne of distant silence, waiting. And Roal knew that to beat the cougar he would have to become the source of the cat's uncertain fear.

While the helicopter hovered in the distance, Roal waved his arms and stepped toward the cougar, allowing himself to become the source of the chopper's wild drum on the air, a sound so large it sounded like the forest was ravenous and howling. Roal grew into it. He opened up his mouth and roared, the sound ripping his throat as he kept his arms held high and took giant, slow steps in the cougar's direction, growling and thundering as he went. The cougar looked from Roal to the sky, from Roal to its chances in the forest behind it. The cougar took a last look at Roal in his giant display of sky crushing madness, and then sprang suddenly backward and disappeared into the forest beyond. The body remained.

Roal was thinking too quickly to separate one idea from the next: he wanted to go home, find the car, smoke for the first time, wear better shoes, fix the screen, check the body's pulse, check his own, buy a jacket to keep out the wind, take an aspirin, tell Chet everything was fine in a voice that could mean it. These thoughts sprang from his mind in explosions, each one replaced by two others. The only thing he knew for sure as the thoughts escaped was the one thing which remained: the cougar had changed things.

The woods were dangerous and whether Dina liked it or not, he wanted her out of them at least until they were safe again. He stepped into the clearing, ready to wave his arms and be rescued.

Roal looked back to where Dina lay at the edge of the clearing "They're coming," he called. "Do you hear me? Everything's fine! I'll taking you home until it's safe, and you can come back later! But for now I'm taking you with me!" There was no response.

Roal positioned himself in the center of the clearing, The helicopter swayed and bobbed in the sky, still a ways away, perhaps too far away to see Roal from their angle. Roal flapped his arms over his head. At first he thought the rumbling of the ground under him was the air's chopping throb.

He jumped and waved, thinking the litter of bark and branches that burst from the trees around him was caused by the wind from the blades as they sliced through the sky. But the helicopter was still too far away for that.

It was not until Roal saw the trees around him shedding minor branches that he understood what was happening. Roal turned to look at Dina, but she was already covered by a thin layer of bark and small branches and lay nearly indistinguishable from the forest floor. The helicopter's noise grew, and Roal felt how the vibration was answered by the air in his lungs, which paused and released in the same staccato beat.

As Roal ran toward Dina so he could drag her into the clearing, a pressure of silence filled Roal's ears, the sound of a breath held until the last possible second before the desperate exhalation. And then the world around him exploded into a rain of branchfall and limbdrop: a tree at the edge of his vision suddenly swept down across him, its branches a jagged tangle that scraped him off his feet and trapped him inside of themselves.

The tree crashed into the ground, its trunk bouncing once, then releasing a series of tremors. It lay still.

The helicopter closed in over him, though Roal could not move to summon it closer. He wanted to whisper something to it. He had seen something in the forest. He was looking right at it. He lay suspended, his face a few inches from the ground as he hung from the center branches of the fallen tree.

The helicopter hovered and a voice called from the sky.

He heard it as a tumult of light throbbed out from his leg which had been put on wrong, and throbbed in his mind until his mind let it go, and then it filled his chest and erased him at the edges, and released him.

CHAPTER 23

In the place of light Roal stretched out his arms, though they had turned to a sediment so fine it sifted endlessly outward. When each particle was nearly out of sight of the others and Roal had thinned himself into the spread of atmosphere, he collected himself into a filament cord of particle and sift, a tendril of reaching that extended and then branched and branched again until he was a multitude of alveolate chambers, each one home to an atom pulsing against its edges.

The crystalline ringing of the chambers crumbled them again into a fine sift, and the atoms combined, then grew and moved outward. From there, the universe was invisible and expanding, was everywhere and attractant.

Those atoms joined with other atoms until there was one form, infinite and becoming.

Everness crushing and bright.

Roal looked for his own hands, and the universe began to contract, focusing him until he again took form and watched his arms pulling back toward him, his hands outstretched but closing as they neared his body. Pain sharpened itself on his ribs.

He heard them calling to him, from outside of his cage in the tree. Their voices felt like small hands patting his face and reminded him of Dina's description of her mother's hands in her hair: the voices were a memory and held him to their calling because it was the kind of holding he needed.

When the people got near to him and eased him out, he told them he had seen something in the forest. He had seen something real. He insisted. They patted him back into stillness.

Then Roal remembered and murmured *Cougar, cougar, the man*. But the officer with the sideburns said he already knew, he understood. Roal had met him before, but could not remember where. The officer said something too. They had found a cougar dead, near the body, and they found the body too: Mike Durango, known in the drug trade as The Insurance Agent.

Roal heard another voice: "Wonder if he had a policy for cougars."

And yet another officer answered: "He had a policy for everything: kill it and check the pockets." They all nodded in grim agreement.

Roal's head lolled to one side and he saw the body too, its face pale and clean, its sandy hair licked neatly to the side as if the cougar had been preparing it to arrive at the table for the dinner of itself, though the neck gaped open, the voice ripped clean away. The officer eased Roal's head back so he faced the sky.

Roal remembered Dina. *I came to find Dina,* he said.

"Where is she?" they asked.

She isn't here any more, he said. *She is gone. She is a gate. She is a boat. She can pass through.*

"It's terrible to have to say goodbye, sir. I'm so sorry for your loss." The officer adjusted a strap, and Roal remembered: the sideburns, Officer Sparks, the father of a boy who would be walking to find a cure for a world held together by cancer.

Roal slumped his head to the other side and squinted. The carpet of needles still lay lightly atop her, and she was nothing they would know how to see. He tried to explain, and the officer leaned in to hear him, *No, her form is now emptiness. She has no perception. It's what she wanted—to enter into the forest. It's her choice, and no one should take her out.* Officer Sparks soothed him, then looked around and told Roal in a low voice not to worry: they had come for Durango, and they had gotten their man. That was all they had come for, and now that they'd found him, that was enough.

The officer kept one hand on his shoulder as they slid him onto a board. And then Roal rose above himself, followed them as they carried him on the board. He felt himself rushing through a lattice work to connect to the next port of connection, and he glided along underground to the edge of the forest. Something happened there, a voice that granted him permission, and that was all.

He woke up again inside of himself and looked back at the forest as they slid him into the helicopter. A tree flickered and moved like a habit of light.

When he tried to focus on that tree, it became a bare strip of air, an attitude of light, and he knew it watched him. He fluttered his hand weakly though his arm was strapped to the board, but something fluttered back from the place of that absence, answering him the way one mirage would rise for another, and then disappearing as Roal focused in.

He closed his eyes and remembered how Helen had once assembled a skeleton for him from a paste of flour and water. *It might be that easy*, he thought. *Our bones could be made from anything.* And he slept.

CHAPTER 24

The letter the press received five days later was from Winter Patent, who had arranged with independent researchers to use noninvasive techniques to measure his results in a Canadian forest that he claimed to have helped restore. Roal knew it was one of Winter's earliest projects. Revealing the old location was Winter's way of diverting attention from the hunt for the current one. The newscaster already seemed bored by Winter's letter—she had covered him last week. It was tiresome that Winter was again seeking publicity for comparing the size of trees by wrapping a piece of string around each and then measuring the difference. Big deal. Time to move on: in fact, it was already coming up on graduation weekend, and the newscaster rushed through Winter's story in order not to be late for the extended forecast: unseasonably warm, with a chance of rain until the weekend, and then the skies were expected to clear.

Chet and Roal sat in Roal's bed watching the news, Chet holding the remote as Roal watched and reentered the stories that wrapped up but never ended, stories that began one after the other, breaking like waves against a shifting shore. The news never got to the actual conclusion, never returned to the scene weeks later to report on the outcome. Points of departure, Roal wrote down in the notebook of what he intended to tell his students next year: the news is good only as a point of departure to find the real story.

The world had kept moving during the days of Roal's absence. In the hospital, it changed—none of the news stories the same as those he'd left. He was almost grateful for the war in which the country fought bravely but no one could remember the reason for because at les tit was consistent. And, of course, the advertisements were still the same, still promising that happiness had a dimension, a weight, and a cost no one could afford to live without.

Since Malva, since the forest, since the days of sleep and pain as they set his leg and wrapped his bruised ribs and scanned his head for swelling, since the day of his return to the house and his settling in, the world had somehow become one which did not merit further mention of the stories he thought he'd cared so much about before he left.

Now the frogs in a local puddle just outside the town where the nerve gas was stored were showing up with five legs and two mouths.

Now the man whose wife gave him divorce papers was suing the city because the police hadn't allowed him back in to get his things, and he hadn't had enough time, he said, to take what belonged to him.

Now a daughter was released from her father's dungeon with children who saw the sun and winced.

Those stories ended, but Roal knew there was a different end which happened after the cameras left and would not be reported: unable to reproduce, the frogs would die while trying to breathe through malformed lungs, and eventually it would happen to the mammals too. The woman who told her husband to leave would remove her clothing carefully and stare at the bruises on her thighs and arms. The children would have to unlearn the fixed positions of the shadows they knew in order to understand the sun.

The story after each story was where the news should start, but because it did not, Roal understood that the next lines were his responsibility, and they could become whatever he would make of them. His own story would be aired shortly, and Roal looked forward to having it told so the world could forget it. The only stories the world wanted were the ones that hadn't been told yet. Though even as that story broke, everyone turned their attention to the one right after, forgetting what they'd been waiting for.

Eventually each person might see something that looked like their own story, and they might remember that somewhere in the world was a person like themselves who wanted to know how it would end, though the news would not be there to help them with that.

Roal turned his head to the side. The blue light of the television required a focus that strained his eyes and it hurt.

Roal waved Chet away when Chet got up to help Roal to the bathroom. Roal would do it himself. He had one good leg and a wheelchair he could use to roll himself to the edge of the door. Then he could grab the sides of the doorframe, pull himself up, and lean on the sink. And it did hurt, and that was another part of the after-story that the news wouldn't mention.

Neither would it mention what he had seen in the forest. Where the tree that fell on him had scraped the ground away, he had seen it: the tiny bent heads of coiled plants, bright green and waiting to unfurl as the spring days heated up and the sun poured in. He tried to explain it, but the interviewer hadn't cared. It was, after all, a forest, she suggested, and growing is what they do.

But Roal had seen it. Had entered it as he hung from the branches of the tree. But what the news needed for their morning segment was a hero. Not a hero who saw a plant, but a hero who was causing a massive outpouring of support for the annual cancer walk.

And in truth he looked the part well enough. Not bad for a man in a leg cast whose wife was gone for good. He wore a pressed blue shirt and tan pants. He was freshly shaved and filled his chair well and kept his shoulders squared and lifted. His name was Roal Bowman, writing professor at Braddock College and inspiration to his students. The students had banded together, agreeing to give up the usual post-graduation parties so they could Walk for the Cure to support Roal in the loss of his wife, a plant lover and book editor who wanted her last days to be spent in the company of trees. Though the story lowered its tempo when it admitted that Roal was still in denial—he couldn't yet use the language of death—it was common, one analyst revealed, for the remaining spouse to use words like the ones Roal chose: "beyond," "passed through," "gone for now." Roal's own mother had died of cancer. No wonder it was hard to accept.

But the other story—the story the news was holding its breath for, was how Mike "The Insurance Agent" Durango had tracked Dina Bowman, thinking she was the same Dina whom Lin Strickland had earlier said she brought to help Winter. Lin had already stated that she had made the name up. But Durango had followed Roal to Dina, and from there he hoped to find Winter. Durango intended to reveal the location of Winter's project to protect the locations of Durango's own hanging marijuana empire. And Lin apologized for her unfortunate mistake: she said she had unwittingly pulled the name of one friend to cover for the name of another. Roal made another note in his notebook, *Call Lin—thank for the story.*

But, as the anchor stated, the story ended as safely as possible: the agents found Durango, killed by a cougar. And fortunately for Roal, if Durango hadn't gone to the forest, it was unlikely anyone would have discovered Roal trapped in the fallen tree. Officer Sparks credited the bright pink shirt—otherwise they might not have seen him, and they certainly wouldn't have stuck around to look. They wanted to get out of the forest quickly—"One more stiff breeze," Officer Sparks said, "and that could have been it. It's not safe to be around tinder in a windstorm."

And then they cut back to Roal Bowman. How did it make him feel to know that this year's graduation speaker would pay tribute to him in her speech? He felt humbled and inspired. What did he feel inspired to do? *Investigate and revise*, Roal said.

Though at graduation, Roal felt afraid. His wheelchair made him feel helpless and irrelevant as Lin Strickland stepped in behind him and pushed him to his place in line with the professors. As they proceeded out of the building and along the sidewalk to the open air of the ceremony, Roal tried to help push his own wheels forward, but they were already turning so fast his hands only burned against the rough wheels as they sped along. Lin pushed him, navigating him around sidewalk bumps and over extension cords that snaked to the microphones and cameras.

A student he had never seen before got up and spoke to the entire assembly. She said she wished she had taken a class from a man she had learned about too late. And she said that this was the best part of her Braddock experience: that she always found out there was more she could have done. This was the lesson she wanted to impart to each of her fellow classmates as they stepped out into a life where the jobs were bleak, educations were expensive, divorce rates were climbing, and the ruined environment was smeared in oil: she wanted them to know that there was always more they could do, and that, therefore, they must.

She said there would always be people like Roal Bowman—quiet, unassuming heroes—people who showed up every day to contribute to the lives of others, and it was up to those others to seek out these quiet heroes and learn from them. There was a lot that no one student could change, the speaker insisted, but they could get to know each other. They could assume that no one's life was simple or perfect, that the professors Braddock had selected to be mentors, professors, and inspirations were just the tip of the iceberg: there was always more. There was always more.

And, she reminded them, today they would put off their parties and take a walk to show that the parties could wait until they had done the serious work before them—the work of doing just a little bit more.

Roal was swept up in the passion of her speech, in the voice rise and voice fall, the cadence and rush of her words. He nearly allowed himself to admire the man she spoke of, though ended up having to be honest that he was slightly afraid by the amount of work it would take to become him. He bowed his head to that man he was obligated to be, and Lin rested her hand reassuringly on his shoulder until he raised his head again.

At the end of the graduation ceremony, the students took off their caps and tossed them, a flutter of dark birds that they shielded themselves against as the caps angled in for a landing. The music began, but the students were not yet done: they opened their robes and then tossed those into the air too. The robes hung over the assembly for a moment, then drifted down onto a sea of bright pink, the students with their arms upraised to catching whomever's gowns fell into them. Every one of them, wearing the pink Stop the War shirt of the afternoon's coming walk. They barely had time to make it.

Once they got to the river's edge where the throng of walkers waited, Jill rushed up to Roal. She leaned over and kissed his cheek. Her boys also ran over, though were too busy checking out Roal's wheelchair to acknowledge him.

"Thank you, Roal," Jill said. "Thank you for everything. This is amazing." Jill gestured to all the people gathered for the walk. They poured in off of the side streets and onto the sidewalk and lawn. A news crew was already set up as the camera lazily surveyed the crowd.

"I had to order more shirts—I actually had to order more every day for about a week. It got a little tense." Jill laughed, then told Roal she had to go—but she turned to thank him again, and told him if he was ever in Chicago, he should join them for dinner.

Roal waited until the crowd in front of him had thinned, insisting to those who held back to walk with him that they should go on ahead. He wanted to do it alone.

Though Rueben and his girlfriend said they would walk behind him, in case he needed anything. When the last of the crowd drifted on down the trail and away, Roal got up from his wheelchair and leaned on his crutches. It would take a long time. For the first hour, Roal heard Rueben and his girlfriend, Amanda, behind him, laughing, talking, playing. When Roal stopped to rest Rueben wanted to know if he should go for a car, if one of them should call for help. But Roal said no, he had only stopped to tell Rueben and Amanda to get a move on, to finish it out quickly so they could get to their parties and then to the rest of summer and, beyond that, their waiting lives. Rueben and Amanda looked at each other, and Rueben reached to shake Roal's hand. Amanda hugged him lightly, and they ran off into their future leaving Roal to the walk in his own time.

He didn't rush it. By the end his arms trembled with the hauled burden of himself.

When he got back to the parking lot, the tables were down, and empty paper cups rolled over the parking lot and littered the grass. The last of the cleanup crew had nothing to offer him and Jill was nowhere to be seen.

Roal leaned against a tree, muscles jittered with fatigue. One of the crew ran to search her car to find a water bottle. Another rolled Roal's chair over and helped him settle in. Roal would call Chet for a ride. But first he wanted to sit by the river, to listen and look out.

The river's course had been carved by the giant floods thirteen thousand years ago, and the waters had followed roughly the same path of that carving ever since. Even so, Roal understood that the river moved its stones around from within, that it rose and churned each year with the spring melt, then dwindled as it ran into autumn, revealing its new-turned stones and the many layers of its falling banks.

Acknowledgments

Large and heartfelt thanks to those who are part of this book's behind-the-scenes story. To this book's early readers—Hilary Barton Billman, Janice King, Nance Van Winckel, and David James Duncan—thank you. Your generous advice (both gentle and seismic) and support make writing feel like the difficult, honest, and connective work that it is—and allowed the book to open further into its path of becoming. Thanks to Sheila Zangar for sharing the neuro-emotional realm with me, and for cheering on the book when that realm was extended to include the trees. To my late father, Thomas Oakes, a planter of trees, my gratitude for sharing your love of what grows; to both you and my mother, Constance Ryan-Oakes, my deep appreciation for recognizing and supporting writing as a fundamental act. Frank and Jane Boyden, thank you for your support and for the sustaining gifts of place and solitude that helped this book find its footing. I also appreciate the expanse of time and concentrated focus made possible during the PLAYA residency. Thanks to Jerrod Macfarlane, for reaching out for this work at just the right moment. It has been a pleasure to work with editors Caroline Russomanno, whose responsive, thorough, and warm replies have made this process a delight, and Alison Strobel and Gavia Boyden, whose wickedly good editorial sensibilities saved me from a perpetuity of mistake-related horror. And finally, Ian and Gavia, because you go to the fierce, bright ends, I thank you for the multitudes you hold, the importance of what you teach, and the love you inspire.